P9-EDQ-242

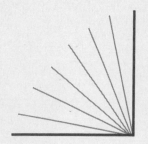

WHAT *the* WORLD *is* READING

Excerpts from a Selection of
Bestselling Paperback Titles from
Penguin Group (USA)

BERKLEY   RIVERHEAD
BOOKS

PENGUIN
BOOKS

NEW
AMERICAN
LIBRARY

PLUME

Published by Penguin, Berkley, Riverhead, Plume and NAL, divisions of
Penguin Group (USA) Inc., 375 Hudson Street, New York, New York 10014, USA
Penguin Group (Canada), 90 Eglinton Avenue East, Suite 700,
Toronto, Ontario M4P 2Y3, Canada (a division of Pearson Penguin Canada Inc.)
Penguin Books Ltd., 80 Strand, London WC2R 0RL, England
Penguin Ireland, 25 St. Stephen's Green, Dublin 2, Ireland (a division of Penguin Books Ltd.)
Penguin Group (Australia), 250 Camberwell Road, Camberwell, Victoria 3124, Australia (a division of Pearson Australia Group Pty. Ltd.)
Penguin Books India Pvt. Ltd., 11 Community Centre, Panchsheel Park, New Delhi - 110 017, India
Penguin Group (NZ), cnr Airborne and Rosedale Roads, Albany, Auckland 1310, New Zealand (a division of Pearson New Zealand Ltd.)
Penguin Books (South Africa) (Pty.) Ltd., 24 Sturdee Avenue, Rosebank, Johannesburg 2196, South Africa

Penguin Books Ltd., Registered Offices:
80 Strand, London WC2R 0RL, England

Excerpt from *The Doctor and the Diva*
© Adrienne McDonnell, 2011

Excerpt from *Fall of Giants*
© Ken Follett, 2010

Excerpt from *The Gendarme*
© Mark T. Mustain, 2010

Excerpt from *The Lake of Dreams*
© Kim Edwards, 2011

Excerpt from *The Weird Sisters*
© Eleanor Brown, 2010

Excerpt from *The House at Tyneford*
© Natasha Solomons, 2011

Excerpt from *A Discovery of Witches*
© Deborah Harkness, 2011

Excerpt from *You Know When the Men Are Gone*
© Siobhan Fallon, 2011

Excerpt from *The Death Instinct*
© Jed Rubenfeld, 2011

Excerpt from *Battle Hymn of the Tiger Mother*
© Amy Chua, 2011

All rights reserved

First published by Penguin, Berkley, Riverhead, Plume, and NAL,
divisions of Penguin Group (USA) Inc.

First Printing, 2011
10 9 8 7 6 5 4 3 2 1

Copyright 2011
All rights reserved

PENGUIN BOOKS · NEW AMERICAN LIBRARY · BERKLEY · RIVERHEAD BOOKS · PLUME · REGISTERED TRADEMARKS—MARCA REGISTRADA

Printed in the United States of America

Without limiting the rights under copyright reserved above, no part of this publication may be reproduced, stored in or introduced into a retrieval system, or transmitted, in any form, or by any means (electronic, mechanical, photocopying, recording, or otherwise), without the prior written permission of both the copyright owner and the above publisher of this book.

PUBLISHER'S NOTE

The Doctor and the Diva, Fall of Giants, The Gendarme, The Lake of Dreams, The Weird Sisters, The House at Tyneford, A Discovery of Witches, You Know When the Men Are Gone, The Death Instinct, and *Battle Hymn of the Tiger Mother* are works of fiction. Names, characters, places, and incidents either are the product of the author's imagination or are used fictitiously, and any resemblance to actual persons, living or dead, business establishments, events, or locales is entirely coincidental.

The publisher does not have any control over and does not assume any responsibility for author or third-party Web sites or their content.

If you purchased this book without a cover you should be aware that this book is stolen property. It was reported as "unsold and destroyed" to the publisher and neither the author nor the publisher has received any payment for this "stripped book."

The scanning, uploading, and distribution of this book via the Internet or via any other means without the permission of the publisher is illegal and punishable by law. Please purchase only authorized electronic editions, and do not participate in or encourage electronic piracy of copyrighted materials. Your support of the author's rights is appreciated.

WHAT *the* WORLD *is* READING

FROM

The Doctor and the Diva

BY

Adrienne McDonnell

"Some novels just naturally enslave you, and this is one of them. . . . Serious and gripping . . . [a] brilliant debut novel."

—*The Washington Post*

It is 1903, and Erika von Kessler has struggled for years to become pregnant. Resigned to childlessness, Erika—a talented opera singer and the wife of a prominent Bostonian—secretly plans to move to Italy to pursue her musical career. When the charismatic Doctor Ravell takes Erika on as a patient, he is mesmerized by her. Impetuously, he takes a shocking risk that could ruin them both.

Inspired by the author's family history, the novel moves from snowy Boston to the gilded balconies of Florence in a stunning tale of opera, longing, and the indomitable power of romantic obsession.

1

⁂

BOSTON

1903

Doctor Ravell had already missed the funeral. The body was being carried from the church as he arrived. Many of Boston's most prominent physicians descended the granite steps in a parade of canes and black silk hats, the modest old man in the casket the most esteemed of them all. Six or seven members of the von Kessler family—all of them doctors—served as pallbearers, and they shouldered the gleaming casket suitable for a king. Ravell wondered how many others, like him, must have deserted patients at their bedsides in order to join the procession.

He heard his name called, a black top hat raised and waved in his direction like a celebratory shout. "Ravell!"

It was Doctor Gerald von Kessler, a homeopath, who greeted him—the nephew of the man they'd come to mourn. His short wife stood beside him, with violets blooming in her hat.

The couple insisted that Ravell ride with them to the cemetery. In the privacy of their carriage, Doctor von Kessler leaned closer to confide.

"Can you help my sister?" von Kessler said. "This is what I am asking."

"We are afraid," his wife added, "that she has grown desperate."

Doctor von Kessler removed his top hat and placed it on the seat. "My sister's husband has become obsessed. He's dragged her to physician after physician, put her through every procedure and humiliation so that she can have a child. He won't relent."

"I'd be honored to help your sister," Ravell said, "in any way I can."

"We heard about your recent triumph in the Hallowell case." Gerald von Kessler gave Ravell a sharp, congratulatory nod.

"After nineteen years in a barren marriage," Mrs. von Kessler said, "thanks to you, they had twins!" The violets jiggled in her hat and her eyes shone at Ravell.

"My sister and her husband have wasted too much time consulting the old guard," Doctor von Kessler said. "They need a younger man—a pioneer in modern techniques, like you."

At the gravesite Ravell stood next to them, one hand clasped over his opposite wrist. He would never have guessed that before his thirtieth birthday, the von Kessler family would be relying on him. In the distance of a valley below, he noticed skaters skimming along a frozen pond. Cold air filled his lungs and he felt an odd elation—so peculiar to sense at a funeral—the buoyancy of knowing that his reputation was on the rise. Lately his practice had expanded at such a rate that he had been forced to turn patients away.

The last time he had seen the legendary physician they would bury today was at a professional dinner just two months previously. It had been the sort of event where eminent men toasted one another, half in jest; they had planted a crown of laurel leaves on Ravell's head to welcome him into their midst. That evening the revered old man had turned to Ravell and said, "You'll be appointed professor of obstetrics at that famous school across the river before we know it. Remember that I made that prediction."

Now the grand old man in the casket was being borne up and carried above their heads to his grave. Mourners settled into respectful poses—heads bowed, feet slightly apart—yet the minister seemed to be delaying for some reason. While they waited, snow flurries began.

Finally a black motorcar drove into the cemetery grounds. A shining black door opened, and a slender woman in a white ermine fur cape stepped out. Two violinists accompanied her. As she clutched her fur and headed for the gravesite, the crush of onlookers parted, making a wide aisle for her.

The woman in the white cape climbed onto a small platform. Above the congregation, she stood dressed entirely in white, and as she raised her oval face to speak, snow fell faster. Flakes dusted her hat and clung to her dark ringlets.

The deceased had been her uncle, she explained to the mourners. "The aria I am about to sing is not religious," she said. "But when my uncle heard me sing Paisiello's 'Il mio ben quando verrà,' he said: 'When they bury me, I want you to send me up to heaven with that song.'"

She loosened the white fur from her throat. For a moment she closed her eyes and gathered herself up, and then she sang.

The sounds were unlike any Ravell had ever heard. It was not an earthly voice; it was a *shimmering*. Falling snow melted on her face as he listened. In the valley below, on the distant pond, skaters circled the ice with the *legato* of her phrases. He wanted those ice skaters to keep going, round and round. He wanted the woman's iridescent voice never to stop.

Who is she? he wondered. Later, when he learned her name—*Erika*—it made him think of the words *aria, air,* as if she breathed melodies.

After her singing ended and the minister had spoken, mourners adjusted their silk top hats and knotted their scarves and shuffled past the open gap in the earth.

"I don't believe you've met my sister, have you?" Gerald von Kessler said to Ravell, and guided him toward the platform. The singer lifted her chin toward him and took his hand and smiled, the light on her face as radiant as snow. Almost immediately she turned to another person. Ravell knew that at that moment, he was nothing to her—only another doctor among scores of them.

2

Ravell watched from an upstairs window in his private quarters as Erika von Kessler and her husband made their way down Commonwealth Avenue. They would be his first appointment of the day. The husband, the one leading the charge to end their childlessness, walked several paces ahead of his wife. She lagged. The husband paused and waited for her to catch up, but when he spoke to her, she turned her head to observe the town houses on the opposite side of the avenue.

Ravell felt a tinge of excitement as he observed them. He was a man drawn to risk; nothing made him feel more alive than the nearness of a gamble. This might—or might not—become a storied case for him.

As the couple moved closer, Ravell saw that the husband, Peter Myrick, was a tall, elegant figure perhaps a few years older than himself. A sandy-haired man with pleasant features, Peter had a narrow face and a blade-thin nose. He looked like a young senator. Later Ravell would learn that on the way to their first meeting, Peter Myrick had urged certain advice upon his wife: *If you want this doctor to dedicate his best efforts to us, we must develop a special rapport with him.*

Ravell had just finished getting dressed, the strands of hair at his neck still damp from his morning bath. Before going downstairs to the street-level suite of rooms that housed his practice, he shook a few drops of musk-scented pomade onto his palms and combed back the wings of his dark hair with his fingers.

When the couple entered, Ravell rose from behind his mahogany desk to greet them. Given his conversation with Erika's brother during the carriage ride to the cemetery, Ravell had not expected to experience any particular warmth toward her husband. But from the moment Peter Myrick came into the room, he seemed lit by optimism, and Ravell felt fondness toward him. Peter was a man of refinement, and yet he had the air of an eager schoolboy.

Like a curious child, Peter glanced around the office. He recognized at once what interested him.

"I see you've got a Morpho!" he said in an accent that was unmistakably British. He lifted the magnifying glass from Ravell's desk to examine three glass cubes. A different butterfly of exquisite colors and dimensions had been preserved inside each.

"Did you capture these yourself?"

Ravell nodded. "A friend has a coconut estate on an island off South America. The wildlife is magnificent there."

"And that?" Peter Myrick pointed to a framed photograph of an anaconda entwined in a mangrove tree. "Is that from the same island?"

Ravell nodded.

"I'm an animal enthusiast myself," Peter said. "Someday I'll show you my collections and my little menagerie."

Erika Myrick (or the mezzo-soprano Erika von Kessler, as she was known professionally) had stepped into his office with the same proud carriage Ravell recalled from the day she'd appeared at the cemetery. Yet she looked very different today, as if she'd been crying earlier, her lids swollen and her eyes small. As she settled herself distantly in a chair, Ravell recalled other things Gerald von Kessler had confided during the ride from the funeral. ("Peter has become fixated to the point of tormenting my sister. If she didn't have such a glorious voice, all this might have destroyed her by now. It's music that has saved her.")

Peter Myrick offered a brief history of their struggles to conceive. They had been married now for six years. He mentioned obstetricians they had previously consulted—all mature gentleman, renowned specialists.

To reassure them that he might have something new to offer, Ravell spoke of his mentor from Harvard Medical School. Together they had designed a series of particularly elegant instruments that were beginning to yield interesting results. "Perhaps you've heard of the famous Doctor Sims? Some people call him 'the Father of Modern Obstetrics.' My mentor was a student of Sims.'"

"A figure of controversy, Sims—wasn't he?" Peter said.

Ravell nodded. Sims had been brilliant, but far too invasive in the eyes of many. "Fertility work is still—" Ravell hesitated. "Well, let's just say this must be handled with the utmost discretion. Few people should be aware of anything except the results."

Peter and Erika nodded. They understood. In a quiet tone she responded to questions about her menstrual cycles. Every gynecologist who had examined her had apparently found her female system healthy and unremarkable.

Ravell put down his pen and turned to Peter to suggest an intrusion that made many men balk. "In such cases, it's standard to inspect a sample of the husband's semen as well."

Peter gave a laugh, as abrupt as a cough. "I can assure you that virility is not of concern here."

"It might provide insight."

"That won't be necessary." Peter crossed one leg over the other.

Ravell knew when a man's dignity must be respected, so instead of pursuing the matter he led Erika von Kessler down a corridor into an examination chamber. Normally a nurse placed a freshly starched sheet on the table, but today he made it up like a little bed for her. She removed her hatpin and set her dove-gray toque on a chair, and smoothed her pompadour.

"I heard you sing at your uncle's funeral," Ravell said. "Afterward, the sound of your voice stayed in my head for days. It was so—so—"

She turned to him with interest. "Do you enjoy opera?"

"My father trained to be a baritone, but he gave it up long before I was born. He managed a large farm in Africa. When I was a little boy, he used to sing from *Figaro,* and I used to dance around and bump against the walls."

Erika von Kessler's lips parted in a faint smile.

A nurse stood in attendance while he examined her. As he reached under the drape of skirts and palpated, he kept his eyes locked on hers, as he had been trained to do, so that a female patient would feel reassured that a doctor had no intention of peering at her private areas. Her eyes were blue-gray, deepened by lavender shadows beneath the lower lashes. Unlike many women, she lay completely relaxed. Her uterus was slightly small—not uncommon for a petite woman—and it tilted to the anterior. The ovaries were healthy, properly positioned. Ravell kept his eyes on hers until she arched her throat backward and switched her gaze to the ceiling, as if returning his stare felt too intimate.

When the examination was over, the nurse left the room. He took Erika von Kessler's hand and helped her sit upright. Her hair had loosened from its knot, with a froth of dark curls sliding down her neck. He smelled whiffs of lilac soap.

As he turned to depart, Erika von Kessler called to him, "It's useless, you realize. My husband doesn't want you to know that every procedure you're about to propose, we've done before—many times. This," she declared gravely, "is the end for me. It's the end for me *of everything*." The anguish in her words made him uneasy.

Yet she did agree to come to the office, accompanied by her husband, for regular visits that winter. Ravell assured Peter that his privacy would be respected; the moment he surrendered a sample of his seed, it would be quickly injected into his wife's body; no one would tamper with the precious substance.

And so, twice a week, Peter retreated into a windowless chamber where a book of photographs taken in a Parisian brothel had been left for him. When Peter Myrick finished, he covered the glass jar and left the specimen there. He then hurried out to the street where a carriage opened its doors and bore him away, wheels rumbling over cobblestones. An importer of textile machinery from Bradford, England, to the mills of New England—and an importer of Egyptian cotton as well—Peter traveled widely. He was a man in a hurry, with numerous transactions to oversee.

After Peter rushed off, twice a week Doctor Ravell completed the procedure on his wife. She was forced to lie for a half hour with her legs raised, knees and calves propped by pillows and bolsters, to allow her husband's seed to flow into her.

"It's hopeless," she said to Ravell every time.

❖

"I'm afraid that she plans to end her life." The wife of Doctor Gerald von Kessler sat in Ravell's office. The worried little woman wore the same crushed violets in her hat that she'd worn that day at the cemetery. "Something dreadful is going to happen to my sister-in-law, I'm certain."

"What makes you think that?"

"Erika asked me, 'If I did something that hurt the family terribly, would you and Gerald ever find it in your hearts to forgive me?' She's asked about wills; she says she wants all of her financial papers in order. She's given away beautiful dresses from her closet, saying that she won't be needing them. She's worried about her maid losing her job. Erika asked me, 'If something happens to me, would you promise to help find another position for Annie?' "

"Thank you for telling me," Ravell said.

He left the room, shaken, and stood behind a door down the hallway to collect himself. He'd once known a patient who had harmed herself under similar circumstances. That had happened during his days as a medical student, while he'd served as an assistant to another obstetrician. Ravell had never forgotten how cheerful the lady had seemed the day before she'd died by her own hand. When he'd passed her on a staircase, she'd smiled and called him by name. As she was leaving the building, she'd thrust her arm upward and waved to him with a flourish, and he heard her calling exuberant good-byes to everyone—the nurse, the head doctor, other patients and acquaintances seated in the waiting room.

The odd cheerfulness. That is what stayed with him most. Later another physician explained to him that a suicidal patient might appear suddenly uplifted just after she'd made her decision, thinking that she'd soon be free from whatever was causing her agony and sorrow. In a last note to her husband, the poor woman had written: *Since I have failed to give you the children you so dearly wanted, it seems only fair to leave you free to remarry more happily, and fruitfully. . . .* If Erika lost her life over this, Ravell knew the news would blind him with regret. He'd never wash the darkness of it from his mind.

❖

At Erika's next appointment, Ravell stepped away after examining her. "So you're having your period," he said. That morning, Erika admitted, she had hidden her bloodstained bloomers from her husband.

"You can tell Peter yourself," Erika told Ravell. Bitterness sharpened her features. "I'm tired of seeing the disappointment in his face."

She was his last appointment of the day. Ravell asked her to come into his office after she'd finished getting dressed. It always took an excruciatingly long while for a patient to rearrange her undergarments and rows of buttons, he'd found, before she was ready to exit with grace.

In the intervening minutes he slipped into the washroom, lathered his hands, and dried them. The small bathroom felt as private as a prayer cell. He tugged hard at the hot and cold water taps to shut off large drops that fell into the porcelain sink. As he combed his dark moustache with his fingers, he wondered what he would to say to her.

In the mirror he stared at himself—a slender man, shorter than most others he passed in the street. People said that if he weren't wearing a fine suit, he might be mistaken for an Arab sheik or a Tartar. His eyes dominated his face—dark eyes like his father's, thoughtful, deep-set. "It's those eyes," a lady had once said, "that make people want to tell you things."

Each woman, each patient, was her own mystery. He tried to listen until he saw distress ease or tears dry on a woman's face. Much depended on their trust in him. Some told him how they shuddered under the weight of their husbands' bodies, shunning and avoiding conjugal duties whenever they could.

When a rare husband or two had pleaded for his advice, Ravell had shown them diagrams and spoken with candor about the importance of a woman's enjoyment. At times he'd needed to be stern with wives, asking: *How do you expect to ever have a child if your husband finds that you keep locking the door to your room?*

❖

He heard a hallway door open. When he returned to his office, Erika was already there, walking around. From his desk, she picked up the glass cube with the big blue Morpho butterfly trapped inside, and she held it up to the light before setting it back down. Then she lifted the magnifying glass. Centering it above her upturned palm, she peered at the lines.

"Are you trying to read your palm?" he asked.

Erika gave a rough shake of her head and put the magnifying glass down, as if she did not believe in palmistry. The walls of his office could not contain her restlessness. She gave a noisy sigh.

When Ravell sat down behind his desk, she took the chair opposite him. "May I ask you something personal?" he said. "A woman's attitude is important. . . . Do you want to become a mother, or is this Peter's—?"

Closing her eyes for a moment, she then opened them and spoke with sharp resolve. "I used to want a child more than anything," she said, "but I've learned not to want a thing I can't have."

She looked sweet and solemn as she said this. Ravell watched her closely. If he did not interrupt and allowed a patient to continue talking, he'd found that she might reveal things she hid from a close friend or sister-in-law. Erika, however, said nothing else.

He leaned toward her, his forearms resting on his desk. "Erika, other people are worried about your state of mind."

She stared at him, then glanced at the closed door. Obviously there was something she was wary of admitting. "You must have a great many patients waiting," she said.

He assured her that this was his last appointment of the day—that he had plenty of time just now to counsel her—but she got up and began fastening her long purple cape.

To delay her, Ravell stepped between her and the doorway. "Don't do anything drastic—will you promise me that?" he said.

She was as tall as he was; her blue-gray eyes looked straight into his, her proud neck growing longer. "My life is my own," she said. "I can do what I like with it."

Had she already rehearsed a ghastly act in her mind? In the darkness of the moment he offered blind assurances. "This will all turn out happily, Erika. I'm certain of it."

"I don't believe you," she said. When she reached for the doorknob, he moved aside. Just before she turned away, he saw the sharp light of tears in her eyes. Drawing her wool cape tighter, she headed into the corridor, and when the front door opened, cold air blew into Ravell's face, lifting the hair off his collar. Long after she had gone out into the winter day, his mind held on to her. Long after the strand of bells jingled and the door banged shut, he saw her dark purple cape make a sweeping turn just above her heels.

Would she keep her next appointment? He worried that something awful would happen before then.

By the time his nurse filed some papers and left for the day, the sky had gone dark outside. Ravell extinguished the lights in his office, went down the corridor, and shut himself into a closet-like room. At medical school—at Harvard—he was hardly the most brilliant, but he had asked bolder questions than most. Since then, he had braved more and taken more risks; he had often gotten results where others had missed.

Now he was about to do something unforgivable. Ravell removed a glass dish from a drawer, set it on the counter, and removed the lid. Less than two hours before, Peter Myrick had departed from this room, leaving a sample of his semen; the specimen was still fresh. Ravell had used only a portion of it; on a hunch, he had saved the rest. Now he adjusted knobs on the microscope.

With nervous hands he took a pipette, and let a drop of fluid splash onto the slide. As he slipped the specimen under the lens, he felt moisture break over his face. He thought of Leeuwenhoek, a man from Holland who had first seen sperm through a microscope in the year 1677. A daring act of discovery then. Before gazing into the eyepiece, Ravell bent his head and held his breath, as Leeuwenhoek must have done.

At first nothing darted past his eye, only a blizzard of grayish-whiteness. He pulled away, changed the magnification, adjusted the focus, and peered again. The results made him feel snow-blind. He saw nothing there, no sperm at all.

3

"Your neck smells marvelous," Ravell said, laughing. His nose nudged the soft place under her earlobe.

Mrs. George Appleton was over forty—a decade older than he. On his bedside table she liked to keep a ring of candles burning while they made love. Wax ran from the tapers. His bedsheets felt moist after their exertions, the air humid with scents from her body and his.

Her hair was half-gray, but her speaking voice was low and deep, with theatre in it. Her laugh had the resonance of an actress's. Her own husband had not touched her in four years.

"I need to leave now," she said. She was a tall woman. When she got up from the bed, in search of the clothing she'd cast across a chair, he saw the large-shouldered, great-breasted silhouette of her, the long lean stilts of her legs, the absence of any tapering at her waist. Her backside fell flat like a cliff, like a man's. ("Where's my derriere?" she liked to jest, grabbing herself there.)

Ravell knew he was not the first man she had sought out, apart from her husband. He loved her hunger. Since he lived on the floors above his practice, he was careful to draw the shades before she came, and he shut every window. She was noisy while being caressed, and in her cries he heard more animals than he could name. When he told her this, she squatted on all fours and dived at his body, snuffling and rooting. That made him laugh. He had to shush her sometimes, because even three stories up, she might be heard from the street.

Prior to Amanda Appleton, he'd never had an affair with a patient.

The idea had appalled him. But from the day she first flung herself across his bed, he'd felt relieved and grateful for all she'd taught him. He'd never had a wife, and when it came to advising married couples, he'd felt secretly embarrassed by the limits of his own experience. He used to worry that he did not know all he felt he should.

She sat at the bed's edge and squeezed Ravell's knee. "What's wrong?" she asked. "You look troubled."

He frowned at the ring of candlelight that wavered on the ceiling. "I've been thinking about a patient. An infertility case." Ravell did not describe to her how he had stolen a bit of Peter Myrick's semen and how, with nervous hands, he had slipped the sample under a microscope. He only said, "It turns out that the husband is azoospermic."

"What's that?"

"That means he has absolutely no hope of fathering a child. He has no sperm in his semen, none whatsoever." Ravell sat up and punched a pillow lightly between his fists. "I don't know how to tell them."

❖

"I have no desire to adopt," Peter Myrick said. "It's not the same, although I admire people who do it."

Ravell and Peter had arranged to lunch at the Algonquin Club. They agreed to meet there as late in the day as possible, after most of the tables had been cleared, to ensure more privacy. They sat in a far corner and kept their voices down. Even their waiter sensed that he ought to stand at a distance, a crisp white towel hung over his bent arm.

Ravell wished he could be frank, but how could he simply blurt out what he'd learned? Peter had never given permission for his manhood to be inspected and counted under a microscope. As a physician, Ravell knew he had committed an invasion of an appalling kind: what husband would trust him in the future if it became known that he had violated a patient's privacy?

"Perhaps it's time we resorted to the dreaded semen analysis," Ravell said briskly.

"What good would it do?" Peter said. "Would it mean that we'd do anything differently?"

"It might help you to stop blaming your wife."

"I'm not finding fault with anybody."

"Do you ever worry," Ravell said, "that your wife may be feeling terribly despondent after all this? There are women who lose their will to live—"

"Not Erika," Peter said. "She has great zest for life. She's indomitable."

Was Peter blinded by his own optimism, by his own gusto? Ravell wondered. Did the man know his own wife at all? Ravell gulped from a glass of ice water, then fingered the tines of his fork. Their white plates shone, clean and ready. The rack of lamb they'd ordered seemed a long time in arriving.

"At this stage," Peter said, "I know some might suggest mixing my seed with another man's. But I won't have it. If I were interested in adopting another man's child, we'd have done that years ago. Besides," he reasoned, "why fool ourselves? If I've fathered a child, I want to know it's mine. I never want to wonder if it's somebody else's."

Their lunch arrived. The waiter replaced the cold white plates before them with hot plates laden with lamb that sizzled and steamed and ran with rich juices. Peter spooned dollops of mint jelly onto each bite with the delight of a boy who relished huge helpings of sweets. "Erika is giving a private recital at our home for my birthday," Peter said. "And she has promised to sing my favorite arias. We'd like to invite you."

Ravell longed to hear her sing again. Peter's enthusiasm welled up as he described the fine musicians he'd hired to accompany her, the turquoise damask dress he'd bought for Erika to wear at the event. "The dress is from Paris," he said. "From Worth. I owe it to her, after all she's endured. Besides, what could give me more pleasure on my birthday than to see my wife looking luscious?" He winked.

After the party, Peter would leave for Egypt, where he had dealings with cotton merchants. From Cairo he would head to England to purchase the latest textile machinery. He would be gone for two months.

Erika would not be joining him because she had singing engagements at the Handel and Haydn Society, as well as at the new palazzo Mrs. Isabella Stewart Gardner had recently opened on the Fenway.

Since he would be gone for many weeks, Peter suggested that he might leave semen samples on ice, ready to be thawed and used on his wife in his absence. "Before I leave"—Peter leaned across the tablecloth and spoke in confidence—"perhaps you might be willing to come to the house? Perhaps on the night of my birthday recital, after the guests are gone? I think my wife and I might be more relaxed there. Things might go better at home, in our own bed, than they have gone at your office. Erika could drift to sleep afterward, and not stir until morning."

The invitation to enter their home intrigued Ravell. The rooms that people inhabited, he'd found, always mirrored unseen aspects of their souls. He was curious to see the paintings they'd chosen, to hear his own steps creak along the staircase they descended every day. He pictured himself opening the lid of Erika's piano and brushing his knuckles across the ivories. He nodded as Peter talked. Ravell agreed to everything, the way one humors a child. What harm could come from pretending—at least for now—that the ghost of Peter's future son or daughter might actually become real? Why crush a man's hopes just before his birthday?

And so Ravell let Peter go on speaking and imagining.

"All I am asking is for a lucky thing to happen once," Peter said. "For one child, boy or girl—I adore small children, their spark. To me, they're like puppies. They're eager to know all they can about the world. Children are always staring," Peter went on. "Have you noticed that? They may stumble, but they pick themselves up and charge ahead."

Like you, Ravell thought.

"If I had a child, I'd never stop teaching it things. . . . Last time I sailed to Europe, a tiny Italian girl saw me on the deck. She must have been about two. She left her mother and came right over to me. I held her in my lap and she opened her little fists and pointed upward. You know what she was after? She wanted me to grab a bird out of the sky and give it to her."

"I have no doubt that you would make a profoundly good father," Ravell said.

They left the Algonquin Club in separate carriages. Ravell headed toward the hospital, Peter toward his offices on Congress Street. Ravell told the driver to let him off early, a few blocks from his destination, so that he could stroll for a few minutes through a park.

On the icy path Ravell's shoes slid against the glaze. A stout nursemaid in uniform wheeled a sleeping baby in a pram, mincing her steps to keep from slipping. Near the pond, two mothers kept watch over young boys who poked and pushed toy boats through the cold water with long sticks. Children ran in circles, their aimless zigzags serving to heat their bodies on this chilly March day. Seeing families on benches, he wondered why he had held himself apart from all of this.

Old dowagers sometimes patted his arm and asked, "Why isn't a handsome young fellow like you married, Doctor Ravell?"

"How can I marry?" he would say, smiling, in response. "It wouldn't be fair to a wife. I'd be up half the night, delivering other ladies' babies."

The truth was that he was fond of all women. He could never believe he had fallen in love for the last time; that was his failing. He looked forward to appointments with a patient so rotund that she barely squeezed through a doorway—because she blurted jokes that made him drop his stethoscope and laugh. Among his favorites were elderly ladies who no longer bothered to gaze at themselves in mirrors; they looked outward, gasping and rejoicing over lapdogs, children, blooming peonies. He missed young mothers whose deaths haunted him—patients whose wrists had gone limp in his hand as he'd searched in vain for a pulse.

How could he ever manage a wife, with so many patients? Their needs sometimes exhausted him. By day's end, he could not have gone upstairs to his rooms and listened to a wife's problems. At suppertime he occasionally took a book and carried his plate into his study just to escape the chatter of his housekeeper.

Still, he wondered if he kept himself from being fully alive by never marrying. At the park a boy held up a baseball glove to catch a ball and missed; the ball landed at Ravell's feet and he reached down and threw it back. Would he never watch his own child being born? Would he remain an observer, in service to others' lives?

He understood Peter's longings more than he dared to say.

4

"It's still a tad early, Doctor," the parlor maid confided in a rough, splintery whisper as she opened the door. "The musicians are upstairs, rehearsing with Madame von Kessler." In the entry hall Ravell took a seat on the velvet cushion of a carved bench. The maid put a finger to her lips as they both heard violins strike up overhead.

The stringed instruments soared in unison, in an exuberance of wings. Erika von Kessler's voice swooped in and caught the air currents of the violins, leading them heavenward. Phrases of the aria she sang—Handel's "Va col canto"—echoed down the wide black walnut staircase.

The thin parlor maid folded Ravell's coat over her arm, her wiry gray hair pinned tightly against her head. Then, with a whimsy Ravell would never have expected from a woman her age, she smiled and rose up on her toes like a ballerina and danced into a dim corridor, out of sight.

It was a stately house—narrow and vertical like the other brick residences on Beacon Street. The entry hall was unusually spacious, with dark wallpaper that had the sheen of gilded leather, imported from somewhere exotic—Morocco, perhaps. While Ravell waited alone, he reached out and touched the wall's leathery paper with its embossed filigree.

Just as the aria ended, Peter appeared from a side staircase that ran five stories from top to bottom of the house. "Forgive me," he said, breathless, pulling on his French cuffs before he clasped Ravell's hand. "When I heard the bell, I put my head out the window and saw you standing on the front steps—but I found myself standing three stories above you with not a stitch of clothing on my body!" He and Ravell both laughed.

After all the guests had arrived, they took their cue and headed upstairs to the music room, where Erika stood near the piano singing "Voi che sapete" from *Le nozze di Figaro,* her shoulders half-exposed in a dress that shimmered like pale turquoise water. She placed one hand on the piano, welcoming everyone with her other arm outstretched.

The fashionable white woodwork made the music room feel larger and more airy than anywhere else in the high, narrow house. As she moved through more Handel and Mozart, to "Caro mio ben," her eyes glittered and skimmed across the audience. *I always search for a face I can sing to,* Erika had told Ravell. Tonight he hoped that face would be his own. When she broke into a flirtatious "Havanaise" and "Près des remparts de Séville" from *Carmen,* she tilted her shoulders and swished her skirts at her husband, and then she glanced at Ravell, as if to say, *After the rest of the guests leave, it will be just us here—Peter, you, and me.* The giddiness in her expression was impossible to miss.

The enthusiasm of the audience was so great that they demanded encore after encore, until she finally refused to sing anymore. Rings of light shone on her half-bared shoulders. Her face was luminous, moist with exertion. How different she seemed here, Ravell thought, than when she sat in his consulting room. He imagined that if they extinguished every light in the house, her face would remain visible in the dark, incandescent. He wondered if she, like so many artists, suffered from periods of manic euphoria—followed by debilitating gloom.

They raised champagne flutes and toasted Peter's birthday; they ate mint ice cream and hazelnut torte. As the party wound to a close, her brother, Doctor Gerald von Kessler, lingered in the entry hall with Ravell. It appeared they would be the last guests to go.

Erika had already declared herself exhausted and she'd bid her brother good night and gone upstairs. For the sake of appearances, she'd also made a show of saying farewell to Ravell, although their business for the evening was hardly finished.

"May I drop you somewhere?" Doctor von Kessler asked Ravell, opening the front door for them to exit together.

Ravell glanced at Peter. Peter stared at him. They had made no firm plan, no excuse for him to remain after the other guests had departed.

"My place isn't far," Ravell told von Kessler. "Just over on Commonwealth Avenue. I'm in the mood for a little brisk exercise."

"I'll walk with you," Doctor von Kessler offered, clearly intent on further conversation. His wife had gone to New Hampshire to visit her sister, who'd recently given birth to a sixth child, so he was alone.

Ravell could think of no graceful way to refuse his company. Under a streetlight near the curb, von Kessler's handsome brougham waited. The driver had dozed off. Doctor von Kessler nudged the man awake, and instructed the driver to meet them over at Ravell's address.

As they walked, von Kessler adjusted his muffler. "So how is the treatment progressing? Are my sister and her husband—?"

Ravell avoided answering. At Clarendon Street, as a cart clattered past in the darkness, he put out an arm to caution his companion before crossing.

"I don't mean to pry," Doctor von Kessler said, "but it's dreadfully hard on Erika, prolonging things."

Ravell sensed the doubts and barely disguised judgments of the other physician. *If you don't feel capable of handling the case—just say so,* von Kessler might as well have been saying, *and we'll move on to another man in the profession who may be.*

"What's the prognosis? Is my sister able to conceive, in your estimation?"

"Your sister is as fertile as any woman in my practice."

"Then *why*—?" von Kessler said, frowning.

"Confidentiality is at stake here," Ravell said. "If you persist in conveying such impatience to your sister, it won't help matters."

Under a lamppost on Marlborough Street, von Kessler stopped midstride. A tall, large man, he loomed over Ravell in the darkness. "Are there techniques you haven't tried? Is there any cause for optimism?"

With all the bravado he could muster, Ravell caught himself uttering words he knew he should not have said. "Of course. Absolutely." At this, the other man's shoulders softened and relaxed, and Ravell felt he had just made an awkward promise.

By the time they reached Ravell's house on Commonwealth Avenue, von Kessler's rig was waiting at the curb. Once again they had to rouse the driver, a man who clearly had a gift for dozing anywhere. The other physician raised his hat to Ravell as they drove off.

The telephone was ringing inside his office as Ravell unlocked the door. He hastened to catch it before the caller hung up.

"Are you coming back to the house?" Peter said. "We are waiting for you. *Knock softly,*" he added, *"so as not to wake the servants."*

❖

It was Peter himself who opened the stout front door as soon as Ravell's knuckles grazed the wood. Peter tightened the belt of his silk dressing gown, which he wore over pajamas. "I thought we'd never be rid of my brother-in-law," he muttered.

As they stole up the grand public staircase (the steps creaked less there than on the second, narrower staircase along the side of the house, Peter confided), Ravell wondered if he ought to be carrying his shoes in his hand. Peter led him into the family's private quarters, careful to lock the bedroom door behind them.

Erika lay on a peach velvet chaise longue in her own silk robe and matching gown, reading a ladies' magazine. "I see you've come to help us out," she remarked, sounding amused.

He'd never seen her hair fully unleashed from its pompadour before; it rippled and streamed across the back of the chaise, the strands reaching her elbows. Contrary to what she'd told her brother, she didn't appear fatigued after her performance. With her body outlined under silk, she looked ready to leap, quite impetuously, from her long chair.

A chambermaid had already turned down the fine linens of their great bamboo bed. The pillows lay smooth, the sheets folded back in parallel triangles, his and hers. The bed had been a wedding gift, built in Japan, they told Ravell.

"This isn't the sort of house call I usually make," Ravell said lightly. He thought of the great Doctor Sims. Back in the 1840s and 1850s, Doctor Sims had not hesitated to bring his newfangled instruments into a married couple's home and stand at the ready, behind a wall, to assist conception—an arrangement that shocked any number of people.

"I suppose we ought to begin," Peter said, his hands hidden in the pockets of his long robe.

The three of them looked at one another. Ravell brought his heels together and stood straighter. He reached into his black bag and gave Peter a special condom, telling him that he should use it with care so that not a drop of his precious seed would be lost. Ravell explained that he would reappear afterward to aim the syringe directly into the opening of the womb. The quick injection might prevent the sperm from tiring on their journey, and from going astray. The syringe might carry the seed more effectively—even faster into a wife's depths—than nature could.

Erika and Peter knew such things by now, of course. "Have you any other advice for us?" Peter joked.

"Enjoy yourselves," Ravell said. "And let me know when you've finished." He took his black leather medical bag and found his own way through the adjoining room, which happened to be a bathroom. From there he wandered into what appeared to be Peter's private study and latched the door.

To distract himself, Ravell picked up a stereoscope. He inserted photographs Peter kept of bazaars in Cairo, and of serpentine streets and arches that might be located, Ravell guessed, in Morocco. Held up to the light, viewed through the stereoscope, the scenes shifted in the brain and became three-dimensional, so that he felt himself step inside dusty North African towns where he had never been.

When he heard the quickening of her breaths in the other room, he put down the slides and the stereoscope and shut his eyes. The door was closed, but he heard them nonetheless. He could not focus on anything else. Not a sound came from Peter, only from her. Her gasps heated up in a mounting crescendo. Something thudded. (A foot or leg against the bamboo bed?)

Ravell walked the circuit of Peter's study, trying to mask the echoes of lovemaking with his own footsteps. He leaned closer to inspect a dozen framed images on the walls—a series of butterflies Peter had painted (Morphos, *Caligos,* extraordinary specimens)—all exquisite miniatures, absolutely true to nature, the colors applied with a hair-thin brush. Normally such paintings would have ensnared Ravell's complete attention.

But not tonight.

Peter's instincts had been good. He had predicted that after a performance, his wife's every pore would open in a kind of radiance. Privately Ravell had to agree: if there was ever a time to impregnate her, tonight was surely it. Was this the same woman who had complained to him—to the point of weeping—about her husband's obsessive tracking of her periods, his habit of picking up undergarments she'd dropped to the floor and turning them inside out, checking for blood?

How relaxed she had seemed tonight when he, her doctor, had entered the bedroom. He'd worried that she might resent his presence, but clearly she wasn't minding the intrusion at all. In the adjacent room, the bamboo wedding bed squeaked like an object vibrating on a factory chassis. Ravell envisioned it shuttling back and forth at a rate faster than the human eye could measure. His chest hurt from the effort of trying not to make a sound, as though something sacred were occurring behind that closed door.

She began to use her voice, issuing more than pants of pleasure. He heard hints of the music they'd all reveled in earlier, her back probably curved, her mouth open as notes leaped from her.

He couldn't recall ever having been in such a position before. In hotels, yes. But not as a physician. No other couple had ever suggested that he embroil himself like this.

Why had he come? He didn't really believe he could help Peter impregnate her, did he?

So why had he come—to torment himself? He rubbed his palm across his face as roughly as if he were washing it. It was unbearable to think, just now, of ruining their hopes. And the elation in Erika that he'd seen tonight—he wanted to keep sparks of that alive. Yet the fact was that Peter's sterility could not be changed. Ravell shut his eyes at the thought. *I will deal with the consequences of that later,* he decided.

In the corner of the study Peter kept a huge birdcage. Either Peter or one of the servants had draped a cover over the bars to help the creature sleep. Ravell lifted the cloth to peek. A gorgeous parrot balanced on a swing, its feathers saturated with scarlet, yellows, and cobalt blue. Ravell removed the cover completely to have a better look.

The parrot's clawed feet shifted on the bar. The cage trembled as the bird awoke.

"Kiss me!" it squawked. "Kiss me!"

Ravell threw the cover back over the bars and the bird went silent.

When Peter appeared, blinking hard against the light, he handed Ravell a small balloon filled with whitish liquid. "Did the parrot wake up?" he asked, incredulous. Ravell quickly turned away and reached into his medical bag, wiping his smile away with his hand.

Erika lay on the bed, fully draped in her silks. Her skin was moist, her cheeks and forehead flushed. The smell of sex filled the room, though she'd tried to disguise it by spraying herself with an atomizer that rested, half-full, on the night table. Her thighs were damp with the spray she'd flashed across them, preparing herself for the doctor. The fragrance was fruity with cherries.

Peter held a bright light for the doctor as Ravell prepared his instruments. He took the condom and siphoned its contents between Erika's open legs. Meticulously he completed his work.

In his dressing robe and slippers, Peter escorted the doctor through the dark house. At the front door, Peter rose up on the balls of his feet, looking pleased. "Maybe tonight will be the turning point," he said.

Ravell had taken care to save the condom that Peter had given him. In

31

the small hours of the night, back in his office, he cut off the end of the rubber he'd tied so precisely, and extracted an unused portion of residue from the condom's interior. He smeared a few drops across a slide, and peered at this second sample. He squinted, watching for anything to float into view, but saw nothing that swam or wiggled or flitted past. The second sample, too, was as lifeless as water siphoned from the Dead Sea.

5

⌘

"I no longer wish to become a mother," Erika said. In his medical office she sat dressed in a smart blue-gray suit with velvet lapels, nipped and tailored to display her slim waist. On her head she wore a matching blue toque, pinned at a fashionable angle against her hair.

She's in despair again, Ravell thought. *She cannot really mean this.*

He listened. Her husband had gone away on business, she said, and when he returned, he would find his life forever changed. "I know I'm about to cause him great sadness," she added.

He kept his eyes on her for so long that she finally glanced away from him—out of embarrassment, perhaps. She tilted her chin upward as if to scan the spines of the medical texts on his shelves. Clearly she had made some sort of decision: he sensed an underlying cheerfulness in her, and that worried him. Yet he still could not be certain that she was a person on the brink of extinguishing her own life. Less than a week previously, Ravell had entered her bedroom and smelled her as she lay in her nest of silks. He'd heard her every inhalation of pleasure. She was a woman of emotions and appetites so strong that she forgot—at least for the duration of lovemaking—why her husband had ever irritated her.

"What are you planning to do that might cause Peter such sadness?"

She would not answer. There was finality in every sharp turn of her head. If she walked out of his practice today, he knew she would not return. (*"I warned you,"* her sister-in-law might rail at him later. *"And you did nothing."*) The prospect that he would disappoint Peter and Erika and all the von Kesslers—that these efforts might provoke a tragedy—sank through him.

Why had he lied to her brother in such a foolhardy way? Insinuating that he could cure what could not be changed? In the end they would believe the failure was his.

He had it in his power to save her life, if that was really what was at stake here. He could satisfy them all. It would be easy enough.

But I cannot do it, he thought. *I would never do such a thing.*

"So—" he said. "You are refusing to seek my help in trying to conceive? Is that what you mean?"

"I've come to say good-bye to you," Erika said.

He felt alarm pulse in his wrists. *I am at my best in times of trouble,* he thought. *At moments of greatest emergency.* Others depended on his ability to rush into a dark room where a dire scene was unfolding and react as if by instinct. It was a gift he had: he could decide a thing quickly, in a flash of light from an opening door. In this way he had pulled forth babies from wombs that might soon have become graves; he had revived half-conscious mothers and staved off more deaths than he could remember.

A doctor is supposed to save lives, he thought, *by any possible means. Erika has been tortured by this situation long enough,* he decided. His leg muscles flexed; he prepared to rise from his chair. Above all, he must keep her from walking through the door and disappearing.

"Erika," he said, and leaned across the desk. "Are you depressed?"

She stared at him. "Of course," she said. "About all this? What else am I supposed to feel?"

"Peter has left frozen samples of his semen," he reminded her. "We've all agreed to work on this in his absence."

She twisted her neck to one side, as if to relieve a crick.

"This is hardly fair to Peter," Ravell argued. "I made a promise to him, and I feel a certain loyalty to the agreement, not only as a physician but as a friend. When Peter returns—if we haven't had any good fortune by then—maybe we can discuss the situation and reconsider matters then.

"I've already thawed the sample for today," Ravell added. "It wouldn't be right to waste it."

At first Erika appeared unmoved, and then a quake of exasperation went through her. "All right," she said, sighing. "But it's futile. And this is going to be the last time."

A radiance carried him then, and his heart beat hard, knowing that he was about to take a terrible chance. *Whatever happens,* he decided, *I'll cope with any unpleasantness that arises.* He ushered her to the examination room where she began, with a few resentful mutters, to undress. Her chest thrust forward as she arched her back and shrugged off her jacket with its velvet lapels.

"I'll be back in a few minutes," Ravell said. He hurried to the closet-like chamber where he kept his microscope and locked the door. The dish containing Peter's specimen waited on the counter. Ravell turned on the tap and carefully washed away every trace of Peter's semen. Then Ravell shut off the light and loosened his suspenders, unfastened his trousers and underwear, and let everything drop to the floor. He took himself in his own hand. Madness! He would never have condoned such a thing before, but now he had no time for self-doubt. He had to hurry. When Peter stood in this space, he'd been given a book illustrated with Parisian prostitutes, but he, the doctor, had no such luxury. He kept the chamber dark, and remembered how her breasts had moved, loose, unleashed under peach silk.

The nurse rapped sharply on every closed door in the corridor, searching, calling his name in a bewildered tone. "Doctor Ravell?"

"Yes!" he managed to answer.

"We're ready for you."

He groped in the darkness and found a dish he knew would be lying on the counter, and replaced Peter's seed with his own. He flicked on a light and buttoned his trousers. His tongue felt swollen in his mouth.

Dutifully the nurse remained in the exam room, a reassuring, motherly presence. Ravell took the dish and suctioned the pale substance into a long instrument. He lifted the drape covering Erika's lower body.

The nurse stood by, a sentry in a corner. She was supposed to serve as a guard of sorts—but what, she and Erika might have wondered, did they need to guard against? Doctor Ravell was a reputable man; he had never done such a thing before, and surely never would. Part of the drape had slid from Erika's thigh, exposing her there, but she did not bother to cover herself.

With his shoulders, Ravell blocked the nurse's view. No one could see inside his mind, but he worried that they might hear how loudly he inhaled and exhaled, the harsh beat of his pulse inside his ears.

"Don't mix mine with another man's," Peter had said. Peter who had read so many articles and obstetrical books.

Ravell had done no mixing. He used only his own.

FROM

Fall of Giants

Book One of the Century Trilogy

BY

Ken Follett

From the #1 *New York Times* bestselling author of *World Without End* and *The Pillars of the Earth*.

"[Ken Follett] is masterly in conveying so much drama and historical information so vividly . . . Grippingly told."
—*New York Times Book Review*

From the danger of a Welsh coal mine to the glittering chandeliers of a Russian palace, and from the boardrooms of power to the bedrooms of the aristocracy, Fall of Giants takes readers into the entangled fates of five families—and into a century we thought we knew, but that will never seem the same again.

January 1914

Earl Fitzherbert, age twenty-eight, known to his family and friends as Fitz, was the ninth-richest man in Britain.

He had done nothing to earn his huge income. He had simply inherited thousands of acres of land in Wales and Yorkshire. The farms made little money, but there was coal beneath them, and by licensing mineral rights Fitz's grandfather had become enormously wealthy.

Clearly God intended the Fitzherberts to rule over their fellow men, and to live in appropriate style; but Fitz felt he had not done much to justify God's faith in him.

His father, the previous earl, had been different. A naval officer, he had been made admiral after the bombardment of Alexandria in 1882, had become the British ambassador to St. Petersburg, and finally had been a minister in the government of Lord Salisbury. The Conservatives lost the general election of 1906, and Fitz's father died a few weeks later—his end hastened, Fitz felt sure, by seeing irresponsible Liberals such as David Lloyd George and Winston Churchill take over His Majesty's government.

Fitz had taken his seat in the House of Lords, the upper chamber of the British Parliament, as a Conservative peer. He spoke good French and he could get by in Russian, and he would have liked one day to be his country's foreign secretary. Regrettably, the Liberals had continued to win elections, so he had had no chance yet of becoming a government minister.

His military career had been equally undistinguished. He had attended the army's officer training academy at Sandhurst, and had spent three years with the Welsh Rifles, ending as a captain. On marriage he had given up full-time soldiering, but had become honorary colonel of the South Wales Territorials. Unfortunately an honorary colonel never won medals.

However, he did have something to be proud of, he thought as the train steamed up through the South Wales valleys. In two weeks' time, the king was coming to stay at Fitz's country house. King George V and Fitz's father had been shipmates in their youth. Recently the king had expressed a wish to know what the younger men were thinking, and Fitz had organized a discreet house party for His Majesty to meet some of them. Now Fitz and his wife, Bea, were on their way to the house to get everything ready.

Fitz cherished traditions. Nothing known to mankind was superior to the comfortable order of monarchy, aristocracy, merchant, and peasant. But now, looking out of the train window, he saw a threat to the British way of life greater than any the country had faced for a hundred years. Covering the once-green hillsides, like a gray-black leaf blight on a rhododendron bush, were the terraced houses of the coal miners. In those grimy hovels there was talk of republicanism, atheism, and revolt. It was only a century or so since the French nobility had been driven in carts to the guillotine, and the same would happen here if some of those muscular black-faced miners had their way.

Fitz would gladly have given up his earnings from coal, he told himself, if Britain could go back to a simpler era. The royal family was a strong bulwark against insurrection. But Fitz felt nervous about the visit, as well as proud. So much could go wrong. With royalty, an oversight might be seen as a sign of carelessness, and therefore disrespectful. Every detail of the weekend would be reported, by the visitors' servants, to other servants and thence to those servants' employers, so that every woman in London society would quickly know if the king were given a hard pillow, a bad potato, or the wrong brand of champagne.

Fitz's Rolls-Royce Silver Ghost was waiting at Aberowen railway station. With Bea at his side he was driven a mile to Tŷ Gwyn, his country house. A light but persistent drizzle was falling, as it so often did in Wales.

"Tŷ Gwyn" was Welsh for White House, but the name had become ironic. Like everything else in this part of the world, the building was covered with a layer of coal dust, and its once-white stone blocks were now a dark gray color that smeared the skirts of ladies who carelessly brushed against its walls.

Nevertheless it was a magnificent building, and it filled Fitz with pride as the car purred up the drive. The largest private house in Wales, Tŷ Gwyn had two hundred rooms. Once when he was a boy he and his sister, Maud, had counted the windows and found 523. It had been built by his grandfather, and there was a pleasing order to the three-story design. The ground-floor windows were tall, letting plenty of light into the grand reception rooms. Upstairs were dozens of guest rooms, and in the attic countless small servants' bedrooms, revealed by long rows of dormer windows in the steep roofs.

The fifty acres of gardens were Fitz's joy. He supervised the gardeners personally, making decisions about planting and pruning and potting. "A house fit for a king to visit," he said as the car stopped at the grand portico. Bea did not reply. Traveling made her bad-tempered.

Getting out of the car, Fitz was greeted by Gelert, his Pyrenean mountain dog—a bear-sized creature that licked his hand, then raced joyously around the courtyard in celebration.

In his dressing room Fitz took off his traveling clothes and changed into a suit of soft brown tweed. Then he went through the communicating door into Bea's rooms.

The Russian maid, Nina, was unpinning the elaborate hat Bea had worn for the journey. Fitz caught sight of Bea's face in the dressing-table mirror, and his heart skipped a beat. He was taken back four years, to the St. Petersburg ballroom where he had first seen that impossibly pretty face framed by blond curls that could not quite be tamed. Then as now she had worn a sulky look that he found strangely alluring. In a heartbeat he had decided that she of all women was the one he wanted to marry.

Nina was middle-aged and her hand was unsteady—Bea often made her servants nervous. As Fitz watched, a pin pricked Bea's scalp, and she cried out.

Nina went pale. "I'm terribly sorry, Your Highness," she said in Russian.

Bea snatched up a hatpin from the dressing table. "See how you like it!" she cried, and jabbed the maid's arm.

Nina burst into tears and ran from the room.

"Let me help you," Fitz said to his wife in a soothing tone.

She was not to be mollified. "I'll do it myself."

Fitz went to the window. A dozen or so gardeners were at work trimming bushes, edging lawns, and raking gravel. Several shrubs were in flower: pink viburnum, yellow winter jasmine, witch hazel, and scented winter honeysuckle. Beyond the garden was the soft green curve of the mountainside.

He had to be patient with Bea, and remind himself that she was a foreigner, isolated in a strange country, away from her family and all that was familiar. It had been easy in the early months of their marriage, when he was still intoxicated by how she looked and smelled and the touch of her soft skin. Now it took an effort. "Why don't you rest?" he said. "I'll see Peel and Mrs. Jevons and find out how their plans are progressing." Peel was the butler and Mrs. Jevons the housekeeper. It was Bea's job to organize the staff, but Fitz was nervous enough about the king's visit to welcome an excuse to get involved. "I'll report back to you later, when you're refreshed." He took out his cigar case.

"Don't smoke in here," she said.

He took that for assent and went to the door. Pausing on his way out, he said: "Look, you won't behave like that in front of the king and queen, will you? Striking the servants, I mean."

"I didn't strike her. I stuck a pin in her as a lesson."

Russians did that sort of thing. When Fitz's father had complained about the laziness of the servants at the British embassy in St. Petersburg, his Russian friends had told him he did not beat them enough.

Fitz said to Bea: "It would embarrass the monarch to have to witness such a thing. As I've told you before, it's not done in England."

"When I was a girl, I was made to watch three peasants being hanged," she said. "My mother didn't like it, but my grandfather insisted. He said: 'This is to teach you to punish your servants. If you do not slap them or flog them for small offenses of carelessness and laziness, they will eventually commit larger sins and end up on the scaffold.' He taught me that indulgence to the lower classes is cruel, in the long run."

Fitz began to lose patience. Bea looked back to a childhood of limitless wealth and self-indulgence, surrounded by troops of obedient servants and thousands of happy peasants. If her ruthless, capable grandfather had still been alive, that life might have continued; but the family fortune had been frittered away by Bea's father, a drunk, and her weak brother, Andrei, who was always selling the timber without replanting the woods. "Times have changed," Fitz said. "I'm asking you—I'm ordering you—not to embarrass me in front of my king. I hope I have left no room for doubt in your mind." He went out and closed the door.

He walked along the wide corridor, feeling irritated and a bit sad. When they were first married, such spats had left him bewildered and regretful; now he was becoming inured to them. Were all marriages like that? He did not know.

A tall footman polishing a doorknob straightened up and stood with his back to the wall and his eyes cast down, as Tŷ Gwyn servants were trained to do when the earl went by. In some great houses the staff had to face the wall, but Fitz thought that was too feudal. Fitz recognized this man, having seen him play cricket in a match between Tŷ Gwyn staff and Aberowen miners. He was a good left-handed batsman. "Morrison," said Fitz, remembering his name. "Tell Peel and Mrs. Jevons to come to the library."

"Very good, my lord."

Fitz walked down the grand staircase. He had married Bea because he had been enchanted by her, but he had had a rational motive, too. He dreamed of founding a great Anglo-Russian dynasty that would rule vast tracts of the earth, much as the Habsburg dynasty had ruled parts of Europe for centuries.

But for that he needed an heir. Bea's mood meant she would not welcome him to her bed tonight. He could insist, but that was never very satisfactory. It was a couple of weeks since the last time. He did not wish for a wife who was vulgarly eager about that sort of thing but, on the other hand, two weeks was a long time.

His sister, Maud, was still single at twenty-three. Besides, any child of hers would probably be brought up a rabid socialist who would fritter away the family fortune printing revolutionary tracts.

He had been married three years, and he was beginning to worry. Bea had been pregnant just once, last year, but she had suffered a miscarriage at three months. It had happened just after a quarrel. Fitz had canceled a planned trip to St. Petersburg, and Bea had become terribly emotional, crying that she wanted to go home. Fitz had put his foot down—a man could not let his wife dictate to him, after all—but then, when she miscarried, he felt guiltily convinced it was his fault. If only she could get pregnant again he would make absolutely sure nothing was allowed to upset her until the baby was born.

Putting that worry to the back of his mind, he went into the library and sat down at the leather-inlaid desk to make a list.

A minute or two later, Peel came in with a housemaid. The butler was the younger son of a farmer, and there was an outdoor look about his freckled face and salt-and-pepper hair, but he had been a servant at Tŷ Gwyn all his working life. "Mrs. Jevons have been took poorly, my lord," he said. Fitz had long ago given up trying to correct the grammar of Welsh servants. "Stomach," Peel added lugubriously.

"Spare me the details." Fitz looked at the housemaid, a pretty girl of about twenty. Her face was vaguely familiar. "Who's this?"

The girl spoke for herself. "Ethel Williams, my lord. I'm Mrs. Jevons's assistant." She had the lilting accent of the South Wales valleys.

"Well, Williams, you look too young to do a housekeeper's job."

"If your lordship pleases, Mrs. Jevons said you would probably bring down the housekeeper from Mayfair, but she hopes I might give satisfaction in the meantime."

Was there a twinkle in her eye when she talked of giving satisfaction? Although she spoke with appropriate deference, she had a cheeky look. "Very well," said Fitz.

Williams had a thick notebook in one hand and two pencils in the other. "I visited Mrs. Jevons in her room, and she was well enough to go through everything with me."

"Why have you got two pencils?"

"In case one breaks," she said, and she grinned.

Housemaids were not supposed to grin at the earl, but Fitz could not help smiling back. "All right," he said. "Tell me what you've got written down in your book."

"Three subjects," she said. "Guests, staff, and supplies."

"Very good."

"From your lordship's letter, we understand there will be twenty guests. Most will bring one or two personal staff, say an average of two, therefore an extra forty in servants' accommodation. All arriving on the Saturday and leaving on the Monday."

"Correct." Fitz felt a mixture of pleasure and apprehension very like his emotions before making his first speech in the House of Lords: he was thrilled to be doing this and, at the same time, worried about doing it well.

Williams went on: "Obviously Their Majesties will be in the Egyptian Apartment."

Fitz nodded. This was the largest suite of rooms. Its wallpaper had decorative motifs from Egyptian temples.

"Mrs. Jevons suggested which other rooms should be opened up, and I've wrote it down by here."

The phrase "by here" was a local expression, pronounced like the Bayeux Tapestry. It was a redundancy, meaning exactly the same as "here." Fitz said: "Show me."

She came around the desk and placed her open book in front of him. House servants were obliged to bathe once a week, so she did not smell as bad as the working class generally did. In fact her warm body had a flowery fragrance. Perhaps she had been stealing Bea's scented soap. He read her list. "Fine," he said. "The princess can allocate guests to rooms—she may have strong opinions."

Williams turned the page. "This is a list of extra staff needed: six girls in the kitchen, for peeling vegetables and washing up; two men with clean hands to help serve at table; three extra chambermaids; and three boys for boots and candles."

"Do you know where we're going to get them?"

"Oh, yes, my lord, I've got a list of local people who've worked here before, and if that's not sufficient we'll ask them to recommend others."

"No socialists, mind," Fitz said anxiously. "They might try to talk to the king about the evils of capitalism." You never knew with the Welsh.

"Of course, my lord."

"What about supplies?"

She turned another page. "This is what we need, based on previous house parties."

Fitz looked at the list: a hundred loaves of bread, twenty dozen eggs, ten gallons of cream, a hundred pounds of bacon, fifty stone of potatoes . . . He began to feel bored. "Shouldn't we leave this until the princess has decided the menus?"

"It's all got to come up from Cardiff," Williams replied. "The shops in Aberowen can't cope with orders of this size. And even the Cardiff suppliers need notice, to be sure they have sufficient quantities on the day."

She was right. He was glad she was in charge. She had the ability to plan ahead—a rare quality, he found. "I could do with someone like you in my regiment," he said.

"I can't wear khaki. It doesn't suit my complexion," she replied saucily.

The butler looked indignant. "Now, now, Williams, none of your cheek."

"I beg your pardon, Mr. Peel."

Fitz felt it was his own fault for speaking facetiously to her. Anyway, he did not mind her impudence. In fact he rather liked her.

Peel said: "Cook have come up with some suggestions for the menus, my lord." He handed Fitz a slightly grubby sheet of paper covered with the cook's careful, childish handwriting. "Unfortunately we're too early for spring lamb, but we can get plenty of fresh fish sent up from Cardiff on ice."

"This looks very like what we had at our shooting party in November," Fitz said. "On the other hand, we don't want to attempt anything new on this occasion—better to stick with tried and tested dishes."

"Exactly, my lord."

"Now, the wines." He stood up. "Let's go down to the cellar."

Peel looked surprised. The earl did not often descend to the basement.

There was a thought at the back of Fitz's mind that he did not want to acknowledge. He hesitated, then said: "Williams, you come as well, to take notes."

The butler held the door, and Fitz left the library and went down the back stairs. The kitchen and servants' hall were in a semibasement. Etiquette was different here, and the skivvies and boot boys curtsied or touched their forelocks as he passed.

The wine cellar was in a subbasement. Peel opened the door and said: "With your permission, I'll lead the way." Fitz nodded. Peel struck a match and lit a candle lamp on the wall, then went down the steps. At the bottom he lit another lamp.

Fitz had a modest cellar, about twelve thousand bottles, much of it laid down by his father and grandfather. Champagne, port, and hock predominated, with lesser quantities of claret and white burgundy. Fitz was not an aficionado of wine, but he loved the cellar because it reminded him of his father. "A wine cellar requires order, forethought, and good taste," the old man used to say. "These are the virtues that made Britain great."

Fitz would serve the very best to the king, of course, but that required a judgment. The champagne would be Perrier-Jouët, the most expensive, but which vintage? Mature champagne, twenty or thirty years old, was less fizzy and had more flavor, but there was something cheerfully delicious about younger vintages. He took a bottle from a rack at random. It was filthy with dust and cobwebs. He used the white linen handkerchief from the breast pocket of his jacket to wipe the label. He still could not see the date in the dim candlelight. He showed the bottle to Peel, who had put on a pair of glasses.

"Eighteen fifty-seven," said the butler.

"My goodness, I remember this," Fitz said. "The first vintage I ever tasted, and probably the greatest." He felt conscious of the maid's presence, leaning close to him and peering at the bottle that was many years older than she. To his consternation, her nearness made him slightly out of breath.

"I'm afraid the fifty-seven may be past its best," said Peel. "May I suggest the eighteen ninety-two?"

Fitz looked at another bottle, hesitated, and made a decision. "I can't read in this light," he said. "Fetch me a magnifying glass, Peel, would you?"

Peel went up the stone steps.

Fitz looked at Williams. He was about to do something foolish, but he could not stop. "What a pretty girl you are," he said.

"Thank you, my lord."

She had dark curls escaping from under the maid's cap. He touched her hair. He knew he would regret this. "Have you ever heard of droit du seigneur?" He heard the throaty tone in his own voice.

"I'm Welsh, not French," she said, with the impudent lift of her chin that he was already seeing as characteristic.

He moved his hand from her hair to the back of her neck, and looked into her eyes. She returned his gaze with bold confidence. But did her expression mean that she wanted him to go further—or that she was ready to make a humiliating scene?

He heard heavy footsteps on the cellar stairs. Peel was back. Fitz stepped away from the maid.

She surprised Fitz by giggling. "You look so guilty!" she said. "Like a schoolboy."

Peel appeared in the dim candlelight, proffering a silver tray on which there was an ivory-handled magnifying glass.

Fitz tried to breathe normally. He took the glass and returned to his examination of the wine bottles. He was careful not to meet Williams's eye.

My God, he thought, what an extraordinary girl.

{ II }

Ethel Williams felt full of energy. Nothing bothered her; she could handle every problem, cope with any setback. When she looked in a mirror she could see that her skin glowed and her eyes sparkled. After chapel on Sunday her father had commented on it, with his usual sarcastic humor. "You're cheerful," he had said. "Have you come into money?"

She found herself running, not walking, along the endless corridors of Tŷ Gwyn. Every day she filled more pages of her notebook with shopping lists, staff timetables, schedules for clearing tables and laying them again, and calculations: numbers of pillowcases, vases, napkins, candles, spoons . . .

This was her big chance. Despite her youth, she was acting housekeeper, at the time of a royal visit. Mrs. Jevons showed no sign of rising from her sickbed, so Ethel bore the full responsibility of preparing Tŷ Gwyn for the king and queen. She had always felt she could excel, if only she were given the chance; but in the rigid hierarchy of the servants' hall there were few opportunities to show that you were better than the rest. Suddenly such an opening had appeared, and she was determined to use it. After this, perhaps the ailing Mrs. Jevons would be given a less demanding job, and Ethel would be made housekeeper, at double her present wages, with a bedroom to herself and her own sitting room in the servants' quarters.

But she was not there yet. The earl was obviously happy with the job she was doing, and he had decided not to summon the housekeeper from London, which Ethel took as a great compliment; but, she thought apprehensively, there was yet time for that tiny slip, that fatal error, that would spoil everything: the dirty dinner plate, the overflowing sewer, the dead mouse in the bathtub. And then the earl would be angry.

On the morning of the Saturday when the king and queen were due to arrive, she visited every guest room, making sure the fires were lit and the pillows were plumped. Each room had at least one vase of flowers, brought that morning from the hothouse. There was Tŷ Gwyn–headed writing paper at every desk. Towels, soap, and water were provided for washing. The old earl had not liked modern plumbing, and Fitz had not yet got around to installing running water in all rooms. There were only three water closets, in a house with a hundred bedrooms, so most rooms also needed chamber pots. Potpourri was provided, made by Mrs. Jevons to her own recipe, to take away the smell.

The royal party was due at teatime. The earl would meet them at Aberowen railway station. There would undoubtedly be a crowd there, hoping for a glimpse of royalty, but at this point the king and queen would not meet the people. Fitz would bring them to the house in his Rolls-Royce, a large closed car. The king's equerry, Sir Alan Tite, and the rest of the royal traveling staff would follow, with the luggage, in an assortment of horse-drawn vehicles. In front of Tŷ Gwyn a battalion from the Welsh Rifles was already assembling either side of the drive to provide a guard of honor.

The royal couple would show themselves to their subjects on Monday morning. They planned a progress around nearby villages in an open carriage, and a stop at Aberowen town hall to meet the mayor and councilors, before going to the railway station.

The other guests began to arrive at midday. Peel stood in the hall and assigned maids to guide them to their rooms and footmen to carry their bags. The first were Fitz's uncle and aunt, the Duke and Duchess of Sussex. The duke was a cousin of the king and had been invited to make the monarch feel more comfortable. The duchess was Fitz's aunt, and like most of the family she was deeply interested in politics. At their London house she held a salon that was frequented by cabinet ministers.

The duchess informed Ethel that King George V was a bit obsessed with clocks and hated to see different clocks in the same house telling different times. Ethel cursed silently: Tŷ Gwyn had more than a hundred clocks. She borrowed Mrs. Jevons's pocket watch and began to go around the house setting them all.

In the small dining room she came across the earl. He was standing at the window, looking distraught. Ethel studied him for a moment. He was the handsomest man she had ever seen. His pale face, lit by the soft winter sunlight, might have been carved in white marble. He had a square chin, high cheekbones, and a straight nose. His hair was dark but he had green eyes, an unusual combination. He had no beard or mustache or even side-whiskers. With a face like that, Ethel thought, why cover it with hair?

He caught her eye. "I've just been told that the king likes a bowl of oranges in his room!" he said. "There's not a single orange in the damn house."

Ethel frowned. None of the grocers in Aberowen would have oranges this early in the season—their customers could not afford such luxuries. The same would apply to every other town in the South Wales valleys. "If I might use the telephone, I could speak to one or two greengrocers in Cardiff," she said. "They might have oranges at this time of year."

"But how will we get them here?"

"I'll ask the shop to put a basket on the train." She looked at the clock she had been adjusting. "With luck the oranges will come at the same time as the king."

"That's it," he said. "That's what we'll do." He gave her a direct look. "You're astonishing," he said. "I'm not sure I've ever met a girl quite like you."

She stared back at him. Several times in the last two weeks he had spoken like this, overly familiar and a bit intense, and it gave Ethel a strange feeling, a sort of uneasy exhilaration, as if something dangerously exciting were about to happen. It was like the moment in a fairy tale when the prince enters the enchanted castle.

The spell was broken by the sound of wheels on the drive outside, then a familiar voice. "Peel! How delightful to see you."

Fitz looked out of the window. His expression was comical. "Oh, no," he said. "My sister!"

"Welcome home, Lady Maud," said Peel's voice. "Though we were not expecting you."

"The earl forgot to invite me, but I came anyway."

Ethel smothered a smile. Fitz loved his feisty sister, but he found her difficult to deal with. Her political opinions were alarmingly liberal: she was a suffragette, a militant campaigner for votes for women. Ethel thought Maud was wonderful—just the kind of independent-minded woman she herself would have liked to be.

Fitz strode out of the room, and Ethel followed him into the hall, an imposing room decorated in the Gothic style beloved of Victorians such as Fitz's father: dark paneling, heavily patterned wallpaper, and carved oak chairs like medieval thrones. Maud was coming through the door. "Fitz, darling, how are you?" she said.

Maud was tall like her brother, and they looked similar, but the sculpted features that made the earl seem like the statue of a god were not so flattering on a woman, and Maud was striking rather than pretty. Contrary to the popular image of feminists as frumpy, she was fashionably dressed, wearing a hobble skirt over button boots, a navy-blue coat with an oversize belt and deep cuffs, and a hat with a tall feather pinned to its front like a regimental flag.

She was accompanied by Aunt Herm. Lady Hermia was Fitz's other aunt. Unlike her sister, who had married a rich duke, Herm had wedded a thriftless baron who died young and broke. Ten years ago, after Fitz and Maud's parents had both died within a few months, Aunt Herm had moved in to mother the thirteen-year-old Maud. She continued to act as Maud's somewhat ineffectual chaperone.

Fitz said to Maud: "What are you doing here?"

Aunt Herm murmured: "I told you he wouldn't like it, dear."

"I couldn't be absent when the king came to stay," Maud said. "It would have been disrespectful."

Fitz's tone was fondly exasperated. "I don't want you talking to the king about women's rights."

Ethel did not think he needed to worry. Despite Maud's radical politics, she knew how to flatter and flirt with powerful men, and even Fitz's Conservative friends liked her.

"Take my coat, please, Morrison," Maud said. She undid the buttons and turned to allow the footman to remove it. "Hello, Williams. How are you?" she said to Ethel.

"Welcome home, my lady," Ethel said. "Would you like the Gardenia Suite?"

"Thank you. I love that view."

"Will you have some lunch while I'm getting the room ready?"

"Yes, please. I'm starving."

"We're serving it club style today, because guests are arriving at different times." Club style meant that guests were served whenever they came into the dining room, as in a gentlemen's club or a restaurant, instead of all at the same time. It was a modest lunch today: hot mulligatawny soup, cold meats and smoked fish, stuffed trout, lamb cutlets, and a few desserts and cheeses.

Ethel held the door and followed Maud and Herm into the large dining room. Already at lunch were the von Ulrich cousins. Walter von Ulrich, the younger one, was handsome and charming, and seemed delighted to be at Tŷ Gwyn. Robert was fussy: he had straightened the painting of Cardiff Castle on his wall, asked for more pillows, and discovered that the inkwell on his writing desk was dry—an oversight that made Ethel wonder fretfully what else she might have forgotten.

They stood up when the ladies walked in. Maud went straight up to Walter and said: "You haven't changed since you were eighteen! Do you remember me?"

His face lit up. "I do, although you *have* changed since you were thirteen."

They shook hands and then Maud kissed him on both cheeks, as if he were family. "I had the most agonizing schoolgirl passion for you at that age," she said with startling candor.

Walter smiled. "I was rather taken with you, too."

"But you always acted as if I was a terrible young pest!"

"I had to hide my feelings from Fitz, who protected you like a guard dog."

Aunt Herm coughed, indicating her disapproval of this instant intimacy. Maud said: "Aunt, this is Herr Walter von Ulrich, an old school friend of Fitz's who used to come here in the holidays. Now he's a diplomat at the German embassy in London."

Walter said: "May I present my cousin the Graf Robert von Ulrich." *Graf* was German for count, Ethel knew. "He is a military attaché at the Austrian embassy."

They were actually second cousins, Peel had explained gravely to Ethel: their grandfathers had been brothers, the younger of whom had married a German heiress and left Vienna for Berlin, which was how come Walter was German whereas Robert was Austrian. Peel liked to get such things right.

Everyone sat down. Ethel held a chair for Aunt Herm. "Would you like some mulligatawny soup, Lady Hermia?" she asked.

"Yes, please, Williams."

Ethel nodded to a footman, who went to the sideboard where the soup was being kept hot in an urn. Seeing that the new arrivals were comfortable, Ethel quietly left to arrange their rooms. As the door was closing behind her, she heard Walter von Ulrich say: "I remember how fond you were of music, Lady Maud. We were just discussing the Russian ballet. What do you think of Diaghilev?"

Not many men asked a woman for her opinion. Maud would like

that. As Ethel hurried down the stairs to find a couple of maids to do the rooms, she thought: That German is quite a charmer.

{ III }

The Sculpture Hall at Tŷ Gwyn was an anteroom to the dining room. The guests gathered there before dinner. Fitz was not much interested in art—it had all been collected by his grandfather—but the sculptures gave people something to talk about while they were waiting for their dinner.

As he chatted to his aunt the duchess, Fitz looked around anxiously at the men in white tie and tails and the women in low-cut gowns and tiaras. Protocol demanded that every other guest had to be in the room before the king and queen entered. Where was Maud? Surely she would not cause an incident! No, there she was, in a purple silk dress, wearing their mother's diamonds, talking animatedly to Walter von Ulrich.

Fitz and Maud had always been close. Their father had been a distant hero, their mother his unhappy acolyte; the two children had got the affection they needed from each other. After both parents died they had clung together, sharing their grief. Fitz had been eighteen then, and had tried to protect his little sister from the cruel world. She, in turn, had worshipped him. In adulthood, she had become independent-minded, whereas he continued to believe that as head of the family he had authority over her. However, their affection for each other had proved strong enough to survive their differences—so far.

Now she was drawing Walter's attention to a bronze cupid. Unlike Fitz, she understood such things. Fitz prayed she would talk about art all evening and keep off women's rights. George V hated liberals; everyone knew that. Monarchs were usually conservative, but events had sharpened this king's antipathy. He had come to the throne in the middle of a political crisis. Against his will he had been forced, by Liberal prime minister H. H. Asquith—strongly backed by public opinion—to curb the power of the House of Lords. This humiliation still rankled. His Majesty knew that Fitz, as a Conservative peer in the House of Lords, had fought to the last ditch against the so-called reform. All the same, if he were harangued by Maud tonight, he would never forgive Fitz.

Walter was a junior diplomat, but his father was one of the kaiser's oldest friends. Robert, too, was well-connected: he was close to the archduke Franz Ferdinand, the heir to the throne of the Austro-Hungarian Empire. Another guest who moved in exalted circles was the tall young American now talking to the duchess. His name was Gus Dewar, and his father, a senator, was intimate adviser to U.S. president Woodrow Wilson. Fitz felt he had done well in assembling such a group of young men, the ruling elite of the future. He hoped the king was pleased.

Gus Dewar was amiable but awkward. He stooped, as if he would have preferred to be shorter and less conspicuous. He seemed unsure of himself, but he was pleasantly courteous to everyone. "The American people are concerned with domestic issues more than foreign policy," he was saying to the duchess. "But President Wilson is a liberal, and as such he is bound to sympathize with democracies such as France and Britain more than with authoritarian monarchies such as Austria and Germany."

At that moment the double doors opened, the room fell silent, and the king and queen walked in. Princess Bea curtsied, Fitz bowed, and everyone else followed suit. There were a few moments of mildly embarrassed silence, for no one was allowed to speak until one of the royal couple had said something. At last the king said to Bea: "I stayed at this house twenty years ago, you know," and people began to relax.

The king was a neat man, Fitz reflected as the four of them made small talk. His beard and mustache were carefully barbered. His hair was receding, but he had enough left on top to comb with a parting as straight as a ruler. Close-fitting evening clothes suited his slim figure: unlike his father, Edward VII, he was not a gourmet. He relaxed with hobbies that required precision: he liked to collect postage stamps, sticking them meticulously into albums, a pastime that drew mockery from disrespectful London intellectuals.

The queen was a more formidable figure, with graying curls and a severe line to her mouth. She had a magnificent bosom, shown off to great advantage by the extremely low neckline that was currently de rigueur. She was the daughter of a German prince. Originally she had been engaged to George's older brother, Albert, but he had died of pneumonia before the wedding. When George became heir to the throne, he also took over his brother's fiancée, an arrangement that was regarded by some people as a bit medieval.

Bea was in her element. She was enticingly dressed in pink silk, and her fair curls were perfectly arranged to look slightly disordered, as if she had suddenly broken away from an illicit kiss. She talked animatedly to the king. Sensing that mindless chatter would not charm George V, she was telling him how Peter the Great had created the Russian navy, and he was nodding interestedly.

Peel appeared in the dining room door, an expectant look on his freckled face. He caught Fitz's eye and gave an emphatic nod. Fitz said to the queen: "Would you care to go in to dinner, Your Majesty?"

She gave him her arm. Behind them, the king stood arm in arm with Bea, and the rest of the party formed up in pairs according to precedence. When everyone was ready, they walked into the dining room in procession.

"How pretty," the queen murmured when she saw the table.

"Thank you," said Fitz, and breathed a silent sigh of relief. Bea had done a wonderful job. Three chandeliers hung low over the long table. Their reflections twinkled in the crystal glasses at each place. All the cutlery was gold, as were the salt and pepper containers and even the small boxes of matches for smokers. The white tablecloth was strewn with hothouse roses and, in a final dramatic touch, Bea had trailed delicate ferns from the chandeliers down to the pyramids of grapes on golden platters.

Everyone sat down, the bishop said grace, and Fitz relaxed. A party that began well almost always continued successfully. Wine and food made people less disposed to find fault.

The menu began with hors d'oeuvres *Russes*, a nod to Bea's home country: little blinis with caviar and cream, triangles of toast and smoked fish, crackers with soused herring, all washed down with the Perrier-Jouët 1892 champagne, which was as mellow and delicious as Peel had promised. Fitz kept an eye on Peel, and Peel watched the king. As soon as His Majesty put down his cutlery, Peel took away his plate, and that was the signal for the footmen to clear all the rest. Any guest who happened to be still tucking into the dish had to abandon it in deference.

Soup followed, a pot-au-feu, served with a fine dry oloroso sherry from Sanlúcar de Barrameda. The fish was sole, accompanied by a mature Meursault Charmes like a mouthful of gold. With the medallions of Welsh lamb Fitz had chosen the Château Lafite 1875—the 1870 was still not ready to drink. The red wine continued to be served with the parfait of goose liver that followed and with the final meat course, quails with grapes baked in pastry.

No one ate all this. The men took what they fancied and ignored the rest. The women picked at one or two dishes. Many plates went back to the kitchen untouched.

There was salad, a dessert, a savory, fruit, and petits fours. Finally, Princess Bea raised a discreet eyebrow to the queen, who replied with an almost imperceptible nod. They both got up, everyone else stood, and the ladies left the room.

The men sat down again, the footmen brought boxes of cigars, and Peel placed a decanter of Ferreira 1847 port at the king's right hand. Fitz drew thankfully on a cigar. Things had gone well. The king was famously unsociable, feeling comfortable only with old shipmates from his happy navy days. But this evening he had been charming and nothing had gone wrong. Even the oranges had arrived.

Fitz had spoken earlier with Sir Alan Tite, the king's equerry, a retired army officer with old-fashioned side-whiskers. They had agreed that tomorrow the king would have an hour or so alone with each of the men around the table, all of whom had inside knowledge of one government or another. This evening, Fitz was to break the ice with some general political conversation. He cleared his throat and addressed Walter von Ulrich. "Walter, you and I have been friends for fifteen years—we were together at Eton." He turned to Robert. "And I've known your cousin since the three of us shared an apartment in Vienna when we were students." Robert smiled and nodded. Fitz liked them both: Robert was a traditionalist, like Fitz; Walter, though not so conservative, was very clever. "Now we find the world talking about war between our countries," Fitz went on. "Is there really a chance of such a tragedy?"

Walter answered: "If talking about war can make it happen, then yes, we will fight, for everyone is getting ready for it. But is there a real reason? I don't see it."

Gus Dewar raised a tentative hand. Fitz liked Dewar, despite his liberal politics. Americans were supposed to be brash, but this one was well-mannered and a bit shy. He was also startlingly well-informed. Now he said: "Britain and Germany have many reasons to quarrel."

Walter turned to him. "Would you give me an example?"

Gus blew out cigar smoke. "Naval rivalry."

Walter nodded. "My kaiser does not believe there is a God-given law that the German navy should remain smaller than the British forever."

Fitz glanced nervously at the king. He loved the Royal Navy and might easily be offended. On the other hand, Kaiser Wilhelm was his cousin. George's father and Willy's mother had been brother and sister, both children of Queen Victoria. Fitz was relieved to see that His Majesty was smiling indulgently.

Walter went on: "This has caused friction in the past, but for two years now we have been in agreement, informally, about the relative size of our navies."

Dewar said: "How about economic rivalry?"

"It is true that Germany is daily growing more prosperous, and may soon catch up with Britain and the United States in economic production. But why should this be a problem? Germany is one of Britain's biggest customers. The more we have to spend, the more we buy. Our economic strength is good for British manufacturers!"

Dewar tried again. "It's said that Germany wants more colonies."

Fitz glanced at the king again, wondering if he minded the conversation being dominated by these two; but His Majesty appeared fascinated.

Walter said: "There have been wars over colonies, notably in your home country, Mr. Dewar. But nowadays we seem able to decide such squabbles without firing our guns. Three years ago Germany, Great Britain, and France quarreled about Morocco, but the argument was settled without war. More recently, Britain and Germany have reached agreement about the thorny issue of the Baghdad Railway. If we simply carry on as we are, we will not go to war."

Dewar said: "Would you forgive me if I used the term *German militarism*?"

That was a bit strong, and Fitz winced. Walter colored, but he spoke smoothly. "I appreciate your frankness. The German Empire is dominated by Prussians, who play something of the role of the English in Your Majesty's United Kingdom."

It was daring to compare Britain with Germany, and England with Prussia. Walter was right on the edge of what was permissible in a polite conversation, Fitz thought uneasily.

Walter went on: "The Prussians have a strong military tradition, but do not go to war for no reason."

Dewar said skeptically: "So Germany is not aggressive."

"On the contrary," said Walter. "I put it to you that Germany is the *only* major power on mainland Europe that is *not* aggressive."

There was a murmur of surprise around the table, and Fitz saw the king raise his eyebrows. Dewar sat back, startled, and said: "How do you figure that?"

Walter's perfect manners and amiable tone took the edge off his provocative words. "First, consider Austria," he went on. "My Viennese cousin Robert will not deny that the Austro-Hungarian Empire would like to extend its borders to the southeast."

"Not without reason," Robert protested. "That part of the world, which the British call the Balkans, has been part of the Ottoman domain for hundreds of years; but Ottoman rule has crumbled, and now the Balkans are unstable. The Austrian emperor believes it is his holy duty to maintain order and the Christian religion there."

"Quite so," said Walter. "But Russia, too, wants territory in the Balkans."

Fitz felt it was his job to defend the Russian government, perhaps because of Bea. "They, too, have good reasons," he said. "Half their foreign trade crosses the Black Sea, and passes from there through the straits to the Mediterranean Sea. Russia cannot allow any other great power to dominate the straits by acquiring territory in the eastern Balkans. It would be like a noose around the neck of the Russian economy."

"Exactly so," said Walter. "Turning to the western end of Europe, France has ambitions to take from Germany the territories of Alsace and Lorraine."

At this point the French guest, Jean-Pierre Charlois, bridled. "Stolen from France forty-three years ago!"

"I will not argue about that," Walter said. "Let us say that Alsace-Lorraine was joined to the German Empire in 1871, after the defeat of France in the Franco-Prussian War. Whether stolen or not, you allow, Monsieur le Comte, that France wants those lands back."

"Naturally." The Frenchman sat back and sipped his port.

Walter said: "Even Italy would like to take, from Austria, the territories of Trentino—"

"Where most people speak Italian!" cried Signor Falli.

"—plus much of the Dalmatian coast—"

"Full of Venetian lions, Catholic churches, and Roman columns!"

"—and Tyrol, a province with a long history of self-government, where most people speak German."

"Strategic necessity."

"Of course."

Fitz realized how clever Walter had been. Not rude, but discreetly provocative, he had stung the representatives of each nation into confirming, in more or less belligerent language, their territorial ambitions.

Now Walter said: "But what new territory is Germany asking for?" He looked around the table, but no one spoke. "None," he said triumphantly. "And the only other major country in Europe that can say the same is Britain!"

Gus Dewar passed the port and said in his American drawl: "I guess that's right."

Walter said: "So why, my old friend Fitz, should we ever go to war?"

FROM

The Gendarme

BY

Mark T. Mustian

**"A harrowing and truly important
novel by a splendid American writer."**
—Robert Olen Butler,
Pulitzer Prize-winning author of *Hell*

*In his dreams he's a gendarme, a soldier marching Armenians
out of Turkey and committing unspeakable acts. Yet he feels
compelled to spare one remarkable woman: Araxie, the girl
with the piercing eyes.*

As the past and present bleed together in The
Gendarme, *Emmett Conn sets out on one final journey
to find Araxie and beg forgiveness before it's too late. With
uncompromising vision and boundless compassion, Mark Y.
Mustain has written a transcendent meditation on the power
of memory—and the dangers of forgetting who we are and
have been.*

1

I awake in a whispering ambulance.

Attendants huddle, a gloved finger withdraws.

Memory makes its way back: the crush of the head-ache, the darkness. I am cold now. My face is numb.

"Can you hear me?"

Başım . . .

"What is your name?"

Speech half forms. In English? At length, "Em . . . Em . . . Emmett Conn."

"Where do you live?"

I think. "Twenty-three fifteen Wisteria Court. Wades-boro, Georgia." The words flow easier.

"When were you born?"

I pause, for I do not truly know. "The year 1898." This is what I have said, for many years now. "I am ninety-two years old."

A light shines in my eyes, twisting the headache's slow thrust. I smell alcohol. Metallic voices flutter. The siren rises—did I not hear it? Then silence, except for a buzzing sound, and darkness. Sleep falls. Is this it?

A sudden burst of coldness comes, then nothing.

I wake. A chill shakes and leaves me, a great wind rushing past. The headache remains, confined now to a solitary spot, perhaps a single nerve ending. I touch my face. A television speaks somewhere, perhaps in a different room. I see no window, no natural light. I am . . . where?

A rustling sounds next to me. Shapes form and dissolve into a woman, a voice.

"You're awake."

For a moment I think I am back there, injured. A prisoner. Unidentified Patient Number A-17.

"How are you feeling?"

I close my eyes. I was a soldier. My injury left me without memory, of the war or much before it.

"A neighbor saw you collapse," the woman whispers. "You had a seizure. They're going to run tests."

"For what?" I try to still myself, even my pulse.

She pauses. "A stroke. Or a brain . . . something."

I attempt a smile, for there is humor in it. A brain something. I shift in her direction, the headache stabbing its response.

"I am an old man."

"They're calling your daughter," she says. My daughter who stays away.

This woman—nurse?—pulls the sheet. "Where are you from?"

I sigh. My foreignness, found at just a few syllables. Despite all the years, all my efforts at English.

"I am an American." I say this. The woman nods.

"We're gonna set you up for an MRI."

She says something more, but a tiredness creeps over me. Arms become elbows become joints, PVC pipe. Plastic tubing spawns hair. I think, How have I lived, for so long now?

I sleep.

Coldness again, and wind. This time I can see—a long, windswept plain, and a train, an ancient steam locomotive, spewing black smoke tossed sideways by the wind. The smoke smells vile and heavy, not the sweet odor of burning wood, but harsher, more primitive. The oddness of smell permeating a dream tugs at me. The train sways. I do not recognize the surroundings.

It looks to be late afternoon, maybe spring or summer. The wind rushes across the plain, barren except for the train and a few dusty trees. The train is barely moving; in fact, I seem to be moving faster, in the same direction, bobbing my head like the mast on a ship. In the distance to my left, at the far end of the plain, red and violet mountains merge with the horizon. The sun stands on my right in what appears to be a sinking posture, placing my bearing as southerly. I hear nothing, which makes it seem surreal, even otherworldly, except for the train, and then the people.

A black line of humanity, several hundred long, trudges in the same direction the train moves. I wonder why I hadn't noticed them before—perhaps the languidness of their pace, perhaps the way they mesh with the shadow. They look to be pilgrims of some sort, dressed mostly in black, with the high collars and shawls of those who seek comfort from the past. A few ride on mules, and here and there a wagon breaks the uniformity of the line, a line that sweeps out to the horizon, longer than I had first noticed, thousands instead of hundreds, maybe more. Figures on horseback pace beside them, erect, dipping, like dogs nudging a herd. I reach down, recognizing my buckle and weave as that of a rider. My hand strikes the hardness of metal and wood, the elongated form of a rifle. For a moment it feels so familiar. Then it trails away, in a blast of cold and wind, the chill condensed to a pinpoint, like after the first headache. Then gone.

The gurney glides along the polished floor. A surgery sign, a black arrow. Post-Op, an arrow. Rumbling, rotating, a large vessel's slow movement. People passing, speaking. Oncology, arrow. Radiology, arrow. A final turn, a slowing.

A heavyset nurse runs a hand through red hair.

"Are you able to sit?"

Lights blink and shimmer. The headache has nearly

vanished, a tenderness in its place like a newly formed bruise. It hurts if I move my head quickly, or if I look at the overhead light. I move slowly, cautiously. I lift a hand to my face.

The nurse prods me onto another gurney, this one attached to a large machine.

"Lie down here, with your head on this headrest."

I move to comply, a man with his fragile egg-head. I think again—I cannot help it—of before, of the hospital. Seven decades before. Almost a year to remember my name. I should have died then. Without Carol I would have.

"Let's scoot you up a bit."

My memory is fine from the hospital forward, but before is still darkness, only speckles of light. I remember almost nothing of the war, the Great War. I rarely dream.

"Lie as still as you can." The voice comes through an earpiece. A plastic object is placed in my hand. "Use the panic button if you need to."

The bench slides inside the machine. The apparatus whooshes and clicks. The machine accelerates to buzzing, then clanging, loud to the point of pain. The earplugs rattle and bounce in my ears. I wonder again at the purpose of this—to add a few breaths to my life? Carol is dead, dead now three years. I am alive. Ninety-two years have passed— for what? For *what*?

I finger the panic button. Then, gently, release it.

2

The horse sways under me, the wind back in my face. It is dark. The light of a campfire flickers off to my right. Sounds carry on the wind, yelps of pain, guttural grunts and moans. Words snap and volley: admonishments to be quiet, directions to get up. A faint sobbing crescendos and lessens, stops. The word *gâvur* sprouts in front of me, hurled as an accusation. *Bahşiş Sigara.* Groupings of consonants, vowels, clips and snorts strung together as symbol, as communication. Snarling, human conversation.

It dawns on me, even through the depths of the dream, that I know this language. I have always known it. It is odd, this, to dream and recognize the dreaming, to dangle beyond the vision like a watchful ghost or god. For an instant I see myself astride the horse, bundled against the wind by a mottled wool blanket, my face scruffy and bearded, my hair long and free. Young, maybe seventeen, thin and upright, dark eyes, heavy brow. Then everything swirls, like a rotating camera, until I find myself back atop the swaying animal, pulling and prodding, peering through darkness at gray things below.

A man straddles a prone form, his bare rump visible in the dim light. He looks up at my approach, smiles in recognition, decouples, extends his arm toward the object beneath. A young girl lies below him, her face darkened with mud. I shake my head, declining, observing his gap-filled grin, his filthy beard, his still-erect *kamış*. Izzet is his name; I knew him somewhere before. Then he is on her again, grunting, the girl whimpering, the slapping sound of flesh on flesh mixed with the wind. I wonder at it a moment, at why I am here, why I seem to know this place yet not to know it, why I understand this language but cannot place it. I smell the smoke of the campfire, hear the shouts and the groans and the rustles. I feel the wind. I touch my own mouth. A certainty strikes that I have been here before, that I have ridden this horse, spoken these words, borne the same silent witness, watching and waiting. And then it is gone, leaving only the dark and the cold, and the wind. I pull the blanket tighter around me, and continue on through the night.

A man fingers my face. I do not know my surroundings, my name. Liquid drips on a hard surface, metal rattles, the smell of medicine floats—all familiar, all strange. Am I among enemies? My hands shake, my body tensed in protection, until the round, smooth face of Dr. Harry Wan registers, like a key clicking true in a lock. I recognize the hospital's bright lights, the static intercom announcements, the smells of plastic and urine. I am Emmett Conn. I am in the United States. It is April 1990.

"How are you this day?"

The dream still tugs at me, the coldness and wind. I smell the sweat of the horse.

"Can you understand me? You may nod yes or no."

I nod affirmatively. My head is sluggish, not my own.

"Good!"

I remember that Dr. Wan is perpetually cheerful, prone to elaborate bows and exclamations of "wonderful." He and I are Rotarians, one of the things Carol tossed me into to acclimate me to Wadesboro. That effort failed, but I remain a member. The others have become used to me, or at best feign indifference. I am an outsider—a Yankee, a foreigner. A transplant. An old man.

"You have what looks to be a brain tumor, Mr. Conn." He smiles as he says this, as if I have won a big prize. "A glioma. It is about the size of a pea, located at the base of the left parietal lobe. We will do a biopsy, confirm the best course of action. We may want to try radiosurgery. It is something new."

He stops to let this sink in. My daughter Violet leans forward, her frown transformed and whisked into a smile. The edge of her mouth curls like Carol's, her mother. I haven't seen her in . . . months? For this I blame myself— we have long had our difficulties. We are in ways so alike.

I am pleased she has come now, even under these circumstances.

"Dr. Wan, at my age . . ."

"Shush." Violet spreads her long fingers. "I spoke to him earlier. Dr. Wan says you are in fantastic shape. He says others older than you have been treated and lived active lives. He is a leader in this field."

I shake my head no. But I think, To be wanted now. Yes.

She leans farther in, exposing dark gums. Has she dreaded this day? She must care for me, comfort me. "Papa. Please."

I nod, confused. Her tone has a hunger. Has she told her sister? The boy Wilfred, her son? For a moment it is 1932, and I am working, working. I realize, as I lie here, that the language in the dream had been Turkish.

The doctor moves closer, speaking in low tones, explaining. There are protocols, possibilities. Malignancy, metastasis, radiation, surgery. My eyes water and I fight welling tears; I cry so easily now, whereas earlier in my life I did not cry at all. The treatment he mentions seems so modern, so unappealing. I see myself: "World's Oldest Patient Receives New Procedure." Dr. Wan's face on a journal. I wonder about payments, insurance. Will someone care for Sultan, my cat? But it is all in the distance. In some strange way I am still in the dream, wounded or dying or already dead.

"Okay," I say.

There are smiles, exhaled breaths.

"You had a head injury once, is that right, Mr. Conn?"

"Yes, in the war." Violet must have told him. Nineteen fifteen. World War I, not II. It led to my marriage, to my coming to America. To the things I remember. To my life.

"Do you have records?"

I look at Violet. "Yes."

He looks at me quizzically. "You fought for the U.S.?"

I shake my head. "No." The headache gains force, like a storm's gathered winds.

Dr. Wan looks on, beaming.

"Wonderful!" he announces, and exits the room.

Dawn approaches in a softening gray. Men mutter, distant, a breeze stifling words and brief bursts of rough laughter. A fire glints and sparks but I am separate, removed. Leaves rustle in trees that shield the starlight spread beyond.

I sit with my back against a trunk's smoothness, watching and listening. Leaves turn and still. Birds twitter, one swooping down to peck in the near darkness. I watch the way its head moves, its tail flicks. It lifts its beak up to gulp food in and swallow. Does it feel pleasure? Know pain? It stares at me one-eyed. Then it flits away.

I turn my head to the campfire, to the dark shapes before it. Beyond lie the others, those permitted no fires, those that sleep on the ground in the cold and dream of home or of death. Some will not wake to this dawn, others may rise but will fall, unable to continue. Some will give up, the older ones or the children, or those who have lost almost everything else. Others will trudge on, stumble to the next campsite, collapse, rise again. At first some cried and complained and begged for water, but most of those are now gone. Only the sturdy remain, and those still with valuables useful for bribes. Maybe seven hundred, from what had once been two thousand. Shuffling, marching, day after day.

I think on how I have come to be here, a tiredness muddling my memory so that bits emerge, almost unwillingly. My name, Ahmet. My father's name, Mehmed. The certainty that the next town is not far. The necessity of reporting to officials in Katma. The days it will take for the return journey home. The fact that my father is dead, that his death sent me here. That I must complete this assignment to gain entry into the army. It all swirls together, then washes away, caught in a blurred exhaustion of dim dream and remembrance. My head nods. I must wake. There are obligations, responsibilities.

I stand, fumbling in my trousers. My urine crackles on dry leaves. Another sound intrudes, or perhaps a smell. I whirl to find a figure standing apart in the gloom. I release myself with one hand, grab my rifle with the other. I adjust my clothing. The figure backs away.

"Who is it?" I ask, pointing the rifle.

The figure continues its retreat.

"Halt!"

The figure stops. I draw closer, the rifle erect in front of me, leaves crunching beneath my feet. I near the edge of the trees.

It is a woman. One of them—the baggy, dark clothes, the braided hair, the large eyes. Out trying to escape, or perhaps murder a guard. I have heard of such things. My charges have been mostly docile, cowed into submission by deprivation and the judicious culling of their men. But I must take care.

I stick the rifle barrel under her chin, lifting her face. I edge her backward, into a plume of glimmering light.

Her face hangs words half formed in my throat. She has mismatched eyes, one dark, the other light, as if neither perfect gene could be denied by her mother. I attribute it at first to the starlight. I even turn her a full rotation to get a better, closer look. The thought strikes that she has been blinded in the light eye, but I know this is not true, as both eyes are alive, reflecting the heavens stretched and glowing above us. I stand silent, struck by this oddity, wondering how I have not seen it before, how she has survived this long march without others taking advantage. She is beautiful beyond the exoticism. She is maybe in her early teens, the small rise of breasts evident beneath the oversized garments.

"What are you doing?" I ask, my voice almost shaky. I could have this girl, now, here on the ground, if I wished.

The eyes stare back, unblinking, as if detached from the body. They resemble, in a way, the blank eyes of a corpse, vacant, almost unseeing. I wonder again if she has suffered some injury.

I finger the rifle. My mouth lathers and dries.

"I was collecting eucalyptus leaves," the girl says quietly. She raises an arm to indicate a bag held in one hand. She does not seem afraid like the others, nor hateful, nor particularly submissive. When I touch my hand to her face, she neither flinches nor cries. Her skin is soft, cooled by the breath of the wind.

I release my hand. We stand for some time, until I step aside to let her pass. I feel confused afterward, as to my actions, as to why I made no move to take her. I convince myself I am merely saving her for later, like a man who saves his sweets for after his meal.

I turn before she vanishes under the trees. "What is your name?" I ask.

She does not respond, or if she does, her name is lost in the leaves.

FROM

The Lake of Dreams

BY

Kim Edwards

**The highly anticipated new novel from
the #1 *New York Times* bestselling author of
*The Memory Keeper's Daughter***

At a crossroads in her life, Lucy Jarrett returns home to upstate New York, only to find herself haunted by her father's unresolved death a decade ago. Late one night, as she paces the hallways of her family's rambling lakeside house, she discovers a collection of objects that first appear to be useless curiosities, but soon reveal a deeper and more complex family past. As Lucy discovers and explores the traces of her lineage, the family story she has always known is shattered; her quest for the truth reconfigures her family's history and yields dramatic insights that embolden her to live freely.

Chapter 1

MY NAME IS LUCY JARRETT, AND BEFORE I KNEW ABOUT THE girl in the window, before I went home and stumbled on the fragments and began to piece the story back together, I found myself living in a village near the sea in Japan. It had been a spring of little earthquakes, and that night I woke abruptly, jarred from a dream. Footsteps faded in the cobblestone lane and distant trains rumbled; I listened harder until I could make out the surge of the sea. But that was all. Yoshi's hand rested on my hip lightly, as if we were still dancing, which we'd been doing earlier in the evening, music from the radio soft in the dark kitchen, our steps slowing until we stopped altogether and stood kissing in the jasmine air.

I lay back down, curving toward his warmth. In the dream I'd gone back to the lake where I'd grown up. I didn't want to go, but I did. The sky was overcast, the faded green cabin—which I'd seen before, but only in dreams—musty and overhung with trees. Its windows were cracked, opaque with dust and snow. I walked past it to the shore, walked out onto the thick, translucent ice. I walked until I came to them. So many people, living their lives just beneath the surface. I caught them in glimpses, fell to my knees, pressed my palms against the glassy surface— so thick, so clear, so cold. I'd put them here, somehow, I knew that. I'd left them for so long. Their hair stirred in underwater currents, and their eyes, when they met mine, were full of a longing that matched my own.

The window shades were trembling. I tensed, caught between the earthquakes and the dream, but it was just a distant train, fading into the mountains. Every night for a week I'd had this same dream, stirred up by the shifting earth, stirring up the past. It took me back to a night when I was seventeen, wild and restless, sliding off the back of Keegan Fall's motorcycle, apple blossoms as pale as stars above us. I fanned my fingers against his chest before he left, the engine ripping through the night. My father was in the garden when I turned toward the house. Moonlight caught the gray in his short hair; the tip of his cigarette burned, rising, falling. Lilacs and early roses floated in the darkness. *Nice of you to show up,* my father said. *I'm sorry you worried,* I told him. A silence, the scents of lake water and compost and green shoots splitting open the dark earth, and then he said, *Want to go fishing with me, Lucy? How about it? It's been a long time.* His words were wistful, and I remembered getting up before dawn to meet him, struggling to carry the tackle box as we crossed the lawn to the boat. I wanted to go fishing, to accept my father's invitation, but I wanted more to go upstairs to think about Keegan Fall. So I turned away, and in a tone as sharp as broken shells I said, *Dad. Really. I'm hardly little anymore.*

Those were the last words I ever spoke to him. Hours later, waking to sunlight and urgent voices, I ran downstairs and across the dew-struck lawn to the shore, where they had pulled my father from the lake. My mother was kneeling in the shallow water, touching his cheek with her fingertips. His lips and skin were bluish. There were traces of foam in the corner of his mouth, and his eyelids were oddly iridescent. *Like a fish,* I thought, a crazy thought, but at least it silenced the other thoughts, which were worse, and which have never left me: *If I'd gone. If I'd been there. If only I'd said yes.*

Beside me on the tatami Yoshi sighed and stirred, his hand slipping from my hip. Moonlight fell in a rectangle across the floor, and the shades rustled faintly with the distant pounding surf, the breeze. Gradually, almost imperceptibly, the shaking grew stronger. It was subtle at first, as soft as the rumble from the train a moment before. Then my Tibetan singing bowls, arranged on the floor, began to hum all by themselves. My collection of small stones began to fall from the bookshelf, hitting the mats with a sound like rain. Downstairs, something crashed, shattered. I held my breath, as if by being still I could still the world, but the trembling grew stronger, and stronger still. The shelves lurched sharply, heaving several books to the floor. Then, in one fluid convulsion, the walls swayed and the floor seemed to roll, as if some great animal had roused and turned, as if the earth itself were alive, the ground mere skin, and volatile.

Abruptly, it stopped. Everything was strangely quiet. Distantly, water dripped into a pool. Yoshi's breathing was calm and even.

I turned and shook his shoulder. He opened his eyes slowly. These little earthquakes left him unfazed, though that season there had been hundreds of tremors, sometimes several dozen in a day, many so tiny they were noted only by seismic machines; others, like this one, strong enough to wake us.

"Earthquake?" he murmured.

"Yes, a big one. Something broke downstairs."

"Really? Well, it is over now. It's quiet, no? Let's go back to sleep."

He closed his eyes and pulled me close. His breathing quickly grew deep and regular again. Through the half-open window, beyond the roof of the house across the street, I glimpsed the scattered stars. "Yoshi?" I said. When he didn't answer, I slid out of bed and went downstairs.

The aloe plant had fallen from the kitchen windowsill, and its pot had shattered. I put water on to boil and swept up the scattered dirt and glass and broken stems. Probably Japanese housewives were doing the same thing all up and down the street, which made me feel uncomfortable and faintly bitter—clearly, I'd been without a job for far too long. I didn't like being dependent on Yoshi, having no income or meaningful work outside the house. I'm a hydrologist, which is to say that I study the movement of water in the world, on the surface and beneath the earth, and I'd been doing research for multinational companies for nearly half a decade by the time I met Yoshi in Jakarta. We'd fallen in love the way it is possible to fall in love overseas, cut off from everything we'd known, so the country we inhabited was of our own making, really, and subject to our own desires. *This is the only continent that matters,* Yoshi used to say, running his hands along my body. *This is the only world that exists.* For a year, then two years, we were very happy. Then our contracts ended. Before I found work, Yoshi was offered what seemed at first like the engineering job of his dreams. That's when we moved to Japan, which had turned out to be another country altogether.

I poured myself a cup of tea and took it to the front room, sliding open the shutters and the windows. Night air flooded in, fresh and cool. It was still dark, but the neighborhood was already stirring; water splashed and plates clattered, near and far. Across the narrow lane the neighbors spoke softly, back and forth.

The house shook lightly with the surf, then settled. I sat at the low table and sipped my tea, letting my thoughts wander to the coming day and our long-planned trip into the mountains. In Indonesia, that other country, Yoshi and I had talked of marriage and even of children, but in those vague fantasies I'd always had satisfying work, or I'd been content to study Japanese and flower arranging and to take long solitary hikes. I hadn't understood how isolating unemployment would be, or how much time Yoshi would end up devoting to his own work. Lately we'd been out of sorts with each other, arguments flaring up over nothing. I hadn't realized how persistent the past would be, either, catching me in its old gravity the minute I slowed down. After three idle months in Japan I started teaching English just to fill my days with voices other than my own. I took my young charges on walks, pausing by the sea to teach concrete nouns: *stone, water, wave,* yearning for the days when I'd used those same words with ease and fluidity in my routine work. Sometimes I found myself saying wilder things, things I was sure they could not understand. *Dinosaurs drank this water, did you know that? Water moves forever in a circle; someday, little ones, your grandchildren may even drink your tears.*

Now, weeks later, I was beginning to wonder if this would be my life, after all, and not simply a brief interlude in the life I had imagined.

Across the room, tiny lights flickered on my laptop. I got up to check e-mail, the glow from the screen casting my hands and arms in pale blue. Sixteen messages, most of them spam, two from friends in Sri Lanka, three others from former colleagues in Jakarta who'd sent photos from their hike in the jungle. I skimmed these messages quickly, remembering a river trip we'd taken with these friends, the lush foliage along the banks and the hats we'd fashioned from water lilies to block the fierce sun, filled with longing for the life Yoshi and I had left.

Three sequential messages were from home. The first, from my mother, surprised me. We were in touch quite often and I tried to visit once a year, even if briefly, but my mother used the Internet like an earlier generation had used the long-distance telephone: seldom, succinctly, and only for matters of certain importance. Mostly, we talked on the phone or sent slim blue air letters, hers posted to wherever my nomadic life had taken me, mine landing in the mailbox outside the rambling house where I'd grown up, in a village called The Lake of Dreams.

Lucy, I was in an accident, but it was minor and you are absolutely not to worry. Take any news from Blake with a grain of salt, please. He means well, of course, but he is being overprotective and kind of driving me crazy. I'm nearly sure my wrist is sprained, not broken. The doctor said the x-rays will confirm one way or the other. There's no need at all for you to come home.

I read this message twice, imagining my mother at her solitary kitchen table, somehow injured. Though it wasn't fair—nearly ten years had passed and we had all moved on, at least on the surface—I felt myself drawn back to the summer after my father's death. We'd gone through our days doing the usual things, trying to create a fragile order. We made meals we hardly touched, and passed in the halls without speaking; my mother started sleeping in the spare room downstairs, and began to close the second floor down, room by room. Her grief was at the center of the stillness in the house, and we all moved carefully, so quietly, around it; if I allowed myself to weep or rage, everything might shatter, so I held still. Even now, when I went back to visit I always felt myself falling into those old patterns, the world circumscribed by loss.

The next e-mail was indeed from Blake, which alarmed me. Blake spent his summers living on his sailboat and working as a pilot for the cruises that left from The Lake of Dreams pier every two hours; he spent his winters in St. Croix doing much the same. He liked Skype, and twice he'd flown across the world to visit me, but he didn't like e-mail and almost never wrote. He gave more details about the accident—someone had run a stop sign, and he described my mother's car as totaled—but he didn't sound overprotective to me, just concerned. It was my cousin Zoe who sounded a little out of control, but then she always did. She had been born when I was nearly fourteen, and she was so much younger than the rest of us that it sometimes seemed she'd grown up in a completely different family. Her older brother, Joey, was about my age, heir to the family name and the family fortunes, and we'd never gotten along. But Zoe, who was fifteen now and adored the Internet, found my life amazing and exotic, and she wrote frequently to relay dramatic events from high school, even though I seldom wrote back.

It was nearly dawn. I got up and went to the window. Outside, the cobblestones were brightening to gray, wooden houses emerging from the night. Across the street, a subdued rattling of pots jarred me from my thoughts, followed by the sound of water running. Mrs. Fujimoro came out to sweep her walk. I stepped out onto the patio, nodding good morning. Her broom made such firm strokes—swish, swish, swish— that until she paused I didn't realize the earth had begun to rumble again. It was ordinary at first, a large wave hitting the shore, a truck passing down the street—but no. I met Mrs. Fujimoro's gaze. She caught my hand as the shaking extended, began to swell.

Leaves quivered and water trembled in a puddle. A tiny crack appeared below the Fujimoros' kitchen window, zigzagging to the foundation. I held her hand, staying very still, thinking of my mother's accident, of the moment she realized she could no more stop the car from smashing into her than she could alter the progress of the moon.

The tremor stopped. A child's questioning voice floated from the house. Mrs. Fujimoro took a deep breath, stepped away from me, and bowed. She picked up her broom. Her expression, so recently unmasked, was already distant again. I stood alone on the worn cobblestones.

"You turned off your gas?" she asked.

"Oh, yes!" I assured her. "Yes, I turned off the gas!" We had this exchange often; it was one of my few phrases of perfect Japanese.

Yoshi was in the doorway by the time I turned, his hair tousled and an old T-shirt pulled on over his running shorts. He had a kind face, and he gave a slight bow to Mrs. Fujimoro, who bowed in turn and spoke to him in rapid Japanese. Her husband had been a schoolmate of Yoshi's father, and we rented the house from them. On the rare occasions when Yoshi's parents visited from London—his mother is British—they stayed in another flat the Fujimoros owned around the corner.

"What were you talking about?" I asked when Yoshi finally bowed again to Mrs. Fujimoro and stepped back inside. He'd grown up bilingual and moved with fluid ease between languages, something I both admired and envied.

"Oh, she was telling me about the Great Kanto Earthquake in the twenties. Some of her family died in it, and she thinks that's why she gets so afraid, even in the little tremors. She's terrified of fires. And she's sorry if she startled you by taking your hand."

"It's all right," I said, following Yoshi to the kitchen, picking up my empty cup on the way. "The earthquakes scare me, too. I don't know how you can be so calm."

"Well, they either stop or they don't. There's not much you can do, is there? Besides, look," he added, gesturing to the paper, which of course I couldn't read. "Front page. It says an island is forming underwater, and then everything will improve. This is just a release of pressure."

"Great. Very reassuring." I watched him add water to the tea, his movements easy, practiced. "Yoshi, my mother was in an accident," I said.

He looked up.

"What happened? Is she okay?"

"A car accident. Not serious, I don't think. Or serious, but she's fine anyway. It depends on whose story you read."

"Ah. That's really too bad. You'll go see her?"

I didn't answer immediately. Did he want me to go? Would that be a relief? "I don't think so," I said, finally. "She says she's okay. Besides, I need to find a job."

Yoshi fixed me with the kind expression that had once drawn me to him and now often made me feel so claustrophobic: as if he understood me, inside out.

"Next week, next month, you can still look for jobs."

I glanced out the kitchen window at the wall of the house next door.

"No, Yoshi. I really don't want to put it off. All this free time is making me a little crazy, I think."

"Well," Yoshi said cheerfully, sitting at the table. "I can't argue with that."

"I've looked hard," I told him tersely. "You have no idea."

Yoshi was peeling a mandarin orange in a skillful way that left the skin almost intact, like an empty lantern, and he didn't look up.

"Well, what about that consultancy—the one on the Chinese dam project on the Mekong? Did you follow through on that?"

"Not yet. It's on my list."

"Your list—Lucy, how long can it be?"

Now I took a deep breath before I answered. We'd been looking forward to this hike in the mountains for weeks, and I didn't want to argue. "I've been researching that firm," I said, finally, trying to remember that just hours ago we'd been dancing in this same room, the air around us dark and fragrant.

Yoshi offered me a segment of his orange. These little oranges, *mikan*s, grew on the trees in the nearby hills and looked like bright ornaments when they ripened. We'd seen them when we visited last fall, back when Yoshi had just been offered this job and everything still seemed full of possibilities.

"Lucy, why not take a break and go see your mother? I could meet you there, too, after this business trip to Jakarta. I'd like to do that. I'd like to meet her."

"But it's such a long way."

"Not unless you're planning to walk."

I laughed, but Yoshi was serious. His eyes, the color of onyx, as dark as the bottom of a lake, were fixed on me. I caught my breath, remembering the night before, how he'd held my gaze without blinking while his fingers moved so lightly across my skin. Yoshi traveled often for his job—an engineer, he designed bridges for a company that had branches in several countries—and this trip had seemed like just one more absence to add to all the others. How ironic if now his job became a way for us to reconnect.

"Don't you ever want me to meet her?" he pressed.

"It's not that," I said, and it really wasn't. I picked up the empty orange skin, light in my palm. "It's just the timing. Besides, my mother's condition isn't serious. It's not exactly an emergency situation."

Yoshi shrugged, taking another orange from the cobalt bowl. "Sometimes loneliness is an emergency situation, Lucy."

"What do you mean?"

"I mean that lately you seem like a very sad and lonely person, that's all."

I looked away, blinking in surprise as my eyes, inexplicably, filled with tears.

"Hey." He touched my hand; his fingertips were sticky. "Look, Lucy,

I'm sorry, okay? Let's not worry about this. Let's just go up to the mountains, like we planned."

So we did. It was muggy near the sea but grew into a high, bright, sunny day as the train switchbacked up the mountain. In early spring, plum trees and cherry trees had blossomed against this landscape, blanketing the ground with white petals, and my vocabulary lessons then had been like poems: *tree, flowers, falling, petals, snow.* Now it was late enough in the season that rice had risen from the watery land near the sea, but in the mountains, spring lingered. The hydrangeas were just beginning to bloom, their clusters of petals faintly green, bleeding into lavender and blue, pressing densely against the windows of the train.

We hiked to an open-air museum beneath a canopy of cedar trees and ate in a mountain village built on the rim of a dormant volcano, and our talk was easy, relaxed, and happy, like our best times together. It was nearly dusk by the time we reached the *rotemboro,* an outdoor hot springs, and parted at the door. The changing room was all clear pine and running water, tranquil, soothing, and almost empty. I scrubbed carefully from head to toe, sluicing warm water to rinse, walking naked to the rock-lined pool. The air was cool, and the moon was rising in the indigo sky. Two other women were lounging against the smooth stones, chatting, their skin white against the wet gray rocks, their pale bodies disappearing into the water at the waist. Their voices were one soft sound; the trickle of water from the spring, another. Farther away, from beyond the wall, came the splashing and the voices of the men.

I slipped into the steaming water, imagining the patterns of underground rivers that fed these springs, thinking how everything was connected, and how our lives here had grown from such a casual decision made during my first weeks in Jakarta well over two years ago. I'd come back tired from a week in the field inspecting a canal system, and I dropped my suitcase on the cool marble floor, imagining nothing beyond a shower, a plate of *nasi goreng,* and a drink. My housemate, who worked at the Irish embassy, was leaving for a party and invited me to go, promising good food and better music. I said no at first, but at the last minute I changed my mind. If I hadn't gone, Yoshi and I would never have met.

The party was in a large house that buzzed with music and laughter. I wore a dark blue silk sheath I'd had made, a perfect fit and a good color for my eyes, and for a while I moved through the rooms, laughing, talking. Then I passed a quiet balcony and, on an impulse, slipped out for some air. Yoshi was leaning against the railing, gazing at the river below. I hesitated, because there was something about his stance that made me wish not to disturb him. But he turned, smiling in that way he has where his whole face is illuminated, warm and welcoming. He asked if I wanted to come and watch the water.

I did. I crossed the tiled floor and stood beside him at the railing. We didn't speak much at first, mesmerized by the swift, muddy currents. When we did start talking, we found we had a lot in common. In addition to our work and love of travel, we were the same age, and we were both allergic to beer. Our conversation flowed so swiftly that we didn't notice the people who came and went, or our empty glasses, or the changing sky, not until the monsoon rain began to pour down with tropical suddenness and intensity. We looked at each other then and started laughing, and Yoshi lifted his hands to the outpouring of the skies. Since we were already drenched, there seemed no point in going inside. We talked on the balcony until the rain ceased as suddenly as it had begun. Yoshi walked me home through the dark and steamy streets. When we reached my house he ran the palms of his hands across my cheeks to smooth away the water, and kissed me.

At first it was easy enough to keep the relationship from gaining traction. I'd had enough of the transitory, long-distance love affairs that happen inevitably for people who travel so much. Then the rains began again. They came early that year, and with an unusual ferocity, overwhelming the city's open canal systems and flooding the streets. Much of Jakarta was low-lying and susceptible to water, and the sprawling development around the city—a loss of trees and green spaces—had left few places to absorb the rain. The water rose, and rose. One morning fish were swimming in the flooded lawn, and by noon water was five inches deep in the living room. My roommate and I watched on the news as the flood washed away cars, the fronts of buildings, and an entire village of 143 people.

As the water began to recede, Yoshi and two coworkers organized a cleanup at an orphanage. He picked me up in an old Nissan truck he'd borrowed and we drove through the drenched and devastated city. The orphanage grounds were awash in mud and filled with debris. It stank. We worked all that day and all the next, and Yoshi was everywhere, shoveling mud and orchestrating volunteers. Once, he paused beside a boy in a worn red shirt who stood crying in the mud, then picked him up and carried him inside.

When he brought me home at the end of that second day, the skies opened again. Running from the car, reaching for my house keys, I slipped and grabbed a mango tree to keep from falling. A cascade of leaves and twigs showered down, scattering seeds and pollen, desiccated stems. I was already a mess from cleaning. Yoshi took my arm and we fumbled our way inside. *You're shivering,* he said, *come here.* We let our wet clothes fall by the steaming shower. *Close your eyes,* he said, stepping behind me, the warm water pouring over us, and then his hands were moving in my hair, working the shampoo through every strand, caressing my scalp, massaging my shoulders, the cold and grime draining away, my tension and uncertainties draining away. My arms eased under his touch, he held my breasts like flowers, and I turned.

And now we were here, all these days and miles away, Yoshi's voice, his laughter, drifting over the wall that divided the hot springs pool. I slid deeper into the water, resting my head on the damp rocks. My limbs floated, faintly luminous, and steam rose; the women across from me chatted softly. They were mother and daughter, I thought, or sisters born years apart, for their bodies were similar in shape, and their gestures mirrored each other's. I thought again of my own mother, sitting alone in her house.

Lately you seem like a very sad and lonely person. The comment still smarted, but I had to wonder if it was true. I'd left for college just weeks after my father died, numb but determined to escape the silence that had descended on the house like a dark enchantment. Keegan Fall had tried again and again to break it, but I'd sent him away harshly, two times, three times, until he stopped calling. In the years since, I'd moved—from college to grad school, from good jobs to better ones and through a whole series of romances, leaving all that grief behind, never letting myself slow down. Until now, unemployed in Japan, I had paused.

One by one, the women stepped out of the pool, water dripping onto the stones, causing little waves. I remembered my dream, the faces just beneath the surface of the ice. My father used to tell me stories where I was always the heroine and the ending was always happy. Nothing had prepared me for the shock of his death. He had fallen, it was determined in the autopsy, and hit his head on the boat and slipped beneath the water, a freak accident that could not fully be explained, or ever undone. His fishing pole had been recovered days later, tangled in the reeds at the edge of the marsh.

I left the pool and dressed, but Yoshi wasn't outside yet, so I started walking idly down a path of stones alone. It followed a narrow stream and opened into a pond, as round as a bowl and silvery with moonlight. I paused at the edge. In the darkness on the other side, something stirred.

Not for the first time that quake-riddled day, I held my breath. A great blue heron stood in the shadows, its long legs disappearing into the dark water, its wings folded closely against its body. Then the pond was still, gleaming like mica. Another, smaller heron stirred beside the first. I thought of the two women in the spring, as if they had stepped outside to the pond and been transformed into these silent, beautiful birds. Then Yoshi called my name, and both herons unfolded their wide wings and lifted off, slowly, gracefully, casting shadows on the water before they disappeared into the trees.

"Lucy," Yoshi called again. "If we hurry, we can catch the next train."

The heat closed in as we lost altitude, and the hydrangea blossoms against the windows grew older and more ragged, as if the slow, incremental season had been compressed into a single hour. By the time we reached our stop by the sea, the blossoms had disappeared completely, leaving only glossy foliage. We walked home along the narrow cobblestone lanes. Crickets hummed and the ground shook slightly with the surf. Twice, I paused.

"Is that the sea?" I asked.

"Maybe."

"Not an earthquake?"

Yoshi sighed, a little wearily, I thought. "I don't know. Maybe a very little one."

A vase of flowers had tipped over on the table. Several books were scattered on the floor. I wiped up the water and gathered the petals. As I stood, there was a single quick, sharp jolt, so strong that even Yoshi reacted, pulling me into the doorway, where we stood for several minutes, alert again to the earth, its shifting, trembling life. I was so tired; I dreaded the night ahead, with its earthquakes and its dreams. I dreaded the next day, too, all the little disagreements flaring out of nothing, and the silence that would press around me once Yoshi left for work. I thought of the herons at the edge of the pond, spreading their dark wings.

"Yoshi," I said. "I think I will go see my family, after all."

Chapter 2

TWO DAYS LATER, WE LEFT FOR THE STATION BEFORE DAWN, the wheels of my carry-on bumping along the cobblestones in the early morning mist. We walked along the curving lane, past the fruit seller and the vending machine that sold sake and beer, past the temple with its garden of little statues and the shop where they made tofu by hand. Yoshi was dressed in his salaryman attire, white shirt, black suit, which I'd once found amusing, but which had begun to seem like a true part of his identity over these past months. Was it just my imagination that with every day we stayed in this place Yoshi was pulled a little further from the person I'd known? Or was he simply becoming more himself, a self I hadn't seen when we lived in that country of our own?

The trip into Tokyo took about an hour, and we were pressed closer and closer together as the train filled. Yoshi slipped his arm through mine so we wouldn't be separated when the doors opened and we poured out with the crowd. We'd been very kind to each other, very formal and polite, but on the platform, in the flow of impatient people, the unending river of mostly men in dark suits, Yoshi stopped and turned to face me, slipping a little package into my purse.

"A Webcam," he explained. "So we can talk while we're traveling.

I'll see you there in two weeks." He took my shoulders in his two hands and kissed me, right there, amid the streaming people. "Travel safe," he said. "Call soon." Then he entered the river of commuters and was gone.

I found a seat on the airport shuttle. Though I tried to hold on to the memory of Yoshi's touch, it faded gradually as the rainy landscape flashed by the windows. I settled into the seat and turned my thoughts to the trip ahead, my family. I tried to visit every year, but the move to Japan had interrupted things, and I hadn't been back in almost two years. Wanderlust was in my blood, I suppose, at least according to the stories I'd heard all my life. My great-grandfather, Joseph Arthur Jarrett, was sixteen years old when Halley's Comet returned in 1910. Despite the worldwide panic around the comet's return, he had a clear head and an adventurous spirit; that night he snuck out of the house and walked to the church on the hill, determined to witness history. He was young, a dreamer, and he had a gift that, like his unusual eyes, he would pass down through generations: he could listen to a lock and understand its secrets. The cylinders in the bell tower door turned and clicked in response to his seeking wire. They fell into place, the door swung open, and he climbed the worn limestone steps to the roof. Above, amid the familiar stars, the comet arced across the sky. He lifted his face to it. *Like a blessing,* is what he thought. *Like a gift.* The word *orbit* came from Latin—from *orbis,* meaning wheel. To my great-grandfather, destined to be a wheelwright like his father and grandfather before him, this strange light seemed to him a sign.

The days that followed turned in familiar cycles of work and meals and sleeping, yet the memory of the comet remained, hidden but present, like a star at noon, like a bright coin in a pocket. When a huge elm was felled by lightning later that summer, my great-grandfather touched its trunk and a dream bloomed, bright and urgent, spreading its leafy arms around him, its thick blossoms luminous, incandescent, soft against his skin. *Build a trunk,* he seemed to hear, and so he took a section of the tree and hid it in his neighbor's barn. For a year he measured and cut and planed, in secret. He bound the new boards with strips of hot iron and fashioned thick straps from leather. His heart sang and trembled on the night he finally left, traveling by ship and then by train to The Lake of Dreams, where a distant cousin, Jesse Evanston, no more than a name on a slip of paper, was standing on the platform in the watery air to meet him.

That was the story, anyway. As I checked in for my flight, I wondered how he'd felt, pinning his dreams on such a faraway unknown—no telephones back then, no e-mails, and no going back. For me, nearly a century later, there was such a careless ease about distance. At almost the same time as our takeoff from Tokyo the day before, we landed at JFK, its corridors bustling with amazing human diversity. After another hour in the air, the lakes came into view, long, narrow, and deep, deep blue—pressed into the low green hills like the slender fingers of a hand. North-flowing rivers once, they had been deepened and widened by the slow work of glaciers. I studied them until they disappeared beneath the silver wing of the plane, remembering the cold, clear shock of the water, the layers of deepening cold and deepening color, the shallows of the shores giving way to the blueness of the depths, turquoise and indigo and finally midnight blue.

I'd e-mailed my brother that I was coming, and as I rode down the escalator to baggage claim I saw Blake waiting, studying the descending people, his hands shoved into the pockets of his jeans. His face opened in a smile when he saw me, and he waved. In some ways Blake had been hit hardest by our father's sudden death. He'd done well at the Maritime College, and he'd taken some good jobs on big boats in the Great Lakes, but he kept circling back to The Lake of Dreams for summers, a kind of holding pattern he couldn't seem to break.

"Hey, Sis," he said, wrapping one arm around me in a hug. He's six foot four, and even as tall as I am, I had to stand on my toes to hug him back. "Mom's at the doctor, or she'd be here, too."

"She's doing okay?"

"She's doing fine. It turned out to be a sprain, after all. She'll have to wear an Aircast for a couple of weeks."

My bag circled by on the belt and I pulled it off, remembering the moment, just a day before, when the luggage service had picked it up from my tiny patio in Japan. A world away, it seemed already. I started toward the car rental area, but Blake caught my arm.

"You can use Dad's old car while you're here," he said. "No need to bother with a rental."

"Really? The Impala?" I asked, as we made our way out the automatic doors to the parking lot. "Has Mom actually started that thing up? It's been sitting in the barn for years."

"I know, but it still runs. Mom had it checked out a couple of months ago, thinking she might sell it, I guess. It's all tuned up and in good shape."

"I'm surprised she'd think of selling it."

Blake glanced at me, his eyes—the family eyes, a changeable blue flecked with green, with long dark lashes—both serious and amused. "Things move on, Luce. You'll see. Lots of changes this time." He tossed my bag into the back of his truck. "How about you? How's your life these days? Do you miss Indonesia at all? I think about my trip there all the time. Especially that park we went to—the one with wild-looking trees, and the volcanoes."

Blake had come to visit me just after I'd met Yoshi, and we'd gone snorkeling on the coral reefs, hiked through the lowland rain forests. It had been Yoshi's idea, actually. He'd gone with some friends a few weeks earlier and thought Blake and I would enjoy it.

"We had a good time, didn't we?"

"We sure did. It was steamy hot, though. What's Japan like? And how's my good friend Yoshi these days? Things okay? I like him, you know."

"I know." They'd hit it off, Yoshi and Blake, drawn together by a love of sailing and all things nautical, as well as by a kind of carefree approach to life that sometimes drove me crazy. They'd both been enamored of rambutans, the hairy red fruits piled high on roadside stands like shaggy Ping-Pong balls, and had pulled over five or six times to buy baskets full, peeling them to reveal the sweet, translucent fruit within. "He's planning to come, you know. In a couple of weeks."

"No joke? That's great, Lucy. I'll be glad to see him again."

"Me, too." I told Blake about my life then, about Yoshi and the geothermal springs, the incessant trembling of the earth, talking in a stream because I was so tired and so happy to see him and so disconcerted, as I always was, to be back in this place I'd known so well, where life had gone on quite steadily without me. Blake filled me in on the businesses that had opened or closed, the classmates who'd had babies or gotten married or divorced, all sorts of local gossip.

We'd left the main roads to climb the low rise between the lakes. The landscape was deeply and comfortingly familiar, the country roads following ancient trails through the lush green hills and fields, broken by white farmhouses, red barns, silos. The Iroquois had lived on this land once, and they had named the lakes: Long Lake, Beautiful Lake, Place of Blessing, Stony Place, Canoe-Landing Place, The Lake of Dreams. After the revolution, their villages were razed and burned to the ground—blue and gold historic signs marking General Sullivan's brutal campaign were scattered every dozen miles or so. The land had then been allotted to the vanquishing soldiers, who carved farms from the forests, braving the long winters for the brief, exquisite months of summer. Along the shores, summer cottages and rough fishing camps had sprouted, and over the years these had been replaced by ever larger and more ostentatious commuter homes. Still, we drove primarily through farms; from the county line at the top of the rise, we followed the road down a long hill, through green fields that ended at the silvery blue edges of the lake.

"Your old friend Keegan is back, by the way."

A pulse then, the familiar quickening I always used to feel.

"Is he? I haven't seen him in years." This was true, though it didn't feel true.

"He is. He opened up a studio in the old Johnson glass insulator factory by the outlet. That whole building's been renovated. Restaurants, galleries. Very trendy." Blake glanced across the cab at me. "You remember Avery, right?"

"*Your* old friend."

Blake smiled, nodded. "Right. We're back together, you know. She's a chef in a new vegetarian place in the Johnson building, too. Did I ever tell you that when we broke up the second time she went to culinary school? She's really good."

By then we had reached the intersection with the lake road, near the entrance to the depot. The lake was deep enough for battleship training, and during World War II hundreds of families had been relocated under eminent domain, their houses and barns razed like the Iroquois villages before them, airstrips and Quonset huts and weapons bunkers rising almost overnight out of the land amid the corn. Usually this stretch was deserted except for the dull green military vehicles that came and went on their mysterious errands, but now dozens of cars were parked on the grassy shoulders, and a small crowd had gathered at the open gates.

"What's going on?"

"That's the other big news," Blake said. "See what happens when you stay away so long? The depot closed, just last week. It was announced three, four months ago."

I was still thinking of Keegan, the way he used to speed his motorcycle flat out on this stretch, the wind tearing at our sleeves, so it took me a minute to process this news.

"Is that possible? I thought the depot was a fact of life."

"Yeah, weird, isn't it? The economy is lousy here anyway, and now it'll only get worse. This place employed a lot of people."

I looked south along the shore at the miles of undeveloped land behind the formidable fences. Our mother's grandparents had been among those evicted when the land was taken and we'd heard stories of that loss all our lives. We'd grown up traveling along the depot's miles-long fence with its barbed-wire summit, the world within a secret place we could never enter. Blake slowed to maneuver through the unexpected traffic, then stopped, waving over a guy wearing jeans and a jacket with the logo of the local television station.

"Hey, Pete. What's happening?"

"Hey there, Blake." Pete was short, with wiry dark hair, and he sprinted across the road, ducking to look in the truck window. "It's a rally—save the black terns, or something." He gestured to the south, toward our land, toward the marshes. "One group is trying to get all of this designated as a protected wetlands area. I don't know what the rest want yet—about six other groups have showed up. You here to watch the fireworks?"

Blake laughed. "Not me. I'm on my way back from the airport. My sister just got in—this is Lucy. Lucy, Pete."

I nodded hello.

"Developers here, too?" Blake asked.

Pete nodded. "Oh, yeah. All kinds. Plus, the Iroquois want it back, and there's a coalition to protect a herd of rare white deer that's living on the land. Some of the descendants of families who got evicted during the war have filed claims, too. You sure you don't have a dog in this fight, Blake? Everyone else seems to."

Blake grinned. "Nah. Haven't even figured out who the dogs are yet."

Pete laughed. "Plenty to choose from, that's for sure. Well, good seeing you. Good to meet you, Lucy."

He slapped the side of the truck as he stepped back. Blake drove slowly through the crowd, picking up speed as the road cleared. Glimpsing the shallow reeds where my father always loved to fish, where herons hid in the rustling grasses, I was pierced suddenly with grief, remembering the long, thin sound of the line flying through mist.

"I used to love it when Dad took us fishing."

Blake took his right hand from the wheel and gripped mine for a second.

"I know," he said. "I did, too."

It was a deep and yet comforting silence that rose between us, one I could have shared with no one else. When we reached the driveway, low-hanging branches of the apple tree scraped the truck roof. The grand house, Italianate, with two wide porches and a cupola, sagged a little, as if it had exhaled a deep breath. Paint was peeling on the trim and the porch. My mother's moon garden had run completely wild. It had once been a magical place, white crocuses, daffodils, and freesia poking from the mulch, the angel trumpets and night-blooming water lilies carried outside once the air had grown as warm as skin, everything fragrant and luminous, the blossoms floating in the dusk. Now, the trellises were broken and leaning at crazy angles; the moonflower vines cascaded over the fence and tangled in the overgrown roses. The peonies were in full bloom, extravagant and beautiful, and the lavender and lamb's ears had spread everywhere, straggly in the center, ragged at the edges.

Our mother was sitting on the side steps in the sun, her legs extended and crossed at the ankles, her right arm in a bright green cast cradled across her ribs. I'd come back to visit many times in the decade since I'd left for college, and she'd been to see me in Seattle and Florida. Each time I was struck by how familiar she looked, and how young. Her face was almost unlined, but her hair had turned a silvery gray when she was still in her twenties. She wore it pulled back, silver at her temples and running in a thick rope down her spine. She stood up when we pulled in and came right over to meet the truck.

"Lucy!" She hugged me with her good arm as I got out, her cheek soft against mine, smelling faintly of oregano and mint. I hugged her lightly in return, remembering her broken ribs. She kept her good hand on my arm as we walked. "I'm so glad to see you, honey. Oh, you look so good, so beautiful. Did you get taller? That's not possible, is it, but you *seem* taller. Come in—are you starving? Thirsty? You must be just exhausted."

We went through the screened-in porch to the kitchen; I dropped my bag near the door. Everything seemed just the same, the wide windows overlooking the garden, the table pressed against the wall, the turquoise-

and-white-checked curtains I'd made in middle school still hanging in the window of the door. My mother filled tall glasses with ice while Blake cut wedges of lemon and poured sun tea from the big glass jar she always kept on the sunny counter in the summer.

"To Lucy," she said, lifting a glass with her good hand. "Welcome home."

"Is that Lucy already?" a voice from the dining room called.

Art, my father's brother, older by a less than a year, came to stand in the doorway. Even as I realized who it was, I was shocked. He had aged, his broad face slackening, and his hair, gone gray at the temples, cut short and bristling. Somehow in this aging he had come to resemble my father so closely it might have been his ghost standing in the doorway. I couldn't speak. Art didn't seem to notice, though. "Here's the wanderer," he said, stepping into the kitchen to give me a quick, tense hug. "Home at last. How long are you staying?"

"A couple of weeks," I said.

"Good. You'll have to come see us—lots of changes afoot."

"I was telling her." Blake was leaning against the counter. "There's a big brouhaha over at the depot today, did you see it?"

Art nodded. "I did. They wanted me to sign a petition. Wetlands— well, damn. I told them that's prime real estate, a once-in-a-lifetime chance to build."

Blake laughed and agreed, and I glanced at my mother, who was standing with her injured arm across her waist. She caught my eye.

"Art was kind enough to replace the bathroom faucet today," she said.

This meant: *Don't make a scene, Lucy, please.*

Undeterred, I was about to tell Art exactly what I thought about losing the wetlands, but then the ancient freezer on the porch shuddered on, forcing me to consider the muttering old house, its demands and complaints, and the kitchen renovation, which had been less than half-finished when my father died, walls torn out, appliances in boxes, dust from the Sheetrock gathered in the corners. Art and my father had never gotten along, but Art had come to finish the kitchen job. Twice in those numb weeks after the funeral I'd walked in and seen my uncle's legs sprawled out from beneath the sink, tools spread out around him as he struggled with the couplings, and thought it was my father.

"Dad loved those marshes," was what I finally said.

Art was a big man, with long arms and hands thickened from years of work. He drummed his fingers on the counter, looking in my direction but not quite at me; his gaze traveled past me, to the scene outside the window, to the lake.

"He did. Your father did love that place, I know, Lucy." He drummed his fingers a little harder, and then slapped his hand flat on the counter. "We used to go there when we were boys. It was our go-to place, I guess you could say, whenever we needed to think something through, or just to get away. Fishing wasn't bad, either," he said, lost in thought for a moment before he shook his head and rejoined the conversation. "Now, Blake," he went on, changing the subject. "I'll see you later today, right?"

"Not today. I can come tomorrow."

"Be early, then. There's plenty of work." Art turned to my mother. "Evie, I fixed the window sash in the bathroom, too. I'll stop back next week to put on a coat of paint. But it should be okay in the meantime. Come and take a look."

"I appreciate it, Art," my mother said, following him into the other room.

"What was that about?" I asked Blake once they'd gone. "Are you working at Dream Master now?"

Dream Master Hardware and Locks was the business our great-grandfather had founded in 1919, turning his intuitions about the internal mechanics of locks into a thriving enterprise. In its heyday the Dream Master factory shipped locks all across the country. Like most of the other industries in the area, it was gone now, but the hardware store remained, and Art owned it. My father had once owned it, too, but in 1986, the year the comet came, when I was almost ten, he had come home one morning with a box full of things from his office, and he'd never gone back, or said a word to me about why he left.

Blake ran one hand through his wild curls and glanced after Art. "Walk me outside," he said.

We went through the porch and down the steps, and then Blake kept right on going across the lawn to the shore. The day was clear but windy, the water punctuated with whitecaps like commas, the buoys singing their hollow metal songs. I caught up with him at the end of the dock.

"What's going on? Did you quit your job on the boat?" I asked.

Blake kept his gaze on the water, watching the rippling patterns change, a distant flock of ducks floating light on the surface.

"Not yet. I've agreed to pilot through the summer, but just the evening cruise. I might quit after that, though. I'm thinking about it. Art offered me a job. A good job. He stopped in a couple of weeks ago to ask me in person. Took me by surprise, I can tell you."

I didn't say anything, trying to sort out why this news felt so upsetting.

"Art's helped Mom out a lot," Blake went on quietly. "I know they always argued, he and Dad, and we were never close to Art growing up. But lately I've been thinking I haven't been quite fair to him. Maybe none of us have."

"Well, so what? When did anything between Dad and Art ever end up fair?"

Blake shrugged. "We were kids, Lucy. We don't really know. Art probably feels bad about the way things turned out. It's got to haunt him, being on such uneasy terms with Dad before he died. Suppose he's just trying to make things right?"

I felt it then, the pull of the family history, an invisible gravity, almost irresistible.

"But what about sailing, Blake? You love to travel. What about winters on St. Croix? You're just giving all that up?"

"Like I said, things change." Blake glanced at me, embarrassed, assessing. "Long story short, Avery is pregnant. The baby's due in October. So, I have to think differently now."

I was too surprised to say anything at all.

"That's right," Blake said. "We're having a baby. Good wishes appreciated."

"Sorry. I'm sorry, Blake. Of course I'm happy for you. It's just a lot to take in."

He gave a small smile, nodded. "That's okay. I had the exact same reaction, actually—stunned silence." We stood in the wind off the lake.

"Are you happy about it?" I asked.

"Sometimes. It's exciting, sure, but a surprise. The timing is bad for us both."

Wind rattled the ropes on the dock, and I tried hard to remember Avery, a slight, energetic girl with dark brown eyes and hair.

"Look," Blake said. "This thing at Dream Master, the way I see it— it's just a job. Not a forever job, just a good-for-right-now kind of job."

"Right, I get it. It makes sense."

He smiled then, his charming old smile, and gave my shoulder a playful push.

"Water looks nice," he said.

"Oh, you wouldn't!"

"Wouldn't I?"

He pushed me harder then, and though I could have kept my balance I grabbed his arm and let myself fall, dragging him in after me. We hit the clear, cold water and came up laughing, shaking bright droplets from our hair.

"Oh! It's freezing!"

"It's June—what did you expect?"

"Not to be swimming." I skimmed my hand across the surface, sending a glittering arc of spray. Blake ducked, then sprayed me back.

"Truce!" I finally called, staggering out of the water onto the gray shale beach. Blake followed me up the lawn, catching my arm before we reached the driveway.

"Mom doesn't know," he said, looking at me seriously with the beautiful dark-lashed family eyes, blue irises mottled with green. "No one else knows. I promised Avery I wouldn't say anything until she's ready, so keep it quiet, okay?"

I nodded slowly. "Okay. I won't say anything."

"Thanks. Hey—it's good to have you home, Luce." He gave me a hug as we reached the driveway, and then headed toward his truck.

"Aren't you even going to dry off?"

"I'll drip dry," he called back. "And I'll see you later, okay? Welcome back."

I waved, watching him pull away and disappear.

Art had gone, too. I found my mother in the kitchen making up plates with chicken salad, lettuce, and grapes, working slowly because she could use only one hand.

"Just a light supper," she said, and then she looked up and saw my wet clothes, my hair. "Oh, the two of you," she said, laughing, biting her lips because it hurt her ribs to laugh. I could tell she was happy, though. "There are towels on the sun porch. And could you pour us some wine? You must be tired, Lucy, but it's so good to see you that I'm not going to let you sleep, not yet."

After I changed we ate on the patio, weighing the napkins down with forks because the breeze was still brisk, cold in my wet hair. The setting sun had emerged below the clouds and the lake had turned from gunmetal gray to the color of sapphires, waves lapping gently at the shore. My mother's face softened in the golden light, her silver hair glinting amber.

"So," she said. "Here you are. And this Yoshi of yours is coming, too, I hear. That would be a first, Lucy, meeting one of your parade of boyfriends. Sounds like it might be serious?"

"Oh, I don't know. I mean, yes, I suppose. We're at kind of a crossroads, I guess." I paused there, surprised at my own words. Was it true?

"Well, you don't want to wait too long," my mother said.

"Too long for what?" I regretted the words the minute I spoke them, because my tone was sharp. My mother averted her gaze, ran her finger around the rim of her glass.

"I'm sorry, honey," she said, her voice mild. She looked up and smiled at me. "I don't mean to pry. And I don't mean that you have to find happiness in a relationship. Not at all. But I do want you to be happy. Wherever you find that happiness, I want it for you. That's all."

Now I had to look away, out to the tranquil waters.

"I think you'll like Yoshi," I said, finally. "He and Blake really hit it off. His job has been really consuming, so that's been kind of hard, especially since I don't have any job at all just now. It seemed like a good time for him to come, that's all."

"I can't wait to meet him."

We talked a little more about work, and then I asked about the car wreck.

"Not serious," she said, waving her good hand. "It could have been, but I was lucky. The ribs are the worst, it hurts to laugh or take a deep breath, and there's nothing I can do but let them heal. Still, I don't know why everyone got quite so upset. Except maybe it reminded us," she added. "About how quickly things can happen."

Again, silence fell between us. I was the first to break it. "I still miss Dad," I said.

"I know."

"What do you think of Blake?" I asked after a moment. "Working for Art, I mean?"

She was looking out at the water with its dancing nets of light, and shook her head slightly. "I try not to get too involved, now that you two are adults. Art has been a terrific help to me, Lucy. You haven't been here to see it, but it's true. I guess your father's death made a powerful impression on him. I think maybe they always imagined they'd have time to patch things up, time to find a way to get along, but then, just like that, it was too late."

"Whatever happened between them, anyway?"

"Oh, honestly, honey, it's hard to pinpoint. There was always tension. I remember when your father brought me here for dinner and announced that we were getting married, Art made a point of taking me aside to tell me all your father's faults. It was strange, almost like he was jealous and wanted to keep things from working out. That didn't really make sense, because he was already dating Austen. But anyway, I didn't think much of Art for doing that, I can tell you. As an only child myself, I always wanted to have siblings, so I've never understood why they couldn't get along. But that's just the way it was for them, growing up, maybe because they were born so close together."

"And Dream Master?" I asked. "That happened later?"

My mother glanced at me, her expression somewhat guarded. "It did."

"Well?"

"You were always such a persistent child," she observed. "No wonder you're such a success around the world."

Long stems of white gladioli stood in a vase on the table. I touched a petal, feeling hurt rather than complimented; my mother had argued against my living overseas, especially after 9/11 happened while I was in Sri Lanka, and it was still a sore point between us. Golden pollen coated my finger.

"These are pretty. Secret admirer?"

To my surprise my mother laughed, color rising briefly in her cheeks. "Not so secret. Someone I met in the emergency room. His name is Andrew. Andrew something or other. I was pretty spacey from the pain pills. We had a lovely conversation, of which I remember almost nothing."

I opened the florist's envelope and pulled out the little card.

"Yes, go ahead," she said. "Feel free."

Dear Evie, thank you for the good conversation on a very bad day. As discussed, these are Apollo gladioli. Hope you like them. Yours, Andrew Stewart.

"Why Apollo gladioli?" I asked, catching the envelope as it skidded across the table in a gust of wind that rattled the wind chimes and slammed waves against the shore.

"Well, we talked about the moon landing, that I do remember. Where we were in 1969, that sort of thing. I suppose I must have mentioned my old moon garden, though it all went to seed years ago. But maybe that's why he sent these."

"Looks like you made a big impression." I put the card back in its envelope, suddenly very sad. My parents had met as volunteers in a community garden just as my father was about to leave for Vietnam. Over the next year, they wrote. My mother savored his letters, the onion-skin pages in their thin envelopes filled with his slanted script. She had known my father so briefly that it was as if she had made him up to suit herself, and when she wrote back it was with a reckless freedom, telling him things she'd never shared before—her secrets, fears, and dreams.

Then one day she had looked up to see my father silhouetted against the door of the greenhouse where she worked. He was so much taller than she remembered, disconcertingly familiar and strange all at once. He crossed the room and stopped in front of her, but didn't speak. The scent of earth gathered in her throat. Water dripped in the sink.

"I'm transplanting zinnias," she'd finally said. As proof she held up her hands, dirt beneath her nails, her fingertips stained brown.

My father had smiled. Then he leaned down and kissed her. She kissed him back, pressing her wrists against his shoulders, her earth-stained hands lifted like wings.

I'd heard this story over and over, growing up, so I didn't really like it, not one bit, that some man I'd never met was sending my mother flowers. Jet lag traveled through me like a wave and the world suddenly seemed vibrant and strange, as if all the colors might burst from their shapes. I put my hand on the table to steady myself.

"You okay?" my mother asked.

"Just a little tired, that's all."

"Of course you are, honey. I'm surprised you lasted this long. I made up the couch on the screened porch for you."

"What about my old room, can't I use that?"

"Do you really want to?"

She sounded reluctant, and I remembered she'd told me once that in the silence of my father's sudden absence, the voices of the house had begun to whisper to her constantly, the trim crying out to be painted, the driveway sputtering about cracks and pits, the faucets leaking a persistent dissatisfaction. *Love,* said the kitchen cabinets my father had built from quarter-sawn oak. The lights in her sewing room, the slate tiles of the patio, the newly sanded floors, all of these persisted, saying *love, love, love,* and when the gutters clogged, when the shutters broke loose, when a windowpane cracked, she could not bear to alter the things he had last tended; nor could she stand to listen to the clamoring of the house. That was why she'd closed off the second floor, turning the glass doorknobs, clicking the metal bolts shut.

"Would you mind? I'll make the bed and everything."

"Of course I don't mind," she said, though I sensed that she did.

I found the key ring hanging inside the kitchen cupboard. The keys made soft metal sounds as I carried them to the second floor, which was warm and stuffy, the doors all closed. When I entered my old room I went from window to window, pushing up the sashes, struggling with the combination storms, letting fresh air pour in. I put a fitted sheet on the narrow bed, unfolded the flat sheet, and tucked it in, fatigue throbbing through me like a pulse.

It was faintly light still, not quite nine o'clock. I lay down without undressing, punched speed dial, and closed my eyes. Yoshi picked up on the second ring, his voice low and smooth, like river stones.

"Moshi Moshi."

"It's me. I got here just fine."

"Good. I miss you, Lucy."

"Me, too. What are you doing?"

"Walking to catch the train. It's raining a little."

I imagined the lane, the river he'd cross before the station. If I were there I'd be lying in bed watching rain drip from the copper eaves, planning my vocabulary lesson for the day.

"I haven't set up the Webcam. Maybe tomorrow. My mother isn't very high-tech."

"How is she?"

"Okay. Fine, really. But the house is very quiet."

"You see. I was right."

"I do see. She's glad you're coming. She wants to meet you."

"Just a few days. I want to meet her, too. How's your brother?"

"He's good. He says hello. He's having a baby."

"What?"

"It's true. Top secret, though. I'll be an aunt in October."

"Congratulations. I didn't know he'd gotten married."

"He didn't. Not yet. I mean, I don't know if he will. It's all a surprise."

"Well, tell him hello."

"I will. Have there been more earthquakes?"

"A few, not so bad."

"Hey. Did you turn off the gas?"

He laughed. "Yes," he said. "Yes. I turned off the gas. Look, I'm almost at the station now, I have to go."

"Okay. Call me tonight?"

"I will. Send me an e-mail if you can, okay?"

"I will."

"Love you."

He really must miss me, I thought, startled—Yoshi wasn't much for endearments, especially on the phone. "Love you, too," I said.

I pressed the button and there was only space, all the miles between us filling up with darkness. I put the phone on the bedside table without opening my eyes, remembering the little concrete house we'd shared in Indonesia, its garden filled with mango trees and lush, swiftly growing plants I couldn't name. We always met there when we got home from work, and shared a drink as the moon rose, listening to the rustling sounds of lizards in the tall grass. I wanted to reach out now and catch Yoshi's hand in mine, to walk with him back into that tranquil life. But he was in the middle of a day and ten thousand miles away. I pulled the blankets up and fell asleep to the sounds and scent of water.

The dream began as a long and wearying journey in the rain, full of airports and frustrations, missed connections and clocks ticking, perilous deadlines. I was being followed, through corridors, first, and then through a forest. My suitcase, old-fashioned and made of leather, hit a tree and broke open, spilling everything. In panic, I started crawling through the foliage, the earth damp and loamy. I searched wildly through the velvet leaves of cyclamen, blossoms flaring around me like birds in startled flight. What I'd lost was important, somehow vital to me, life or death, and even though footsteps and voices were approaching, growing louder and more menacing, I couldn't stop, pushing leaves away and digging in the earth with my hands, until the voices were upon me.

I woke, so frightened and disoriented I could not move.

Gradually, slowly, I remembered where I was. Still, I had to take several deep breaths before I could swing my legs over the edge of the bed and stand up. In the glaring light of the bathroom I splashed water on my face, studying my pale reflection in the mirror. My eyes, like Blake's, were large and blue, but shadowed with fatigue.

The house was still, the closed doors in the hallway like blank faces. I unlocked them all. Everything was caught in time, as if the world had stopped the summer after my father died. In my parents' room, the bed was neatly made. Blake's room still had its posters of the moon and the earth, our luminous blue-green planet floating in the interstellar space of his walls. In the guest room, packed boxes were stacked high against one wall, so perhaps my mother had been up here after all, starting to go through the old things. When I opened the door to the cupola, stale, hot air spilled down the narrow steps, as if nothing had stirred in it for decades. It was like a tower in a fairy tale, where the princess pricked her finger, or spun straw into gold, or lowered her thick hair to her lover below.

No breath in that tiny rooftop room. Here, too, I opened all the windows, sweeping away the dead flies that had collected in the sills. When the room was full of the lapping sounds of the lake, full of wind, I sat on one of the window seats, breathing in the fresh air. The lake was calm and smooth, almost opalescent. I watched dawn come, the sun catching on the ring of keys I'd left splayed out against the painted seat: new keys and ancient keys, formed for locks that no longer existed, kept because they were beautifully fashioned, or because no one could remember what they opened and thought they might be needed someday.

My father's lock-picking tools hung from the ring, too, folded like a Swiss Army knife into a compact metal case. They were a kind of inheritance, passed down from my great-grandfather, Joseph Arthur Jarrett. I opened them, wondering when my father had used them last. As a girl I would sometimes go to his office at Dream Master after school and do my homework in the corner, happy to be near the swirl of conversation and the scents of metal and sawdust, customers coming in for nails or tools or chicken wire or a special order of tile. Sometimes they came with their secrets, too, stored in metal boxes from which the keys had been lost. My father's expression was always intent and focused as he worked, his scalp visible beneath his cropped hair in the harsh light, his face breaking open in satisfaction, finally, as the tumblers clicked and fell into place. He charged five dollars for this service, ten dollars for house calls, and people paid happily, so eager that they almost never waited to open their boxes in private: Bonds or jewelry or wills; a few times, nothing at all.

My father had taught me what he knew, letting me sit in his chair and press my ear against the smooth wood or metal of a shuttered box on his desk, instructing me how to listen to the whisper of metal shifting, something like a wave, smooth and uninterrupted, until suddenly the frequency changed slightly, became weighted, suspenseful. What was or wasn't inside never really mattered; it was the whisper of metal on metal that he wanted me to hear. The first time I succeeded, the box springing open beneath my touch, he'd let out a cheer of delight and lifted me up in a hug.

Beneath the lip of the window seat, almost hidden beneath layers of paint, but visible now that the cushions had been stripped away, was a little keyhole. I slid down and squatted on the floor amid the dust motes and the carcasses of flies, slipping a thin metal tool into the keyhole and pressing my ear against the wood. I closed my eyes, imagining my father on those long ago days, making the same motions I was making now, listening in this same intent way. When the last tumbler clicked into place I exhaled a breath I didn't realize I'd been holding, feeling a relief so intense it was almost like joy, and pulled open the cupboard door.

The space seemed empty. In the soft glow of sunrise, I reached inside and felt along the floor, worrying about dead mice or, worse, finding nothing but grit. Then my wrist grazed a stack of papers and I pulled it out. Dust streaked my hands and permeated the papers. At first I felt a rush of excitement; surely, if someone had taken such pains to hide these, they must be important. Yet aside from the mild scholarly interest they immediately evoked—they were mostly flyers and little magazines that seemed to have been written by or for suffragettes—the pamphlets were disappointing, more like insulation than a true find. I closed the cupboard, the lock clicking back into place, and carried the keys and dusty papers back to my room. I lay down on the bed, meaning to read through them, but I got caught in the mysterious tides of jet lag, and fell asleep instead.

The Weird Sisters

BY

Eleanor Brown

"Delightful...pulls us into the heart of the family circle."
—*The Miami Herald*

Three sisters have returned to their childhood home, reuniting the eccentric Andreas family. Here, books are a passion (there is no problem a library card can't solve) and TV is something other people watch. Their father—a professor of Shakespeare who speaks almost exclusively in verse—named them after the Bard's heroines. It's a lot to live up to.

The sisters have a hard time communicating with their parents and their lovers, but especially with one another. What can the shy homebody eldest sister, the fast-living middle child, and the bohemian youngest sibling have in common? Only that none has found life to be what was expected; and now, faced with their parents' frailty and their own personal disappointments, not even a book can solve what ails them...

PROLOGUE

We came home because we were failures. We wouldn't admit that, of course, not at first, not to ourselves, and certainly not to anyone else. We said we came home because our mother was ill, because we needed a break, a momentary pause before setting off for the Next Big Thing. But the truth was, we had failed, and rather than let anyone else know, we crafted careful excuses and alibis, and wrapped them around ourselves like a cloak to keep out the cold truth. The first stage: denial.

For Cordelia, the youngest, it began with the letters. They arrived the same day, though their contents were so different that she had to look back at the postmarks to see which one had been sent first. They seemed so simple, paper in her hands, vulnerable to rain, or fire, or incautious care, but she would not destroy them. These were the kind you save, folded into a memory box, to be opened years later with fingers against crackling age, heart pounding with the sick desire to be possessed by memory.

We should tell you what they said, and we will, because their contents affect everything that happened afterward, but we first have to explain how our family communicates, and to do that, we have to explain our family.

Oh, man.

Perhaps we had just better explain our father.

If you took a college course on Shakespeare, our father's name might be resident in some dim corner of your mind, under layers of unused telephone numbers, forgotten dreams, and the words that never seem to make it to the tip of your tongue when you need them. Our father is Dr. James Andreas, professor of English literature at Barnwell College, singular focus: The Immortal Bard.

The words that might come to mind to describe our father's work are insufficient to convey to you what it is like to live with someone with such a singular preoccupation. Enthusiast, expert, obsessed—these words all thud hollow when faced with the sandstorm of Shakespeare in which we were raised. Sonnets were our nursery rhymes. The three of us were given advice and instruction in couplets; we were more likely to refer to a hated playmate as a "fat-kidneyed rascal" than a jerk; we played under the tables at Christmas parties where phrases like "deconstructionist philosophy" and "patriarchal malfeasance" drifted down through the heavy tablecloths with the carols.

And this only begins to describe it.

But it is enough for our purposes.

The first letter was from Rose: precise pen on thick vellum. From *Romeo and Juliet*; Cordy knew it at once. *We met, we woo'd and made exchange of vow, I'll tell thee as we pass; but this I pray, That thou consent to marry us to-day.*

And now you will understand this was our oldest sister's way of telling us that she was getting married.

The second was from our father. He communicates almost exclusively through pages copied from *The Riverside Shakespeare*. The pages are so heavily annotated with decades of thoughts, of interpretations, that we can barely make out the lines of text he highlights. But it matters not; we have been nursed and nurtured on the plays, and the slightest reminder brings the language back.

Come, let us go; and pray to all the gods/For our beloved mother in her pains. And this is how Cordy knew our mother had cancer. This is how she knew we had to come home.

ONE

❧

Cordy had never stolen anything before. As a matter of pride, when our friends were practicing their light-fingered shuffles across the shelves of Barnwell's stores in our teens, she had refused to participate, refused even to wear the cheap earrings and clumpy lipstick or listen to the shoplifted music. But here she was in this no-name desert town, facing off against the wall of pregnancy tests, knowing full well she didn't have the money to pay for one. A Wild West shootout: Cordy versus the little pink sticks at high noon.

She'd wanted to do this somewhere anonymous, in a wide-aisled store that hummed with soft, inoffensive music and belonged to a company, not a person, but those stores had long ago gotten smart, put anti-theft devices like hunch-shouldered guardians at the doors. So she was in this dusty little mom and pop drugstore, her stomach churning, cheeks bright with fire.

"Strike up the drum; cry 'Courage!' and away," she whispered to herself, and then giggled, one thin hand sneaking out to grab one of the boxes—any one, it didn't matter. They'd all tell her the thing she already knew but refused to admit.

She slipped the box into her gaping shoulder bag with one hand, the other rooting around at the bottom for the remnants of her last, months-ago paycheck, the few loose coins buried in a grave of stale breath mints, lint, and broken pens. Along the way, she grabbed a toffee bar off the shelf and presented it to the cashier, digging for a few more pennies, her hand burning when she brushed against the box hidden in the loose depths.

Outside the store, a rush of elation. "Too easy," she said aloud to the empty street, her skirt whispering against the sidewalk, already gone hot and sullen in the rise of spring, her sandals so worn that she could feel the insistent warmth against her heels. The pleasure of the forbidden lasted until she had made it back to the house, ramshackle and dark, where she was staying, a few people crashed on the broken furniture in the living room, sleeping off last night's excess. She yanked open the box, tossing the instructions in the direction of the trash can, and did the deed. Huddled on the toilet in the bathroom, tile cracked and shredding beneath her feet, staring at the pink line, pale as fading newsprint, her conscience caught up with her.

"It doesn't get much lower than this, old Cordy, old sock," she could hear Bean telling her cheerfully.

"How are you going to take care of a baby if you can't even afford a pregnancy test?" Rose harped.

Cordy brushed our imaginary voices aside and buried the evidence in the trash can. It didn't make a difference, really, she told herself. She'd been headed home anyway, wandering a circuitous loop, going where the wind or the next ride took her. This just confirmed what she'd already known—that after seven years of floating like a dandelion seed, it was time to settle down.

Settle down. She shuddered.

Those words were a bell ringing inside her. That was, after all, why she'd left. Just before exams in the spring of her junior year at Barnwell College, she'd been in the study lounge in the psychology department, lying on the industrial carpet, her arms locked as she held a textbook above her face. Two women, seniors, were talking nearby—one of them was getting married, the other going to graduate school. Cordy lowered the book to her chest, its weight pressing harder and harder against her heart as she listened to the litany of What Was to Come. Wedding favors and student loans. Mortgages and health insurance. Careers and taxes. Unable to breathe, she shoved the book onto the floor and walked out of the lounge. If that was the future, she wanted no part of it.

It was our fault, probably, the way we'd always babied her. Or maybe it was our father's fault—Cordelia had always been his favorite. He'd never said no to her, not to her breathless baby cries, not to her childhood entreaties for ballet lessons (dropped before they got to fourth position, though she did wear the tutu for an awful long time after that, so it wasn't a total waste), and not to the desperate late-night calls for cash infusions in the years she'd spent drifting around the country, accomplishing nothing in particular. She was the Cordelia to his Lear, legendary in her devotion. *He always lov'd our sister most.* But whoever's fault it was, Cordy had thus far refused to grow up, and we'd indulged that in the same way we'd indulged every other whim she'd had for nearly her entire life. After all, we could hardly blame her. We were fairly certain that if anyone made public the various and variegated ways in which being an adult sucked eggs, more people might opt out entirely.

But now? Growing up didn't seem so much like a choice anymore. Cordy fumbled around through one of the bedrooms until she found a calendar, counting backward. It was almost June now, she was fairly certain. And she'd left Oregon, the last stop on that long, strange trip, in, what, February? She rubbed her knuckles on her forehead, thinking. It had been so long since things like dates mattered.

But she could trace the journey back, before she'd started feeling so empty and nauseated in the mornings, before her breasts had grown tender enough that even the material of a T-shirt seemed like it was scraping against her skin, before the endless fatigue that swept over her at the strangest times, before she'd known. Washington, California, Arizona. Her period had come in Arizona; she dimly remembered a tussle with a recalcitrant tampon dispenser in a rest stop bathroom. And then she'd gone to New Mexico, where there'd been a painter, much older, his hair painted with shocking strands of white, his skin wrinkled from the sun, his hands broad and calloused. She'd paused there for a few weeks, waitressing a handful of shifts to make money for the rest of the trip home, not that it had lasted. He'd come into the restaurant to eat, all by himself, and it had been so late, and his eyes were so lonely. For a week she'd stayed with him, spending the days curled on a couch in his studio, reading and staring out over the arroyos while he painted in silence: strange, contorted swirls of color that dripped off the canvases onto the floor. But he'd been gentle, and blessedly quiet, and after so much *Sturm und Drang*, she'd nearly been sad to leave. The last night, there'd been a broken condom, a hushed argument, dark dreams, and the next morning she had been gone.

Slumping on the bed, Cordy let the calendar fall from her hands. What was she supposed to do now? Go back to New Mexico and tell the painter? She doubted he'd be excited to hear the news. She wasn't exactly thrilled herself. Maybe she'd have a miscarriage. Heroines in novels were always having serendipitously timed miscarriages that saved them from having to make sticky decisions. And Cordy had always been awfully lucky.

Until now.

Cordy stepped over the piles of dirty clothes on the floor and back into the hallway. The crashers in the living room were still snoring as she tiptoed through to the kitchen, where she'd left her backpack. She'd lived here one winter—it seemed like years ago, but it couldn't have been that long, since this was the address the letters had come to. Had it been years ago? Had it really been years since she had been in one place long enough to have an address?

Gritting her teeth, Cordy began shoving things into the bag. She didn't know what to do. But that was okay. Someone would figure this out for her. Someone would take care of her. Someone always took care of her.

No problem.

B ean absolutely and positively did not believe in anything even vaguely paranormal. But for the past week or so, she'd had the strangest feeling that something bad was coming. She woke up in the morning with a hard pit in her stomach, as though she'd swallowed something malignant, growing, and the weight stayed with her all day, making her heels clack more sharply on the subway steps, her body ache after only a few minutes of running on the treadmill, jewel-toned cocktails simmer in her stomach until she left them in their glasses to sweat into water on the mahogany bars of the city's trendiest watering holes.

Nothing in her bag of tricks made the feeling go away—not seducing a hapless investment banker over the din of a club, not a punishing spin class that left her so rubbery and tired that she vomited into the toilet at the gym, not a new pair of shoes that cost as much as the rent she paid for her tiny closet of a bedroom in a shared apartment in Manhattan. As a matter of fact, that last one made the rock inside her turn into steel.

When the moment she had been dreading finally came, the managing partner of the law firm she worked at arriving at her desk and asking to see her in his office, it was almost a relief. *"If it were done, when 'tis done, then 'twere well it were done quickly,"* she quoted to herself, following his wizened steps into his office.

"Have a seat, Bianca," he said.

In New York, everyone called her Bianca. Men, upon asking for her number in a terminally hip watering hole, would have to ask her to repeat it, and then, upon comprehension, would smile. Something about the name—and, honestly, few of them had the synapses to rub together at that point in the evening to make any sort of literary connections, so it must have been something else—made her even more attractive to them.

To us, however, she would always be Bean. And it was still the way she spoke to herself. "Nice going, Bean," she would say when she dropped something, and her roommates in the city would look at her curiously. But being Bianca was a part she played well, and she wondered if part of the sickness she felt inside was knowing that performance was coming to an end. Forever.

She perched on the edge of one of the leather wing chairs in his sitting area. He sat in the other. "We've been doing a bit of an accounting audit, you see," he said without preamble.

Bean stared at him. The pit inside her stomach was turning into fire. She stared at him, his beetled, bushy eyebrows, his soft, wrinkled hands, and wanted to cry.

"We've found a number of . . . shall we say, anomalies in the payroll records. In your favor. I'd like to think they're errors." He looked almost hopeful.

She said nothing.

"Can you tell me what's been happening, Bianca?"

Bean looked down at the bracelet on her wrist. She'd bought it at Tiffany months ago, and she remembered the strange seizing in her stomach as she'd handed over her credit card, the same feeling she'd gotten lately when she bought anything, from groceries to a handbag. The feeling that her luck was running out, that she couldn't go on, and maybe (most terrifying of all), maybe she didn't want to.

"They aren't errors," Bean said, but her voice caught on the last word, so she cleared her throat and tried again, louder. "They aren't errors." She folded her hands in her lap.

The managing partner looked unsurprised, but disappointed. Bean wondered why they'd chosen him for this particular dirty work—he was practically emeritus, holding on to this corner office for no good reason other than to have a place to escape from his wife and while away the hours until he died. She considered trying to sleep with him, but he was looking at her with such grandfatherly concern the idea withered on the vine before she could even fully imagine it. Truthfully, she felt something that could only be described as gratitude that it was him, not one of the other partners whose desperation to push themselves to the top had made their tongues sharp as teeth, whose bellows of frustration came coursing down the hallways like a swelling tide when things dared not go their way.

"Are you well?" he asked, and the kindness in his voice made her heart twist. She bit her tongue hard, blinked back tears. She would not cry. Not in front of him, anyway. Not here. "It's a great deal of money, Bianca. Was there some reason . . . ?" His question trailed off hopefully.

She could have lied. Maybe she should have been picturing this scene all along, planning for it. She was good at the theater of life, our Bean, she could have played any part she wanted. But lying seemed desperate and weak, and she was suddenly exhausted. She wanted nothing more than to lie down and sleep for days.

"No," she said. She couldn't meet his eyes. "No good reason."

He sighed at that, a long, slow exhale that seemed to make the air move differently in the room. "We could call the police, you know."

Bean's eyes widened. She'd never thought about that. Why had she never thought about that? She'd known stealing from her employers was wrong, but somehow she'd never let herself think that it was actually criminal (criminal! how had it come to that?). God, she could go to jail. She saw herself in a cell, in an orange jumpsuit, stripped of her bracelet and her makeup and all the armor that living in the city required of her. She was speechless.

"But I don't think that's entirely necessary. You've done good work for us. And I know what it's like to be young in this city. And it's so unpleasant, involving the police. I'd imagine that your resignation will be enough. And, of course, you'll repay your debt."

"Of course," Bean said. She was still frozen, wondering how she'd managed to miscalculate so badly, wondering if she really was going to squeak out of here with nothing but a slap on the wrist, or if she'd be nabbed halfway out of the lobby, handcuffs on her wrists, her box of personal effects scattering on the marble floor while everyone looked on at the spectacle.

"It might be worthwhile for you to take a little time. Go home for a bit. You're from Kentucky, aren't you?"

"Ohio," Bean said, and it was only a whisper.

"Right. Go back to the Buckeye State. Spend a little time. Reevaluate your priorities."

Bean forced back the tears that were, again, welling out of control. "Thank you," she said, looking up at him. He was, miraculously, smiling.

"We've all done foolish, foolish things, dear. In my experience, good people punish themselves far more than any external body can manage. And I believe you are a good person. You may have lost your way more than a little bit, but I believe you can find your way back. That's the trick. Finding your way back."

"Sure," Bean said, and her tongue was thick with shame. It might have been easier if he had been angry, if he'd taken her to task the way he really should have, called the police, started legal proceedings, done something that equaled the horrible way she'd betrayed their trust and pissed on everything she knew to be good and right in the service of nothing more than a lot of expensive clothes and late-night cab rides. She wanted him to yell, but his voice remained steady and quiet.

"I don't recommend you mention your employment here when you do seek another job."

"Of course not," Bean said. He was about to continue, but she pushed her hair back and interrupted him. "I'm sorry. I'm so, so sorry."

His hands were steepled in front of him. He looked at her, the way her makeup was smudging around her eyes, despite her impressive ability to hold back the tears. "I know," he said. "You have fifteen minutes to get out of the building."

Bean fled.

She took nothing from work. She cared about nothing there anyway, had never bothered to make the place her own. She went home and called a friend with a car he'd been trying to sell for junk, though even that would take nearly the last of her ill-gotten gains, and while he drove over, she packed up her clothes, and she wondered how she could have spent all that money and have nothing but clothes and accessories and a long list of men she never wanted to see again to show for it, and the thought made her so ill she had to go into the bathroom and vomit until she could bring up nothing but blood and yellow bile, and she took as much money as she could from the ATM and threw everything she owned into that beater of a car and she left right then, without even so much as a fare-thee-well to the city that had given her . . . well, nothing.

Because Cordelia was the last to find out, she was the last to arrive, though we understand this was neither her intention nor her fault. It was simply her habit. Cordy, last born, came a month later than expected, lazily sweeping her way out of our mother's womb, putting a lie to the idea that labor gets shorter every time. She has been late to everything since then, and is fond of saying she will be late to her own funeral, haw haw haw.

We forgive her for her tardiness, but not for the joke.

Would we all have chosen to come back, knowing that it would be the three of us again, that all those secrets squeezed into one house would be impossible to keep? The answer is irrelevant—it was some kind of sick fate. We were destined to be sisters at birth, and apparently we were destined to be sisters now, when we thought we had put all that behind us.

While Bean and Cordy were dragging their baggage (literal and meta-phorical) across the country, Rose was already safely ensconced in our childhood home. Unlike Bean and Cordy, Rose had never been away for very long. For years she had been in the habit of having dinner with our parents once or twice a week, coming home on Sundays. Someone, after all, had to keep an eye on them. They were getting older, Rose told Bean on the phone, with exactly the right amount of sighing to convey that she felt she was doing Bean and Cordy's duty as well as her own. And usually her visits to our house for Sunday dinner felt like duty, equal parts frustration and triumph as she reminded our father that he had to mow the lawn before the neighbors complained, as she bustled around the living room putting bookmarks in books left open, their spines strain-ing under the weight, as she reminded our mother that she actually had to open the mail, not just bring it inside. It was a good thing, Rose invari-ably told herself when she left (with not a little satisfaction on her face) that she was here. Who knows what kind of disarray they'd fall into with-out her?

But moving home? At the advanced age of thirty-three? Like, for per-manent, as Cordy might say?

She should have been living in the city with her fiancé, Jonathan, hav-ing recently signed her first contract as a tenured professor, waving her engagement ring around wildly whenever she came back to Barnwell just to show that she was, in fact, not just the smart one, that Bean was not the only one who could land a man, and our father was not the only professorial genius in the family. This is how it should have been. This is how it was:

ACT I

Setting: Airport interior, and Jonathan's apartment, just after winter break

Characters: Jonathan, Rose, travelers

Rose had changed positions a dozen times as the passengers on Jonathan's flight came streaming through the airport gates. She was looking for the right position for him to catch her in; the right balance of careless inattention and casual beauty, neither of which would betray how much she had missed him.

But when he finally did emerge, cresting over the gentle grade of the ramp that led from the gate, when she could see his rumpled hair bobbing above the heads of the other passengers, the graceful way his tall, reedy shoulders were bent forward as though he were walking into an insistent wind, she forgot her artifice and stood, dropping her book by her side and smoothing her clothes and her hair until he was in front of her and she was in his arms, his mouth warm against her own.

"I missed you," she said, running her hand down his cheek, marveling at the fact of his presence. Light stubble brushed against her palm as he moved his chin against her touch, catlike. "Don't ever go away again."

He laughed, tipping his head back slightly, and then dropped a kiss on her forehead, shifting his bag over his shoulder to keep it from slipping. "I've come back," he said.

"Yes, and you are never allowed to leave again," Rose said. She'd think back on that later and wonder if his expression had changed, but at the time she didn't notice a thing. She picked up her book and slipped her hand into his as they headed to pick up his luggage.

"Was it that awful? Your sisters didn't come home when they got your father's letter?" He turned to face her so he was standing backward on the escalator, his hands spread over the rails.

"No, they didn't come home, and thank heavens, because that would have been even worse. It's just been me and Mom and Dad."

"Lonely?" He turned back and stepped off the escalator, holding his hand out to help her step off. Swoon-worthy, as Cordy would have said.

"Ugh. I don't want to talk about it. How was your trip?"

Jonathan had been gone for two weeks, nearly the entire break, presenting at a conference in Germany and stopping on the way back to visit friends in England. Rose had carefully crossed each passing day off in her day planner, feeling like a ridiculous schoolgirl with a crush but unable to stop herself. Ridiculous, she knew. When they had been a couple for only a few months, she'd been the one to utter the magical four-letter word first, breathless and laughing as they lay on his bed and he alternated between kissing her neck and tickling her mercilessly. She'd been thinking that this was love for weeks, but she couldn't say it first, and then the words slipped out in a rush of giddiness. She'd frozen, horrified at her own lack of control, but then he'd whispered back that he loved her, too, and her relief and happiness made her feel faint. Being without him had felt like a cruel amputation, and she reached out for his hand to remind herself that he was there, after all.

He took her hand in his and lifted it to his mouth, kissing her fingertips. "You look lovely," he said. "I'd forgotten how beautiful you are."

Rose blushed and shook her head, smoothing her clothes again with her free hand. "I look awful. I didn't have time to change and—"

Jonathan cut her off with another kiss, this time in the center of her palm. "I wish you could see yourself through my eyes," he said softly. "My vision is better."

She drove them back to his apartment and they hauled his suitcase inside. She hadn't been here since he'd left—he had no pets, no plants, and there was no reason for her to visit unless he was there—and the air was thick and stale. She opened the windows and turned on the fan, and they sat together on the sofa, fingers entwined, until he cleared his throat awkwardly. "I've got a little news."

"Good or bad?" Rose wasn't quite listening. She reached out with her free hand and stroked a wayward lock of hair behind his ear. It had gotten long—she'd have to make an appointment for him to have it cut.

"Excellent, actually. While I was in Oxford with Paul and Shari—"

"How are they, by the way?" Paul had been Jonathan's roommate in their doctoral program, and many of Jonathan's best stories revolved around their misadventures.

"Great—sleep-deprived, you know, but head over heels with the baby, and they seem happy. I've got pictures. They'd love to meet you."

Rose laughed. "Not likely, unless they're considering a transatlantic flight with a newborn."

Jonathan swallowed awkwardly. "Well, that's the thing, love. When I was over there, Paul and I had lunch with his dean." He paused, searching for the next words, and Rose felt her heart growing colder, a thin sheet of ice covering its surface like frost on a windowpane.

"He's very interested in my research. He wants me to join the faculty there—a lab of my own, graduate students to work with me. It's ideal. A perfect opportunity."

Rose reached for the glass of water he'd left for her on the coffee table. Her mouth was painfully dry, her throat ached. Alone again. It seemed it was Just Her Luck to have finally found her Orlando, her perfect love, only to have him leave her. Shakespeare's Rosalind had never had this kind of problem; she was too busy cross-dressing and frolicking around in forests with her servant. Rough life. Rose set the glass back on the table and slipped her other hand from his.

"So you're leaving," she said dully, when she could push her parched lips into words again.

"I'd like to," he said softly. He reached for her hand again, but she moved so she was facing forward, away from him, her ankles crossed primly, hands folded in her lap, as though she were waiting to be served at a particularly stuffy tea party.

"But we were supposed to get married," she whispered.

"And we will, of course we will. I'm not saying that at all. But I'd be a fool to turn this down. You can see that, can't you?" His voice was pleading, but she turned away.

"When are you going?"

"I haven't said I am, as of yet. But I could start at the beginning of the third term, just after Easter."

"Your contract here goes through the end of the year, doesn't it? You're just going to break your contract?"

"Rose, don't be like that. Please hear me out. I want you to come with me."

Rose turned her head toward him and barked a short, harsh laugh. "To England? You want me to come to England with you? You have got to be kidding, Jonathan. I have a job. I have a life here. I'm not like you. I don't get to go globe-hopping every time I get a whim."

"That's a bit harsh, don't you think?" he asked, recoiling from the bite. Our Rose, *whose tongue more poisons than the adder's tooth*! He rubbed his hands quickly on his knees and stood up, rumpling his hair impatiently. "It could be good for us—for both of us. For me, yes, but for you, too. You haven't got a job past next year, right?"

"Is this supposed to make me feel better?" Rose had been told this spring, in no uncertain terms, that her adjunct contract wouldn't be renewed after this year. No hard feelings, nothing personal, but they hadn't any tenure-track positions open, and it was so important to keep the department adjuncts fresh, to keep the curriculum vital, you know. Yes, Rose had thought sourly, and because you can keep milling through those brand-new Ph.D.s and never have to give them a penny more than you think you can get away with. The thought of having to find a new job paralyzed her, the thought of being without a job paralyzed her, and she was highly tempted to stick her fingers in her ears and sing until the entire thing blew over.

"I don't know about better. But I'd hoped you'd be at least a little happy for me."

She looked up at him, his eyes sad and wounded, and she crumbled a little. "I am. I'm sorry. But it's so big. . . . It's such a huge change from what we were planning."

"We always knew we'd have to consider it, love. My position here is only temporary, you know that."

"But I thought maybe . . ." Rose didn't want to say what she had thought. She'd just assumed that he would give up this fancy academic jet-setting and find something nearby, something where she wouldn't have to go anywhere. Where she wouldn't have to change at all. "I'm sorry," she said again.

"Oh, Rose, I'm sorry, too. Let's not talk about it anymore. Let's just enjoy being together for a bit."

He came over to her and put his arms around her and kissed her, and that did only a little to soothe the ache inside where her heart had been bruised. So that was it. He wouldn't stay, and she wouldn't—couldn't—go. It was ridiculous to even think about it.

His hands were in her hair, slowly pulling the pins out and letting it fall down her back the way he liked it, stroking the tresses the way she liked it, the gentle pull against her scalp so soothing. She wasn't paying attention. Bean and Cordy were sitting on her shoulders, whispering in her ears like a cartoon devil and angel. Or two devils, really. "You could go if you wanted to, Rosie," our youngest sister said. "Just pick up and go. It's not so hard. I do it all the time."

"What are you afraid of?" Bean mocked. "Don't want to leave your glamorous life behind?"

Okay, so it wasn't a glamorous life. But it was important. She was important. We needed her. Didn't we?

Bean and Cordy didn't answer. Bean was adjusting her horns, and Cordy was chasing her own forked tail. You need me, Rose thought fiercely. They turned away.

"Hush," Jonathan said, as though he could hear the busy spinning of Rose's thoughts, and he kissed her, and we fell off her shoulders as though we'd been physically brushed aside.

ACT II

Setting: Interior, the Golden Dragon, a small Chinese restaurant a few towns over, famed more for its convenience than its cuisine. Also the site of an infamous embarrassment for Bean, aged eight, in which she devoured a sweet and sour pork entrée all by herself and then regurgitated the entire thing tidily into the mouth of a fake dragon hidden behind a plant, certain it would never be found there.
Characters: Rose, Jonathan, our father, our mother.

They sat around the table, the four of them, sharing dishes and companionable chatter. Tea steamed in tiny cups, and Rose was fumbling with her chopsticks, envying Jonathan's easy grace with the infernal things.

"We have something to tell you," our father said, clearing his throat.

Rose looked up quickly, warily. This was the sort of announcement that had preceded the game-changing births of both Bean and Cordy. Whatever the news was, it wasn't bound to be good.

Our father cleared his throat again, but it was our mother who spoke, leaping in, tearing off the conversational Band-Aid. "I have breast cancer," she said.

The ice in Rose's throat grew solid, and she grabbed for her still-scalding cup of tea, taking a long swallow, letting the liquid burn away the freeze inside her, leaving a bubble on her tongue she would feel every time she spoke for the next few days. There was silence. The few other diners in the restaurant kept eating, oblivious.

"Mom," Rose finally said. "Are you sure?"

Our mother nodded. "It's early, you see. But I found a lump—what was it, a month ago?" She looked at our father for confirmation, the quiet ease of cooperative conversation they had developed years ago. He nodded.

"A month ago?" Rose's voice cracked. She set down her teacup, hand shaking. "Why didn't you call me? I could have . . ." She trailed off, unsure of what she could have done. But she could have done something. She could have taken care of this. She took care of everything. How had she missed this? A month, they'd been going to doctors and having quiet conversations between themselves, and she hadn't seen it at all?

"We've been to the oncologist, and it's malignant. It doesn't look like it's spread, but it's quite large. So they're going to do a round of chemotherapy before surgery. Shrink it down a bit. And then . . ." Our mother's voice caught and trembled for a moment, as though the meaning behind the clinical words had only just become clear to her, and she swallowed and took a breath. "And then a mastectomy. You know, just get the whole problem dealt with." She said this as though it were something she had woken up and decided to do on a relative lark. Like going on a cruise, say, or taking up tennis.

"I'm so sorry," Jonathan said. He reached across the table and put his hand over our mother's, squeezed. He was so elegant in his sympathy. "What can we do?"

Rose stared wildly around the restaurant, at the gilt and red and paper placemats. This is what she would remember, she knew, not the fear in our mother's eyes, or the pounding of her own heart, but how desperately tacky this place was, how cheap it looked, how the chopsticks had not broken properly when she had separated them but splintered along the center. This is what she would remember.

But when the shock passed, it had become something, forgive her for saying it, something of a relief. Thank God, a purpose. An excuse to be needed. A reason to turn Jonathan's abandonment into something important. So the next day she broke her lease, packed up her things, and moved back home, uninvited.

It wasn't until she had been home for a while, had straightened out the little messes around the house and helped our mother through the first rounds of chemotherapy that the shame of her situation had hit her. How humiliating to be living at home again. If she told people that she had moved back to help care for our mother, of course they would nod and sigh sympathetically. But still, where was she? Living with our parents? At her age? She felt like a swimmer who had been earnestly beating back the waves only to find herself exhausted and just as far from shore as when she had begun. She was lonely and tired.

Embarrassed even by the thought of herself in this rudderless life, she flushed and stood impatiently from the window seat, where she'd been staring in irritation at our mother's wildflower garden. The garden had, in the way of wildflower gardens, grown out of control. Our mother loved it—the way it drew butterflies and fat bees, the dizzy

way the purples and yellows blurred together as the stems tangled—
but Rose preferred her gardens to be more obedient.

She turned to look back into the living room, one dim light behind
our father's favorite sun-paled orange wing-back chair spreading
shadows over the opened books that covered every surface despite
her attempts to keep them orderly. Our family's vices—disorder and
literature—captured in evening tableau. We were never organized
readers who would see a book through to its end in any sort of logical
order. We weave in and out of words like tourists on a hop-on, hop-off
bus tour. Put a book down in the kitchen to go to the bathroom and
you might return to find it gone, replaced by another of equal interest.
We are indiscriminate. Our father, of course, limits his reading to
things by, of, and about our boy Bill, but our mother brought diversity
to our readings and therefore our education. It was never really
a problem for any of us to read a children's biography of Amelia
Earhart followed by a self-help book on alcoholism (from which no
one in the family suffered), followed by Act III of *All's Well That Ends
Well*, followed by a collection of Neruda sonnets. Cordy claims this is
the source of her inability to focus on anything for more than a few
minutes at a time, but we do not believe her. It is just our way.

And it wasn't that Rose regretted being home, exactly. Our parents' house and Barnwell in general were far more pleasant than the
anonymous apartment she'd rented in Columbus—thin carpet over
concrete floors, neighbors moving in and out so quickly she'd
stopped bothering to learn their names—but after she filled our parents' pill cases and straightened the living room, after she had finally
hired a lawn service and balanced the checkbook, after she went with
our parents to our mother's chemo treatments, sitting in the waiting
room because they didn't need her there, not really, they would have
been fine just the two of them, her life was almost as empty as it had
been before.

The tiny clock on the mantelpiece chimed ten, and Rose sighed in relief. Ten was a perfectly acceptable hour to go to bed without feeling like a complete loafer. She walked toward the stairs and then paused by the mirror, warped and pale, that had hung there since any of us could remember. Rose stared at her reflection and spoke six words none of us had ever said before.

"I wish my sisters were here."

*T*he fox, the ape and the humble-bee, Were still at odds, being but three.

Our father once wrote an essay on the importance of the number three in Shakespeare's work. A little bit of nothing, he said, a bagatelle, but it was always our favorite. The Father, the Son, the Holy Spirit. The Billy Goats Gruff, the Three Blind Mice, *Three Men in a Boat (To Say Nothing of the Dog)*. *King Lear*—Goneril, Regan, Cordelia. *The Merchant of Venice*—Portia, Nerissa, Jessica.

And us—Rosalind, Bianca, Cordelia.

The Weird Sisters.

We have, while trapped in the car with our father behind the wheel, been subjected to extended remixes of the history of the word "weird" in *Macbeth* with a special encore set of Norse and Scottish Sources Shakespeare Used in Creating This Important Work. These indignities we will spare you.

But it is worth noting, especially now that "weird" has evolved from its delicious original meaning of supernatural strangeness into something depressingly critical and pedestrian, as in, "'Don't you think Rose's outfit looks *weird*?' Bean asked," that Shakespeare didn't really mean the sisters were weird at all.

The word he originally used was much closer to "wyrd," and that has an entirely different meaning. "Wyrd" means fate. And we might argue that we are not fated to do anything, that we have chosen everything in our lives, that there is no such thing as destiny. And we would be lying.

Rose always first, Bean never first, Cordy always last. And if we don't accept it, don't see, like Shakespeare's Weird Sisters did, that we cannot fight our family and cannot fight our fates, well, whose failing is that but our own? Our destiny is in the way we were born, in the way we were raised, in the sum of the three of us.

The history of this trinity is fractious—a constantly shifting dividing line, never equal, never equitable. Two against one, or three opposed, but never all together. Upon Cordy's birth, Rose took Bean into her, two against one. And when Bean rebelled, refused any longer to play Rose's games, Rose and Cordy found each other, and Cordy became the willing follower. Two against one.

Until Rose went away and we were three apart.

And then Bean and Cordy found each other sneaking out of their respective windows onto the broad-limbed oak trees one hot summer night, and we were two against one again.

And now here we are, measuring our distance an arm's length away, staying far apart and cold. For what? To hold the others at bay? To protect ourselves?

We see stories in magazines or newspapers sometimes, or read novels, about the deep and loving relationships between sisters. Sisters are supposed to be tight and connected, sharing family history and lore, laughing over misadventures. But we are not that way. We never have been, really, because even our partnering was more for spite than for love. Who *are* these sisters who act like this, who treat each other as their best friends? We have never met them. We know plenty of sisters who get along well, certainly, but wherefore the myth?

We don't think Cordy minds, really, because she tends to take things as they come. Rose minds, certainly, because she likes things to align with her mental image. And Bean? Well, it comes and goes with Bean, as does everything with her. To forge such an unnatural friendship would just require so much *effort*.

Our estrangement is not drama-laden—we have not betrayed one another's trust, we have not stolen lovers or fought over money or property or any of the things that irreparably break families apart. The answer, for us, is much simpler.

See, we love one another. We just don't happen to like one another very much.

A Discovery of Witches

BY

Deborah Harkness

"A wonderfully imaginative grown-up fantasy with all the magic of *Harry Potter* or *Twilight*."
—*People*

Deep in the stacks of Oxford's Bodleian Library, young scholar Diana Bishop unwittingly calls up a bewitched alchemical manuscript in the course of her research. Descended from an old and distinguished line of witches, Diana wants nothing to do with sorcery; so after a furtive glance and a few notes, she banishes the book to the stacks. But her discovery sets a fantastical underworld stirring, and a horde of daemons, witches, and vampires soon descends upon the library. Diana has stumbled upon a coveted treasure lost for centuries—and she is the only creature who can break its spell.

Chapter 1

The leather-bound volume was nothing remarkable. To an ordinary historian, it would have looked no different from hundreds of other manuscripts in Oxford's Bodleian Library, ancient and worn. But I knew there was something odd about it from the moment I collected it.

Duke Humfrey's Reading Room was deserted on this late-September afternoon, and requests for library materials were filled quickly now that the summer crush of visiting scholars was over and the madness of the fall term had not yet begun. Even so, I was surprised when Sean stopped me at the call desk.

"Dr. Bishop, your manuscripts are up," he whispered, voice tinged with a touch of mischief. The front of his argyle sweater was streaked with the rusty traces of old leather bindings, and he brushed at it self-consciously. A lock of sandy hair tumbled over his forehead when he did.

"Thanks," I said, flashing him a grateful smile. I was flagrantly disregarding the rules limiting the number of books a scholar could call in a single day. Sean, who'd shared many a drink with me in the pink-stuccoed pub across the street in our graduate-student days, had been filling my requests without complaint for more than a week. "And stop calling me Dr. Bishop. I always think you're talking to someone else."

He grinned back and slid the manuscripts—all containing fine examples of alchemical illustrations from the Bodleian's collections—over his battered oak desk, each one tucked into a protective gray cardboard box. "Oh, there's one more." Sean disappeared into the cage for a moment and returned with a thick, quarto-size manuscript bound simply in mottled calfskin. He laid it on top of the pile and stooped to inspect it. The thin gold rims of his glasses sparked in the dim light provided by the old bronze reading lamp that was attached to a shelf. "This one's not been called up for a while. I'll make a note that it needs to be boxed after you return it."

"Do you want me to remind you?"

"No. Already made a note here." Sean tapped his head with his fingertips.

"Your mind must be better organized than mine." My smile widened.

Sean looked at me shyly and tugged on the call slip, but it remained where it was, lodged between the cover and the first pages. "This one doesn't want to let go," he commented.

Muffled voices chattered in my ear, intruding on the familiar hush of the room.

"Did you hear that?" I looked around, puzzled by the strange sounds.

"What?" Sean replied, looking up from the manuscript.

Traces of gilt shone along its edges and caught my eye. But those faded touches of gold could not account for a faint, iridescent shimmer that seemed to be escaping from between the pages. I blinked.

"Nothing." I hastily drew the manuscript toward me, my skin prickling when it made contact with the leather. Sean's fingers were still holding the call slip, and now it slid easily out of the binding's grasp. I hoisted the volumes into my arms and tucked them under my chin, assailed by a whiff of the uncanny that drove away the library's familiar smell of pencil shavings and floor wax.

"Diana? Are you okay?" Sean asked with a concerned frown.

"Fine. Just a bit tired," I replied, lowering the books away from my nose.

I walked quickly through the original, fifteenth-century part of the library, past the rows of Elizabethan reading desks with their three ascending bookshelves and scarred writing surfaces. Between them, Gothic windows directed the reader's attention up to the coffered ceilings, where bright paint and gilding picked out the details of the university's crest of three crowns and open book and where its motto, "God is my illumination," was proclaimed repeatedly from on high.

Another American academic, Gillian Chamberlain, was my sole companion in the library on this Friday night. A classicist who taught at Bryn Mawr, Gillian spent her time poring over scraps of papyrus sandwiched between sheets of glass. I sped past her, trying to avoid eye contact, but the creaking of the old floor gave me away.

My skin tingled as it always did when another witch looked at me.

"Diana?" she called from the gloom. I smothered a sigh and stopped.

"Hi, Gillian." Unaccountably possessive of my hoard of manuscripts, I remained as far from the witch as possible and angled my body so they weren't in her line of sight.

"What are you doing for Mabon?" Gillian was always stopping by my desk to ask me to spend time with my "sisters" while I was in town. With the Wiccan celebrations of the autumn equinox just days away, she was redoubling her efforts to bring me into the Oxford coven.

"Working," I said promptly.

"There are some very nice witches here, you know," Gillian said with prim disapproval. "You really should join us on Monday."

"Thanks. I'll think about it," I said, already moving in the direction of the Selden End, the airy seventeenth-century addition that ran perpendicular to the main axis of Duke Humfrey's. "I'm working on a conference paper, though, so don't count on it." My aunt Sarah had always warned me it wasn't possible for one witch to lie to another, but that hadn't stopped me from trying.

Gillian made a sympathetic noise, but her eyes followed me.

Back at my familiar seat facing the arched, leaded windows, I resisted the temptation to dump the manuscripts on the table and wipe my hands. Instead, mindful of their age, I lowered the stack carefully.

The manuscript that had appeared to tug on its call slip lay on top of the pile. Stamped in gilt on the spine was a coat of arms belonging to Elias Ashmole, a seventeenth-century book collector and alchemist whose books and papers had come to the Bodleian from the Ashmolean Museum in the nineteenth century, along with the number 782. I reached out, touching the brown leather.

A mild shock made me withdraw my fingers quickly, but not quickly enough. The tingling traveled up my arms, lifting my skin into tiny goose pimples, then spread across my shoulders, tensing the muscles in my back and neck. These sensations quickly receded, but they left behind a hollow feeling of unmet desire. Shaken by my response, I stepped away from the library table.

Even at a safe distance, this manuscript was challenging me—threatening the walls I'd erected to separate my career as a scholar from my birthright as the last of the Bishop witches. Here, with my hard-earned doctorate, tenure, and promotions in hand and my career beginning to blossom, I'd renounced my family's heritage and created a life that depended on reason and scholarly abilities, not inexplicable hunches and spells. I was in Oxford to complete a research project. Upon its conclusion, my findings would be published, substantiated with extensive analysis and footnotes, and presented to human colleagues, leaving no room for mysteries and no place in my work for what could be known only through a witch's sixth sense.

But—albeit unwittingly—I had called up an alchemical manuscript that I needed for my research and that also seemed to possess an otherworldly power that was impossible to ignore. My fingers itched to open it and learn more. Yet an even stronger impulse held me back: Was my curiosity intellectual, related to my scholarship? Or did it have to do with my family's connection to witchcraft?

I drew the library's familiar air into my lungs and shut my eyes, hoping that would bring clarity. The Bodleian had always been a sanctuary to me, a place unassociated with the Bishops. Tucking my shaking hands under my elbows, I stared at Ashmole 782 in the growing twilight and wondered what to do.

My mother would instinctively have known the answer, had she been standing in my place. Most members of the Bishop family were talented witches, but my mother, Rebecca, was special. Everyone said so. Her supernatural abilities had manifested early, and by the time she was in grade school, she could outmagic most of the senior witches in the local coven with her intuitive understanding of spells, startling foresight, and uncanny knack for seeing beneath the surface of people and events. My mother's younger sister, my Aunt Sarah, was a skilled witch, too, but her talents were more mainstream: a deft hand with potions and a perfect command of witchcraft's traditional lore of spells and charms.

My fellow historians didn't know about the family, of course, but everyone in Madison, the remote town in upstate New York where I'd lived with Sarah since the age of seven, knew all about the Bishops. My ancestors had moved from Massachusetts after the Revolutionary War. By then more than a century had passed since Bridget Bishop was executed at Salem. Even so, rumors and gossip followed them to their new home. After pulling up stakes and resettling in Madison, the Bishops worked hard to demonstrate how useful it could be to have witchy neighbors for healing the sick and predicting the weather. In time the family set down roots in the community deep enough to withstand the inevitable outbreaks of superstition and human fear.

But my mother had a curiosity about the world that led her beyond the safety of Madison. She went first to Harvard, where she met a young wizard named Stephen Proctor. He also had a long magical lineage and a desire to experience life outside the scope of his family's New England history and influence. Rebecca Bishop and Stephen Proctor were a charming couple, my mother's all-American frankness a counterpoint to my father's more formal, old-fashioned ways. They became anthropologists, immersing themselves in foreign cultures and beliefs, sharing their intellectual passions along with their deep devotion to each other. After securing positions on the faculty in area schools—my mother at her alma mater, my father at Wellesley—they made research trips abroad and made a home for their new family in Cambridge.

I have few memories of my childhood, but each one is vivid and surprisingly clear. All feature my parents: the feel of corduroy on my father's elbows, the lily of the valley that scented my mother's perfume, the clink of their wineglasses on Friday nights when they'd put me to bed and dine together by candlelight. My mother told me bedtime stories, and my father's brown briefcase clattered when he dropped it by the front door. These memories would strike a familiar chord with most people.

Other recollections of my parents would not. My mother never seemed to do laundry, but my clothes were always clean and neatly folded. Forgotten permission slips for field trips to the zoo appeared in my desk when the teacher came to collect them. And no matter what condition my father's study was in when I went in for a good-night kiss (and it usually looked as if something had exploded), it was always perfectly orderly the next morning. In kindergarten I'd asked my friend Amanda's mother why she bothered washing the dishes with soap and water when all you needed to do was stack them in the sink, snap your fingers, and whisper a few words. Mrs. Schmidt laughed at my strange idea of housework, but confusion had clouded her eyes.

That night my parents told me we had to be careful about how we spoke about magic and with whom we discussed it. Humans outnumbered us and found our power frightening, my mother explained, and fear was the strongest force on earth. I hadn't confessed at the time that magic—my mother's especially—frightened me, too.

By day my mother looked like every other kid's mother in Cambridge: slightly unkempt, a bit disorganized, and perpetually harassed by the pressures of home and office. Her blond hair was fashionably tousled even though the clothes she wore remained stuck in 1977—long billowy skirts, oversize pants and shirts, and men's vests and blazers she picked up in thrift stores the length and breadth of Boston in imitation of Annie Hall. Nothing would have made you look twice if you passed her in the street or stood behind her in the supermarket.

In the privacy of our home, with the curtains drawn and the door locked, my mother became someone else. Her movements were confident and sure, not rushed and hectic. Sometimes she even seemed to float. As she went around the house, singing and picking up stuffed animals and books, her face slowly transformed into something otherworldly and beautiful.

When my mother was lit up with magic, you couldn't tear your eyes away from her.

"Mommy's got a firecracker inside her," was the way my father explained it with his wide, indulgent grin. But firecrackers, I learned, were not simply bright and lively. They were unpredictable, and they could startle and frighten you, too.

My father was at a lecture one night when my mother decided to clean the silver and became mesmerized by a bowl of water she'd set on the dining-room table. As she stared at the glassy surface, it became covered with a fog that twisted itself into tiny, ghostly shapes. I gasped with delight as they grew, filling the room with fantastic beings. Soon they were crawling up the drapes and clinging to the ceiling. I cried out for my mother's help, but she remained intent on the water. Her concentration didn't waver until something half human and half animal crept near and pinched my arm. That brought her out of her reveries, and she exploded into a shower of angry red light that beat back the wraiths and left an odor of singed feathers in the house. My father noticed the strange smell the moment he returned, his alarm evident. He found us huddled in bed together. At the sight of him, my mother burst into apologetic tears. I never felt entirely safe in the dining room again.

Any remaining sense of security evaporated after I turned seven, when my mother and father went to Africa and didn't come back alive.

I shook myself and focused again on the dilemma that faced me. The manuscript sat on the library table in a pool of lamplight. Its magic pulled on something dark and knotted inside me. My fingers returned to the smooth leather. This time the prickling sensation felt familiar. I vaguely remembered experiencing something like it once before, looking through some papers on the desk in my father's study.

Turning resolutely away from the leather-bound volume, I occupied myself with something more rational: searching for the list of alchemical texts I'd generated before leaving New Haven. It was on my desk, hidden among the loose papers, book call slips, receipts, pencils, pens, and library maps, neatly arranged by collection and then by the number assigned to each text by a library clerk when it had entered into the Bodleian. Since arriving a few weeks ago, I had been working through the list methodically. The copied-out catalog description for Ashmole 782 read, "*Anthropologia, or a treatis containing a short description of Man in two parts: the first Anatomical, the second Psychological.*" As with most of the works I studied, there was no telling what the contents were from the title.

My fingers might be able to tell me about the book without even cracking open the covers. Aunt Sarah always used her fingers to figure out what was in the mail before she opened it, in case the envelope contained a bill she didn't want to pay. That way she could plead ignorance when it turned out she owed the electric company money.

The gilt numbers on the spine winked.

I sat down and considered the options.

Ignore the magic, open the manuscript, and try to read it like a human scholar?

Push the bewitched volume aside and walk away?

Sarah would chortle with delight if she knew my predicament. She had always maintained that my efforts to keep magic at arm's length were futile. But I'd been doing so ever since my parents' funeral. There the witches among the guests had scrutinized me for signs that the Bishop and Proctor blood was in my veins, all the while patting me encouragingly and predicting it was only a matter of time before I took my mother's place in the local coven. Some had whispered their doubts about the wisdom of my parents' decision to marry.

"Too much power," they muttered when they thought I wasn't listening. "They were bound to attract attention—even without studying ancient ceremonial religion."

This was enough to make me blame my parents' death on the supernatural power they wielded and to search for a different way of life. Turning my back on anything to do with magic, I buried myself in the stuff of human adolescence—horses and boys and romantic novels—and tried to disappear among the town's ordinary residents. At puberty I had problems with depression and anxiety. It was all very normal, the kindly human doctor assured my aunt.

Sarah didn't tell him about the voices, about my habit of picking up the phone a good minute before it rang, or that she had to enchant the doors and windows when there was a full moon to keep me from wandering into the woods in my sleep. Nor did she mention that when I was angry the chairs in the house rearranged themselves into a precarious pyramid before crashing to the floor once my mood lifted.

When I turned thirteen, my aunt decided it was time for me to channel some of my power into learning the basics of witchcraft. Lighting candles with a few whispered words or hiding pimples with a time-tested potion—these were a teenage witch's habitual first steps. But I was unable to master even the simplest spell, burned every potion my aunt taught me, and stubbornly refused to submit to her tests to see if I'd inherited my mother's uncannily accurate second sight.

The voices, the fires, and other unexpected eruptions lessened as my hormones quieted, but my unwillingness to learn the family business remained. It made my aunt anxious to have an untrained witch in the house, and it was with some relief that Sarah sent me off to a college in Maine. Except for the magic, it was a typical coming-of-age story.

What got me away from Madison was my intellect. It had always been precocious, leading me to talk and read before other children my age. Aided by a prodigious, photographic memory—which made it easy for me to recall the layouts of textbooks and spit out the required information on tests—my schoolwork was soon established as a place where my family's magical legacy was irrelevant. I'd skipped my final years of high school and started college at sixteen.

There I'd first tried to carve out a place for myself in the theater department, my imagination drawn to the spectacle and the costumes—and my mind fascinated by how completely a playwright's words could conjure up other places and times. My first few performances were heralded by my professors as extraordinary examples of the way good acting could transform an ordinary college student into someone else. The first indication that these metamorphoses might not have been the result of theatrical talent came while I was playing Ophelia in *Hamlet*. As soon as I was cast in the role, my hair started growing at an unnatural rate, tumbling down from shoulders to waist. I sat for hours beside the college's lake, irresistibly drawn to its shining surface, with my new hair streaming all around me. The boy playing Hamlet became caught up in the illusion, and we had a passionate though dangerously volatile affair. Slowly I was dissolving into Ophelia's madness, taking the rest of the cast with me.

The result might have been a riveting performance, but each new role brought fresh challenges. In my sophomore year, the situation became impossible when I was cast as Annabella in John Ford's *'Tis Pity She's a Whore*. Like the character, I attracted a string of devoted suitors—not all of them human—who followed me around campus. When they refused to leave me alone after the final curtain fell, it was clear that whatever had been unleashed couldn't be controlled. I wasn't sure how magic had crept into my acting, and I didn't want to find out. I cut my hair short. I stopped wearing flowing skirts and layered tops in favor of the black turtlenecks, khaki trousers, and loafers that the solid, ambitious prelaw students were wearing. My excess energy went into athletics.

After leaving the theater department, I attempted several more majors, looking for a field so rational that it would never yield a square inch to magic. I lacked the precision and patience for mathematics, and my efforts at biology were a disaster of failed quizzes and unfinished laboratory experiments.

At the end of my sophomore year, the registrar demanded I choose a major or face a fifth year in college. A summer study program in England offered me the opportunity to get even farther from all things Bishop. I fell in love with Oxford, the quiet glow of its morning streets. My history courses covered the exploits of kings and queens, and the only voices in my head were those that whispered from books penned in the sixteenth and seventeenth centuries. This was entirely attributable to great literature. Best of all, no one in this university town knew me, and if there were witches in the city that summer, they stayed well away. I returned home, declared a major in history, took all the required courses in record time, and graduated with honors before I turned twenty.

When I decided to pursue my doctorate, Oxford was my first choice among the possible programs. My specialty was the history of science, and my research focused on the period when science supplanted magic—the age when astrology and witch-hunts yielded to Newton and universal laws. The search for a rational order in nature, rather than a supernatural one, mirrored my own efforts to stay away from what was hidden. The lines I'd already drawn between what went on in my mind and what I carried in my blood grew more distinct.

My Aunt Sarah had snorted when she heard of my decision to specialize in seventeenth-century chemistry. Her bright red hair was an outward sign of her quick temper and sharp tongue. She was a plain-speaking, no-nonsense witch who commanded a room as soon as she entered it. A pillar of the Madison community, Sarah was often called in to manage things when there was a crisis, large or small, in town. We were on much better terms now that I wasn't subjected to a daily dose of her keen observations on human frailty and inconsistency.

Though we were separated by hundreds of miles, Sarah thought my latest attempts to avoid magic were laughable—and told me so. "We used to call that alchemy," she said. "There's a lot of magic in it."

"No, there's not," I protested hotly. The whole point of my work was to show how scientific this pursuit really was. "Alchemy tells us about the growth of experimentation, not the search for a magical elixir that turns lead into gold and makes people immortal."

"If you say so," Sarah said doubtfully. "But it's a pretty strange subject to choose if you're trying to pass as human."

After earning my degree, I fought fiercely for a spot on the faculty at Yale, the only place that was more English than England. Colleagues warned that I had little chance of being granted tenure. I churned out two books, won a handful of prizes, and collected some research grants. Then I received tenure and proved everyone wrong.

More important, my life was now my own. No one in my department, not even the historians of early America, connected my last name with that of the first Salem woman executed for witchcraft in 1692. To preserve my hard-won autonomy, I continued to keep any hint of magic or witchcraft out of my life. Of course there were exceptions, like the time I'd drawn on one of Sarah's spells when the washing machine wouldn't stop filling with water and threatened to flood my small apartment on Wooster Square. Nobody's perfect.

Now, taking note of this current lapse, I held my breath, grasped the manuscript with both hands, and placed it in one of the wedge-shaped cradles the library provided to protect its rare books. I had made my decision: to behave as a serious scholar and treat Ashmole 782 like an ordinary manuscript. I'd ignore my burning fingertips, the book's strange smell, and simply describe its contents. Then I'd decide—with professional detachment— whether it was promising enough for a longer look. My fingers trembled when I loosened the small brass clasps nevertheless.

The manuscript let out a soft sigh.

A quick glance over my shoulder assured me that the room was still empty. The only other sound was the loud ticking of the reading room's clock.

Deciding not to record "Book sighed," I turned to my laptop and opened up a new file. This familiar task—one that I'd done hundreds if not thousands of times before—was as comforting as my list's neat checkmarks. I typed the manuscript name and number and copied the title from the catalog description. I eyed its size and binding, describing both in detail.

The only thing left to do was open the manuscript.

It was difficult to lift the cover, despite the loosened clasps, as if it were stuck to the pages below. I swore under my breath and rested my hand flat on the leather for a moment, hoping that Ashmole 782 simply needed a chance to know me. It wasn't magic, exactly, to put your hand on top of a book. My palm tingled, much as my skin tingled when a witch looked at me, and the tension left the manuscript. After that, it was easy to lift the cover.

The first page was rough paper. On the second sheet, which was parchment, were the words *"Anthropologia, or a treatis containing a short description of Man,"* in Ashmole's handwriting. The neat, round curves were almost as familiar to me as my own cursive script. The second part of the title—*"in two parts: the first Anatomical, the second Psychological"*—was written in a later hand, in pencil. It was familiar, too, but I couldn't place it. Touching the writing might give me some clue, but it was against the library's rules and it would be impossible to document the information that my fingers might gather. Instead I made notes in the computer file regarding the use of ink and pencil, the two different hands, and the possible dates of the inscriptions.

As I turned the first page, the parchment felt abnormally heavy and revealed itself as the source of the manuscript's strange smell. It wasn't simply ancient. It was something more—a combination of must and musk that had no name. And I noticed immediately that three leaves had been cut neatly out of the binding.

Here, at last, was something easy to describe. My fingers flew over the keys: *"At least three folios removed, by straightedge or razor."* I peered into the valley of the manuscript's spine but couldn't tell whether any other pages were missing. The closer the parchment to my nose, the more the manuscript's power and odd smell distracted me.

I turned my attention to the illustration that faced the gap where the missing pages should be. It showed a tiny baby girl floating in a clear glass vessel. The baby held a silver rose in one hand, a golden rose in the other. On its feet were tiny wings, and drops of red liquid showered down on the baby's long black hair. Underneath the image was a label written in thick black ink indicating that it was a depiction of the philosophical child—an allegorical representation of a crucial step in creating the philosopher's stone, the chemical substance that promised to make its owner healthy, wealthy, and wise.

The colors were luminous and strikingly well preserved. Artists had once mixed crushed stone and gems into their paints to produce such powerful colors. And the image itself had been drawn by someone with real artistic skill. I had to sit on my hands to keep them from trying to learn more from a touch here and there.

But the illuminator, for all his obvious talent, had the details all wrong. The glass vessel was supposed to point up, not down. The baby was supposed to be half black and half white, to show that it was a hermaphrodite. It should have had male genitalia and female breasts—or two heads, at the very least.

Alchemical imagery was allegorical, and notoriously tricky. That's why I was studying it, searching for patterns that would reveal a systematic, logical approach to chemical transformation in the days before the periodic table of the elements. Images of the moon were almost always representations of silver, for example, while images of the sun referred to gold. When the two were combined chemically, the process was represented as a wedding. In time the pictures had been replaced by words. Those words, in turn, became the grammar of chemistry.

But this manuscript put my belief in the alchemists' logic to the test. Each illustration had at least one fundamental flaw, and there was no accompanying text to help make sense of it.

I searched for something—anything—that would agree with my knowledge of alchemy. In the softening light, faint traces of handwriting appeared on one of the pages. I slanted the desk lamp so that it shone more brightly.

There was nothing there.

Slowly I turned the page as if it were a fragile leaf.

Words shimmered and moved across its surface—hundreds of words—invisible unless the angle of light and the viewer's perspective were just right.

I stifled a cry of surprise.

Ashmole 782 was a palimpsest—a manuscript within a manuscript. When parchment was scarce, scribes carefully washed the ink from old books and then wrote new text on the blank sheets. Over time the former writing often reappeared underneath as a textual ghost, discernible with the help of ultraviolet light, which could see under ink stains and bring faded text back to life.

There was no ultraviolet light strong enough to reveal these traces, though. This was not an ordinary palimpsest. The writing hadn't been washed away—it had been hidden with some sort of spell. But why would anyone go to the trouble of bewitching the text in an alchemical book? Even experts had trouble puzzling out the obscure language and fanciful imagery the authors used.

Dragging my attention from the faint letters that were moving too quickly for me to read, I focused instead on writing a synopsis of the manuscript's contents. *"Puzzling,"* I typed. *"Textual captions from the fifteenth to seventeenth centuries, images mainly fifteenth century. Image sources possibly older? Mixture of paper and vellum. Colored and black inks, the former of unusually high quality. Illustrations are well executed, but details are incorrect, missing. Depicts the creation of the philosopher's stone, alchemical birth/creation, death, resurrection, and transformation. A confused copy of an earlier manuscript? A strange book, full of anomalies."*

My fingers hesitated above the keys.

Scholars do one of two things when they discover information that doesn't fit what they already know. Either they sweep it aside so it doesn't bring their cherished theories into question or they focus on it with laserlike intensity and try to get to the bottom of the mystery. If this book hadn't been under a spell, I might have been tempted to do the latter. Because it was bewitched, I was strongly inclined toward the former.

And when in doubt, scholars usually postpone a decision.

I typed an ambivalent final line: *"Needs more time? Possibly recall later?"*

Holding my breath, I fastened the cover with a gentle tug. Currents of magic still thrummed through the manuscript, especially fierce around the clasps.

Relieved that it was closed, I stared at Ashmole 782 for a few more moments. My fingers wanted to stray back and touch the brown leather. But this time I resisted, just as I had resisted touching the inscriptions and illustrations to learn more than a human historian could legitimately claim to know.

Aunt Sarah had always told me that magic was a gift. If it was, it had strings attached that bound me to all the Bishop witches who had come before me. There was a price to be paid for using this inherited magical power and for working the spells and charms that made up the witches' carefully guarded craft. By opening Ashmole 782, I'd breached the wall that divided my magic from my scholarship. But back on the right side of it again, I was more determined than ever to remain there.

I packed up my computer and notes and picked up the stack of manuscripts, carefully putting Ashmole 782 on the bottom. Mercifully, Gillian wasn't at her desk, though her papers were still strewn around. She must be planning on working late and was off for a cup of coffee.

"Finished?" Sean asked when I reached the call desk.

"Not quite. I'd like to reserve the top three for Monday."

"And the fourth?"

"I'm done with it," I blurted, pushing the manuscripts toward him. "You can send it back to the stacks."

Sean put it on top of a pile of returns he had already gathered. He walked with me as far as the staircase, said good-bye, and disappeared behind a swinging door. The conveyor belt that would whisk Ashmole 782 back into the bowels of the library clanged into action.

I almost turned and stopped him but let it go.

My hand was raised to push open the door on the ground floor when the air around me constricted, as if the library were squeezing me tight. The air shimmered for a split second, just as the pages of the manuscript had shimmered on Sean's desk, causing me to shiver involuntarily and raising the tiny hairs on my arms.

Something had just happened. Something magical.

My face turned back toward Duke Humfrey's, and my feet threatened to follow.

It's nothing, I thought, resolutely walking out of the library.

Are you sure? whispered a long-ignored voice.

Chapter 2

Oxford's bells chimed seven times. Night didn't follow twilight as slowly as it would have a few months ago, but the transformation was still lingering. The library staff had turned on the lamps only thirty minutes before, casting small pools of gold in the gray light.

It was the twenty-first day of September. All over the world, witches were sharing a meal on the eve of the autumn equinox to celebrate Mabon and greet the impending darkness of winter. But the witches of Oxford would have to do without me. I was slated to give the keynote address at an important conference next month. My ideas were still unformed, and I was getting anxious.

At the thought of what my fellow witches might be eating somewhere in Oxford, my stomach rumbled. I'd been in the library since half past nine that morning, with only a short break for lunch.

Sean had taken the day off, and the person working at the call desk was new. She'd given me some trouble when I requested one crumbling item and tried to persuade me to use microfilm instead. The reading room's supervisor, Mr. Johnson, overheard and came out of his office to intervene.

"My apologies, Dr. Bishop," he'd said hurriedly, pushing his heavy, dark-rimmed glasses over the bridge of his nose. "If you need to consult this manuscript for your research, we will be happy to oblige." He disappeared to fetch the restricted item and delivered it with more apologies about the inconvenience and the new staff. Gratified that my scholarly credentials had done the trick, I spent the afternoon happily reading.

I pulled two coiled weights from the upper corners of the manuscript and closed it carefully, pleased at the amount of work I'd completed. After encountering the bewitched manuscript on Friday, I'd devoted the weekend to routine tasks rather than alchemy in order to restore a sense of normalcy. I filled out financial-reimbursement forms, paid bills, wrote letters of recommendation, and even finished a book review. These chores were interspersed with more homey rituals like doing laundry, drinking copious amounts of tea, and trying recipes from the BBC's cooking programs.

After an early start this morning, I'd spent the day trying to focus on the work at hand, rather than dwelling on my recollections of Ashmole 782's strange illustrations and mysterious palimpsest. I eyed the short list of to-dos jotted down over the course of the day. Of the four questions on my follow-up list, the third was easiest to resolve. The answer was in an arcane periodical, *Notes and Queries,* which was shelved on one of the bookcases that stretched up toward the room's high ceilings. I pushed back my chair and decided to tick one item off my list before leaving.

The upper shelves of the section of Duke Humfrey's known as the Selden End were reachable by means of a worn set of stairs to a gallery that looked over the reading desks. I climbed the twisting treads to where the old buckram-covered books sat in neat chronological rows on wooden shelves. No one but me and an ancient literature don from Magdalen College seemed to use them. I located the volume and swore softly under my breath. It was on the top shelf, just out of reach.

A low chuckle startled me. I turned my head to see who was sitting at the desk at the far end of the gallery, but no one was there. I was hearing things again. Oxford was still a ghost town, and anyone who belonged to the university had left over an hour earlier to down a glass of free sherry in their college's senior common room before dinner. Given the Wiccan holiday, even Gillian had left in the late afternoon, after extending one final invitation and glancing at my pile of reading material with narrowed eyes.

I searched for the gallery's stepstool, which was missing. The Bodleian was notoriously short on such items, and it would easily take fifteen minutes to locate one in the library and haul it upstairs so that I could retrieve the volume. I hesitated. Even though I'd held a bewitched book, I'd resisted considerable temptations to work further magic on Friday. Besides, no one would see.

Despite my rationalizations, my skin prickled with anxiety. I didn't break my rules very often, and I kept mental accounts of the situations that had spurred me to turn to my magic for assistance. This was the fifth time this year, including putting the spell on the malfunctioning washing machine and touching Ashmole 782. Not too bad for the end of September, but not a personal best either.

I took a deep breath, held up my hand, and imagined the book in it.

Volume 19 of *Notes and Queries* slid backward four inches, tipped at an angle as if an invisible hand were pulling it down, and fell into my open palm with a soft thwack. Once there, it flopped open to the page I needed.

It had taken all of three seconds. I let out another breath to exhale some of my guilt. Suddenly two icy patches bloomed between my shoulder blades.

I had been seen, and not by an ordinary human observer.

When one witch studies another, the touch of their eyes tingles. Witches aren't the only creatures sharing the world with humans, however. There are also daemons—creative, artistic creatures who walk a tightrope between madness and genius. "Rock stars and serial killers" was how my aunt described these strange, perplexing beings. And there are vampires, ancient and beautiful, who feed on blood and will charm you utterly if they don't kill you first.

When a daemon takes a look, I feel the slight, unnerving pressure of a kiss.

But when a vampire stares, it feels cold, focused, and dangerous.

I mentally shuffled through the readers in Duke Humfrey's. There had been one vampire, a cherubic monk who pored over medieval missals and prayer books like a lover. But vampires aren't often found in rare-book rooms. Occasionally one succumbed to vanity and nostalgia and came in to reminisce, but it wasn't common.

Witches and daemons were far more typical in libraries. Gillian Chamberlain had been in today, studying her papyri with a magnifying glass. And there were definitely two daemons in the music reference room. They'd looked up, dazed, as I walked by on the way to Blackwell's for tea. One told me to bring him back a latte, which was some indication of how immersed he was in whatever madness gripped him at the moment.

No, it was a vampire who watched me now.

I'd happened upon a few vampires, since I worked in a field that put me in touch with scientists, and there were vampires aplenty in laboratories around the world. Science rewards long study and patience. And thanks to their solitary work habits, scientists were unlikely to be recognized by anyone except their closest co-workers. It made a life that spanned centuries rather than decades much easier to negotiate.

These days vampires gravitated toward particle accelerators, projects to decode the genome, and molecular biology. Once they had flocked to alchemy, anatomy, and electricity. If it went bang, involved blood, or promised to unlock the secrets of the universe, there was sure to be a vampire around.

I clutched my ill-gotten copy of *Notes and Queries* and turned to face the witness. He was in the shadows on the opposite side of the room in front of the paleography reference books, lounging against one of the graceful wooden pillars that held up the gallery. An open copy of Jane Roberts's *Guide to Scripts Used in English Handwriting Up to 1500* was balanced in his hands.

I had never seen this vampire before—but I was fairly certain he didn't need pointers on how to decipher old penmanship.

Anyone who has read paperback bestsellers or even watched television knows that vampires are breathtaking, but nothing prepares you to actually see one. Their bone structures are so well honed that they seem chiseled by an expert sculptor. Then they move, or speak, and your mind can't begin to absorb what you're seeing. Every movement is graceful; every word is musical. And their eyes are arresting, which is precisely how they catch their prey. One long look, a few quiet words, a touch: once you're caught in a vampire's snare you don't stand a chance.

Staring down at this vampire, I realized with a sinking feeling that my knowledge on the subject was, alas, largely theoretical. Little of it seemed useful now that I was facing one in the Bodleian Library.

The only vampire with whom I had more than a passing acquaintance worked at the nuclear particle accelerator in Switzerland. Jeremy was slight and gorgeous, with bright blond hair, blue eyes, and an infectious laugh. He'd slept with most of the women in the canton of Geneva and was now working his way through the city of Lausanne. What he did after he seduced them I had never wanted to inquire into too closely, and I'd turned down his persistent invitations to go out for a drink. I'd always figured that Jeremy was representative of the breed. But in comparison to the one who stood before me now, he seemed raw-boned, gawky, and very, very young.

This one was tall—well over six feet even accounting for the problems of perspective associated with looking down on him from the gallery. And he definitely was not slight. Broad shoulders narrowed into slender hips, which flowed into lean, muscular legs. His hands were strikingly long and agile, a mark of physiological delicacy that made your eyes drift back to them to figure out how they could belong to such a large man.

As my eyes swept over him, his own were fixed on me. From across the room, they seemed black as night, staring up under thick, equally black eyebrows, one of them lifted in a curve that suggested a question mark. His face was indeed striking—all distinct planes and surfaces, with high-angled cheekbones meeting brows that shielded and shadowed his eyes. Above his chin was one of the few places where there was room for softness—his wide mouth, which, like his long hands, didn't seem to make sense.

But the most unnerving thing about him was not his physical perfection. It was his feral combination of strength, agility, and keen intelligence that was palpable across the room. In his black trousers and soft gray sweater, with a shock of black hair swept back from his forehead and cropped close to the nape of his neck, he looked like a panther that could strike at any moment but was in no rush to do so.

He smiled. It was a small, polite smile that didn't reveal his teeth. I was intensely aware of them anyway, sitting in perfectly straight, sharp rows behind his pale lips.

The mere thought of *teeth* sent an instinctive rush of adrenaline through my body, setting my fingers tingling. Suddenly all I could think was, *Get out of this room NOW.*

The staircase seemed farther away than the four steps it took to reach it. I raced down to the floor below, stumbled on the last step, and pitched straight into the vampire's waiting arms.

Of course he had beaten me to the bottom of the stairs.

His fingers were cool, and his arms felt steelier than flesh and bone. The scent of clove, cinnamon, and something that reminded me of incense filled the air. He set me on my feet, picked *Notes and Queries* off the floor, and handed it to me with a small bow. "Dr. Bishop, I presume?"

Shaking from head to toe, I nodded.

The long, pale fingers of his right hand dipped into a pocket and pulled out a blue-and-white business card. He extended it. "Matthew Clairmont."

I gripped the edge of the card, careful not to touch his fingers in the process. Oxford University's familiar logo, with the three crowns and open book, was perched next to Clairmont's name, followed by a string of initials indicating he had already been made a member of the Royal Society.

Not bad for someone who appeared to be in his mid- to late thirties, though I imagined that his actual age was at least ten times that.

As for his research specialty, it came as no surprise that the vampire was a professor of biochemistry and affiliated with Oxford Neuroscience at the John Radcliffe Hospital. Blood and anatomy—two vampire favorites. The card bore three different laboratory numbers in addition to an office number and an e-mail address. I might not have seen him before, but he was certainly not unreachable.

"Professor Clairmont." I squeaked it out before the words caught in the back of my throat, and I quieted the urge to run screaming toward the exit.

"We've not met," he continued in an oddly accented voice. It was mostly Oxbridge but had a touch of softness that I couldn't place. His eyes, which never left my face, were not actually dark at all, I discovered, but dominated by dilated pupils bordered with a gray-green sliver of iris. Their pull was insistent, and I found myself unable to look away.

The vampire's mouth was moving again. "I'm a great admirer of your work."

My eyes widened. It was not impossible that a professor of biochemistry would be interested in seventeenth-century alchemy, but it seemed highly unlikely. I picked at the collar of my white shirt and scanned the room. We were the only two in it. There was no one at the old oak card file or at the nearby banks of computers. Whoever was at the collection desk was too far away to come to my aid.

"I found your article on the color symbolism of alchemical transformation fascinating, and your work on Robert Boyle's approach to the problems of expansion and contraction was quite persuasive," Clairmont continued smoothly, as if he were used to being the only active participant in a conversation. "I've not yet finished your latest book on alchemical apprenticeship and education, but I'm enjoying it a great deal."

"Thank you," I whispered. His gaze shifted from my eyes to my throat. I stopped picking at the buttons around my neck.

His unnatural eyes floated back to mine. "You have a marvelous way of evoking the past for your readers." I took that as a compliment, since a vampire would know if it was wrong. Clairmont paused for a moment. "Might I buy you dinner?"

My mouth dropped open. Dinner? I might not be able to escape from him in the library, but there was no reason to linger over a meal—especially one he would not be sharing, given his dietary preferences.

"I have plans," I said abruptly, unable to formulate a reasonable explanation of what those plans might involve. Matthew Clairmont must know I was a witch, and I was clearly not celebrating Mabon.

"That's too bad," he murmured, a touch of a smile on his lips. "Another time, perhaps. You are in Oxford for the year, aren't you?"

Being around a vampire was always unnerving, and Clairmont's clove scent brought back the strange smell of Ashmole 782. Unable to think straight, I resorted to nodding. It was safer.

"I thought so," said Clairmont. "I'm sure our paths will cross again. Oxford is such a small town."

"Very small," I agreed, wishing I had taken leave in London instead.

"Until then, Dr. Bishop. It has been a pleasure." Clairmont extended his hand. With the exception of their brief excursion to my collar, his eyes had not drifted once from mine. I didn't think he had blinked either. I steeled myself not to be the first to look away.

My hand went forward, hesitating for a moment before clasping his. There was a fleeting pressure before he withdrew. He stepped backward, smiled, then disappeared into the darkness of the oldest part of the library.

I stood still until my chilled hands could move freely again, then walked back to my desk and switched off my computer. *Notes and Queries* asked me accusingly why I had bothered to go and get it if I wasn't even going to look at it; my to-do list was equally full of reproach. I ripped it off the top of the pad, crumpled it up, and tossed it into the wicker basket under the desk.

"'Sufficient unto the day is the evil thereof,'" I muttered under my breath.

The reading room's night proctor glanced down at his watch when I returned my manuscripts. "Leaving early, Dr. Bishop?"

I nodded, my lips closed tightly to keep myself from asking whether he knew there had been a vampire in the paleography reference section.

He picked up the stack of gray cardboard boxes that held the manuscripts. "Will you need these tomorrow?"

"Yes," I whispered. "Tomorrow."

Having observed the last scholarly propriety of exiting the library, I was free. My feet clattered against the linoleum floors and echoed against the stone walls as I sped through the reading room's lattice gate, past the books guarded with velvet ropes to keep them from curious fingers, down the worn wooden stairs, and into the enclosed quadrangle on the ground floor. I leaned against the iron railings surrounding the bronze statue of William Herbert and sucked the chilly air into my lungs, struggling to get the vestiges of clove and cinnamon out of my nostrils.

There were always things that went bump in the night in Oxford, I told myself sternly. So there was one more vampire in town.

No matter what I told myself in the quadrangle, my walk home was faster than usual. The gloom of New College Lane was a spooky proposition at the best of times. I ran my card through the reader at New College's back gate and felt some of the tension leave my body when the gate clicked shut behind me, as if every door and wall I put between me and the library somehow kept me safe. I skirted under the chapel windows and through the narrow passage into the quad that had views of Oxford's only surviving medieval garden, complete with the traditional mound that had once offered a green prospect for students to look upon and contemplate the mysteries of God and nature. Tonight the college's spires and archways seemed especially Gothic, and I was eager to get inside.

When the door of my apartment closed behind me, I let out a sigh of relief. I was living at the top of one of the college's faculty staircases, in lodgings reserved for visiting former members. My rooms, which included a bedroom, a sitting room with a round table for dining, and a decent if small kitchen, were decorated with old prints and warm wainscoting. All the furniture looked as if it had been culled from previous incarnations of the senior common room and the master's house, with down-at-the-heels late-nineteenth-century design predominant.

In the kitchen I put two slices of bread in the toaster and poured myself a cold glass of water. Gulping it down, I opened the window to let cool air into the stuffy rooms.

Carrying my snack back into the sitting room, I kicked off my shoes and turned on the small stereo. The pure tones of Mozart filled the air. When I sat on one of the maroon upholstered sofas, it was with the intention to rest for a few moments, then take a bath and go over my notes from the day.

At half past three in the morning, I woke with a pounding heart, a stiff neck, and the strong taste of cloves in my mouth.

I got a fresh glass of water and closed the kitchen window. It was chilly, and I shivered at the touch of the damp air.

After a glance at my watch and some quick calculations, I decided to call home. It was only ten-thirty there, and Sarah and Em were as nocturnal as bats. Slipping around the rooms, I turned off all the lights except the one in my bedroom and picked up my mobile. I was out of my grimy clothes in a matter of minutes—how do you get so filthy in a library?—and into a pair of old yoga pants and a black sweater with a stretched-out neck. They were more comfortable than any pajamas.

The bed felt welcoming and firm underneath me, comforting me enough that I almost convinced myself a phone call home was unnecessary. But the water had not been able to remove the vestiges of cloves from my tongue, and I dialed the number.

"We've been waiting for your call" were the first words I heard.

Witches.

I sighed. "Sarah, I'm fine."

"All signs to the contrary." As usual, my mother's younger sister was not going to pull any punches. "Tabitha has been skittish all evening, Em got a very clear picture of you lost in the woods at night, and I haven't been able to eat anything since breakfast."

The real problem was that damn cat. Tabitha was Sarah's baby and picked up any tension within the family with uncanny precision. "I'm *fine*. I had an unexpected encounter in the library tonight, that's all."

A click told me that Em had picked up the extension. "Why aren't you celebrating Mabon?" she asked.

Emily Mather had been a fixture in my life for as long as I could remember. She and Rebecca Bishop had met as high-school students working in the summer at Plimoth Plantation, where they dug holes and pushed wheelbarrows for the archaeologists. They became best friends, then devoted pen pals when Emily went to Vassar and my mother to Harvard. Later the two reconnected in Cambridge when Em became a children's librarian. After my parents' death, Em's long weekends in Madison soon led to a new job in the local elementary school. She and Sarah became inseparable partners, even though Em had maintained her own apartment in town and the two of them had made a big deal of never being seen heading into a bedroom together while I was growing up. This didn't fool me, the neighbors, or anyone else living in town. Everybody treated them like the couple they were, regardless of where they slept. When I moved out of the Bishop house, Em moved in and had been there ever since. Like my mother and my aunt, Em came from a long line of witches.

"I was invited to the coven's party but worked instead."

"Did the witch from Bryn Mawr ask you to go?" Em was interested in the classicist, mostly (it had turned out over a fair amount of wine one summer night) because she'd once dated Gillian's mother. "It was the sixties" was all Em would say.

"Yes." I sounded harassed. The two of them were convinced I was going to see the light and begin taking my magic seriously now that I was safely tenured. Nothing cast any doubt on this wishful prognostication, and they were always thrilled when I had any contact with a witch. "But I spent the evening with Elias Ashmole instead."

"Who's he?" Em asked Sarah.

"You know, that dead guy who collected alchemy books" was Sarah's muffled reply.

"Still here, you two," I called into the phone.

"So who rattled your cage?" Sarah asked.

Given that both were witches, there was no point in trying to hide anything. "I met a vampire in the library. One I've never seen before, named Matthew Clairmont."

There was silence on Em's end as she flipped through her mental card file of notable creatures. Sarah was quiet for a moment, too, deciding whether or not to explode.

"I hope he's easier to get rid of than the daemons you have a habit of attracting," she said sharply.

"Daemons haven't bothered me since I stopped acting."

"No, there was that daemon who followed you into the Beinecke Library when you first started working at Yale, too," Em corrected me. "He was just wandering down the street and came looking for you."

"He was mentally unstable," I protested. Like using witchcraft on the washing machine, the fact that I'd somehow caught the attention of a single, curious daemon shouldn't count against me.

"You draw creatures like flowers draw bees, Diana. But daemons aren't half as dangerous as vampires. Stay away from him," Sarah said tightly.

"I have no reason to seek him out." My hands traveled to my neck again. "We have nothing in common."

"That's not the point," Sarah said, voice rising. "Witches, vampires, and daemons aren't supposed to mix. You know that. Humans are more likely to notice us when we do. No daemon or vampire is worth the risk." The only creatures in the world that Sarah took seriously were other witches. Humans struck her as unfortunate little beings blind to the world around them. Daemons were perpetual teenagers who couldn't be trusted. Vampires were well below cats and at least one step below mutts within her hierarchy of creatures.

"You've told me the rules before, Sarah."

"Not everyone obeys the rules, honey," Em observed. "What did he want?"

"He said he was interested in my work. But he's a scientist, so that's hard to believe." My fingers fiddled with the duvet cover on the bed. "He invited me to dinner."

"To *dinner*?" Sarah was incredulous.

Em just laughed. "There's not much on a restaurant menu that would appeal to a vampire."

"I'm sure I won't see him again. He's running three labs from the look of his business card, and he holds two faculty positions."

"Typical," Sarah muttered. "That's what happens when you have too much time on your hands. And stop picking at that quilt—you'll put a hole in it." She'd switched on her witch's radar full blast and was now seeing as well as hearing me.

"It's not as if he's stealing money from old ladies and squandering other people's fortunes on the stock market," I countered. The fact that vampires were reputed to be fabulously wealthy was a sore spot with Sarah. "He's a biochemist and a physician of some sort, interested in the brain."

"I'm sure that's fascinating, Diana, but what did he *want?*" Sarah matched my irritation with impatience—the one-two punch mastered by all Bishop women.

"Not dinner," Em said with certainty.

Sarah snorted. "He wanted something. Vampires and witches don't go on dates. Unless he was planning to dine on you, of course. They love nothing more than the taste of a witch's blood."

"Maybe he was just curious. Or maybe he does like your work." Em said it with such doubt that I had to laugh.

"We wouldn't be having this conversation at all if you'd just take some elementary precautions," Sarah said tartly. "A protection spell, some use of your abilities as a seer, and—"

"I'm not using magic or witchcraft to figure out why a vampire asked me to dinner," I said firmly. "Not negotiable, Sarah."

"Then don't call us looking for answers when you don't want to hear them," Sarah said, her notoriously short temper flaring. She hung up before I could think of a response.

"Sarah does worry about you, you know," Em said apologetically. "And she doesn't understand why you won't use your gifts, not even to protect yourself."

Because the gifts had strings attached, as I'd explained before. I tried again.

"It's a slippery slope, Em. I protect myself from a vampire in the library today, and tomorrow I protect myself from a hard question at a lecture. Soon I'll be picking research topics based on knowing how they'll turn out and applying for grants that I'm sure to win. It's important to me that I've made my reputation on my own. If I start using magic, nothing would belong entirely to me. I don't want to be the next Bishop witch." I opened my mouth to tell Em about Ashmole 782, but something made me close it again.

"I know, I know, honey." Em's voice was soothing. "I do understand. But Sarah can't help worrying about your safety. You're all the family she has now."

My fingers slid through my hair and came to rest at my temples. Conversations like this always led back to my mother and father. I hesitated, reluctant to mention my one lingering concern.

"What is it?" Em asked, her sixth sense picking up on my discomfort.

"He knew my name. I've never seen him before, but he knew who I was."

Em considered the possibilities. "Your picture's on the inside of your latest book cover, isn't it?"

My breath, which I hadn't been aware I was holding, came out with a soft whoosh. "Yes. That must be it. I'm just being silly. Can you give Sarah a kiss from me?"

"You bet. And, Diana? Be careful. English vampires may not be as well behaved around witches as the American ones are."

I smiled, thinking of Matthew Clairmont's formal bow. "I will. But don't worry. I probably won't see him again."

Em was quiet.

"Em?" I prompted.

"Time will tell."

Em wasn't as good at seeing the future as my mother was reputed to have been, but something was niggling at her. Convincing a witch to share a vague premonition was almost impossible. She wasn't going to tell me what worried her about Matthew Clairmont. Not yet.

Battle Hymn of the Tiger Mother

BY

Amy Chua

"Readers will alternately gasp at and empathize with Chua's struggles and aspirations, all the while enjoying her writing, which, like her kid-rearing philosophy, is brisk, lively and no-holds-barred."

—Elizabeth Chang, *The Washington Post*

All decent parents want to do what is best for their children. What Battle Hymn of the Tiger Mother *reveals is that the Chinese just have a totally different idea of how to do that. Western parents try to respect their children's individuality, encouraging them to pursue their true passions and providing a nurturing environment. The Chinese believe that the best way to protect your children is by preparing them for the future and arming them with skills, strong work habits, and inner confidence.* Battle Hymn of the Tiger Mother *chronicles Chua's iron-willed decision to raise her daughters, Sophia and Lulu, her way—the Chinese way—and the remarkable results her choice inspires.*

I

The Chinese Mother

A lot of people wonder how Chinese parents raise such stereo-typically successful kids. They wonder what these parents do to produce so many math whizzes and music prodigies, what it's like inside the family, and whether they could do it too. Well, I can tell them, because I've done it. Here are some things my daughters, Sophia and Louisa, were never allowed to do:

- attend a sleepover
- have a playdate
- be in a school play
- complain about not being in a school play
- watch TV or play computer games
- choose their own extracurricular activities
- get any grade less than an A

- not be the #1 student in every subject except gym and drama
- play any instrument other than the piano or violin
- not play the piano or violin.

I'm using the term "Chinese mother" loosely. I recently met a supersuccessful white guy from South Dakota (you've seen him on television), and after comparing notes we decided that his working-class father had definitely been a Chinese mother. I know some Korean, Indian, Jamaican, Irish, and Ghanaian parents who qualify too. Conversely, I know some mothers of Chinese heritage, almost always born in the West, who are *not* Chinese mothers, by choice or otherwise.

I'm also using the term "Western parents" loosely. Western parents come in all varieties. In fact, I'll go out on a limb and say that Westerners are far more diverse in their parenting styles than the Chinese. Some Western parents are strict; others are lax. There are same-sex parents, Orthodox Jewish parents, single parents, ex-hippie parents, investment banker parents, and military parents. None of these "Western" parents necessarily see eye to eye, so when I use the term "Western parents," of course I'm not referring to all Western parents—just as "Chinese mother" doesn't refer to all Chinese mothers.

All the same, even when Western parents think they're being strict, they usually don't come close to being Chinese mothers. For example, my Western friends who consider themselves strict make their children practice their instruments thirty minutes every day. An hour at most. For a Chinese mother, the first hour is the easy part. It's hours two and three that get tough.

Despite our squeamishness about cultural stereotypes, there are tons of studies out there showing marked and quantifiable differences between Chinese and Westerners when it comes to parenting. In one study of 50 Western American mothers and 48 Chinese immigrant mothers, almost 70% of the Western mothers said either that "stressing academic success is not good for children" or that "parents need to foster the idea that learning is fun." By contrast, roughly 0% of the Chinese mothers felt the same way. Instead, the vast majority of the Chinese mothers said that they believe their children can be "the best" students, that "academic achievement reflects successful parenting," and that if children did not excel at school then there was "a problem" and parents "were not doing their job." Other studies indicate that compared to Western parents, Chinese parents spend approximately ten times as long every day drilling academic activities with their children. By contrast, Western kids are more likely to participate in sports teams.

This brings me to my final point. Some might think that the American sports parent is an analog to the Chinese mother. This is so wrong. Unlike your typical Western overscheduling soccer mom, the Chinese mother believes that (1) schoolwork always comes first; (2) an A-minus is a bad grade; (3) your children must be two years ahead of their classmates in math; (4) you must never compliment your children in public; (5) if your child ever disagrees with a teacher or coach, you must always take the side of the teacher or coach; (6) the only activities your children should be permitted to do are those in which they can eventually win a medal; and (7) that medal must be gold.

2

Sophia

Sophia

Sophia is my firstborn daughter. My husband, Jed, is Jewish, and I'm Chinese, which makes our children Chinese-Jewish-American, an ethnic group that may sound exotic but actually forms a majority in certain circles, especially in university towns.

Sophia's name in English means "wisdom," as does Si Hui, the Chinese name my mother gave her. From the moment Sophia was born, she displayed a rational temperament and exceptional powers of concentration. She got those qualities from her father. As an infant Sophia quickly slept through the night, and cried only if it achieved a purpose. I was struggling to write a law article at the time—I was on leave from my Wall Street law firm and desperate to get a teaching job so I wouldn't have to go back—and at two months Sophia understood this. Calm and contemplative, she basically slept, ate, and watched me have writer's block until she was a year old.

Sophia was intellectually precocious, and at eighteen months she knew the alphabet. Our pediatrician denied that this was neurologically possible, insisting that she was only mimicking sounds. To prove his point, he pulled out a big tricky chart, with the alphabet disguised as snakes and unicorns. The doctor looked at the chart, then at Sophia, and back at the chart. Cunningly, he pointed to a toad wearing a nightgown and a beret.

"*Q*," piped Sophia.

The doctor grunted. "No coaching," he said to me.

I was relieved when we got to the last letter: a hydra with lots of red tongues flapping around, which Sophia correctly identified as "*I*."

Sophia excelled in nursery school, particularly in math. While the other kids were learning to count from 1 to 10 the creative American way—with rods, beads, and cones—I taught Sophia addition, subtraction, multiplication, division, fractions, and decimals the rote Chinese way. The hard part was displaying the right answer using the rods, beads, and cones.

The deal Jed and I struck when we got married was that our children would speak Mandarin Chinese and be raised Jewish. (I was brought up Catholic, but that was easy to give up.

Catholicism has barely any roots in my family, but more of that later.) In retrospect, this was a funny deal, because I myself don't speak Mandarin—my native dialect is Hokkien Chinese—and Jed is not religious in the least. But the arrangement somehow worked. I hired a Chinese nanny to speak Mandarin constantly to Sophia, and we celebrated our first Hanukkah when Sophia was two months old.

As Sophia got older, it seemed like she got the best of both cultures. She was probing and questioning, from the Jewish side. And from me, the Chinese side, she got skills—lots of skills. I don't mean inborn skills or anything like that, just skills learned the diligent, disciplined, confidence-expanding Chinese way. By the time Sophia was three, she was reading Sartre, doing simple set theory, and could write one hundred Chinese characters. (Jed's translation: She recognized the words "No Exit," could draw two overlapping circles, and okay maybe on the Chinese characters.) As I watched American parents slathering praise on their kids for the lowest of tasks—drawing a squiggle or waving a stick—I came to see that Chinese parents have two things over their Western counterparts: (1) higher dreams for their children, and (2) higher regard for their children in the sense of knowing how much they can take.

Of course, I also wanted Sophia to benefit from the best aspects of American society. I did not want her to end up like one of those weird Asian automatons who feel so much pressure from their parents that they kill themselves after coming in second on the national civil service exam. I wanted her to be well rounded and to have hobbies and activities. Not just any activity, like "crafts," which can lead nowhere—or even worse, playing the drums, which leads to drugs—but rather a hobby that was meaningful and highly difficult with the potential for depth and virtuosity.

And that's where the piano came in.

In 1996, when she was three, Sophia got two new things: her first piano lesson, and a little sister.

3

Louisa

Louisa

There's a country music song that goes, "She's a wild one with an angel's face." That's my younger daughter, Lulu. When I think of her, I think of trying to tame a feral horse. Even when she was in utero she kicked so hard it left visible imprints on my stomach. Lulu's real name is Louisa, which means "famous warrior." I'm not sure how we called that one so early.

Lulu's Chinese name is Si Shan, which means "coral" and connotes delicacy. This fits Lulu too. From the day she was born,

Lulu had a discriminating palate. She didn't like the infant formula I fed her, and she was so outraged by the soy milk alternative suggested by our pediatrician that she went on a hunger strike. But unlike Mahatma Gandhi, who was selfless and meditative while he starved himself, Lulu had colic and screamed and clawed violently for hours every night. Jed and I were in earplugs and tearing our hair out when fortunately our Chinese nanny Grace came to the rescue. She prepared a silken tofu braised in a light abalone and shiitake sauce with a cilantro garnish, which Lulu ended up quite liking.

It's hard to find the words to describe my relationship with Lulu. "All-out nuclear warfare" doesn't quite capture it. The irony is that Lulu and I are very much alike: She inherited my hot-tempered, viper-tongued, fast-forgiving personality.

Speaking of personalities, I don't believe in astrology—and I think people who do have serious problems—but the Chinese Zodiac describes Sophia and Lulu *perfectly*. Sophia was born in the Year of the Monkey, and Monkey people are curious, intellectual, and "generally can accomplish any given task. They appreciate difficult or challenging work as it stimulates them." By contrast, people born in the Year of the Boar are "willful" and "obstinate" and often "fly into a rage," although they "never harbor a grudge," being fundamentally honest and warmhearted. That's Lulu exactly.

I was born in the Year of the Tiger. I don't want to boast or anything, but Tiger people are noble, fearless, powerful, authoritative, and magnetic. They're also supposed to be lucky. Beethoven and Sun Yat-sen were both Tigers.

I had my first face-off with Lulu when she was about three. It was a freezing winter afternoon in New Haven, Connecticut, one of the coldest days of the year. Jed was at work—he was a professor at Yale Law School—and Sophia was at kindergarten. I decided that it would be a perfect time to introduce Lulu to the piano. Excited about working together—with her brown curls, round eyes, and china doll face, Lulu was deceptively cute—I put her on the piano bench, on top of some comfortable pillows. I then demonstrated how to play a single note with a single finger, evenly, three times, and asked her to do the same. A small request, but Lulu refused, preferring instead to smash at many notes at the same time with two open palms. When I asked her to stop, she smashed harder and faster. When I tried to pull her away from the piano, she began yelling, crying, and kicking furiously.

Fifteen minutes later, she was still yelling, crying, and kicking, and I'd had it. Dodging her blows, I dragged the screeching demon to our back porch door, and threw it open.

The wind chill was twenty degrees, and my own face hurt from just a few seconds' exposure to the icy air. But I was determined to raise an obedient Chinese child—in the West, obedience is associated with dogs and the caste system, but in Chinese culture, it is considered among the highest of virtues—if it killed me. "You can't stay in the house if you don't listen to Mommy," I said sternly. "Now, are you ready to be a good girl? Or do you want to go outside?"

Lulu stepped outside. She faced me, defiant.

A dull dread began seeping though my body. Lulu was wearing only a sweater, a ruffled skirt, and tights. She had stopped crying. Indeed, she was eerily still.

"Okay good—you've decided to behave," I said quickly. "You can come in now."

Lulu shook her head.

"Don't be silly, Lulu." I was panicking. "It's freezing. You're going to get sick. Come in *now*."

Lulu's teeth were chattering, but she shook her head again. And right then I saw it all, as clear as day. I had underestimated Lulu, not understood what she was made of. She would sooner freeze to death than give in.

I had to change tactics immediately; I couldn't win this one. Plus I might be locked up by Child Services. My mind racing, I reversed course, now begging, coddling, and bribing Lulu to come back into the house. When Jed and Sophia arrived home, they found Lulu contentedly soaking in a hot bath, dipping a brownie in a steaming cup of hot chocolate with marshmallows.

But Lulu had underestimated me too. I was just rearming. The battle lines were drawn, and she didn't even know it.

4

The Chuas

My last name is Chua—Cài in Mandarin—and I love it. My family comes from southern China's Fujian Province, which is famous for producing scholars and scientists. One of my direct ancestors on my father's side, Chua Wu Neng, was the royal astronomer to Emperor Shen Zong of the Ming Dynasty, as well as a philosopher and poet. Obviously wide-ranging in his skills, Wu Neng was appointed by the emperor to be the chief of military staff in 1644, when China faced a Manchu invasion. My family's most prized heirloom—in fact, our only heirloom—is a 2000-page treatise, handwritten by Wu Neng, interpreting the *I Ching,* or *Book of Changes,* one of the oldest of the classic Chinese texts. A leather-bound copy of Wu Neng's treatise—with the character for "Chua" on the cover—now sits prominently on my living room coffee table.

All of my grandparents were born in Fujian, but at different points in the 1920s and 1930s they boarded boats for the Philippines, where there was said to be more opportunity. My mother's father was a kind, mild-mannered schoolteacher who became a rice merchant to support his family. He was not religious and not particularly good at business. His wife, my grandmother, was a great beauty and devout Buddhist. Despite the antimaterialistic teachings of the Bodhisattva Guanyin, she always wished her husband were more successful.

My father's father, a good-natured fish-paste merchant, was also not religious and not particularly good at business. His wife, my Dragon Lady grandmother, made a fortune after World War II by going into plastics, then investing her profits in gold bars and diamonds. After she became wealthy—securing an account to produce containers for Johnson & Johnson was key—she moved into a grand hacienda in one of Manila's most prestigious neighborhoods. She and my uncles started buying up Tiffany glass, Mary Cassatts, Braques, and condos in Honolulu. They also converted to Protestantism and began using forks and spoons instead of chopsticks, to be more like Americans.

Born in China in 1936, my mother arrived in the Philippines with her family when she was two. During the Japanese occupation of the Philippines, she lost her infant brother, and I'll never forget her description of Japanese soldiers holding her uncle's jaws open, forcing water down his throat, and laughing about how he was going to burst like an overfilled balloon. When General Douglas MacArthur liberated the Philippines in 1945, my mother remembers running after American jeeps, cheering wildly, as U.S. troops tossed out free cans of Spam. After the war, my mother attended a Dominican high school, where she was converted to Catholicism. She eventually graduated from the

University of Santo Tomas first in her class, summa cum laude, with a degree in chemical engineering.

My father was the one who wanted to immigrate to America. Brilliant at math, in love with astronomy and philosophy, he hated the grubbing, backstabbing world of his family's plastics business and defied every plan they had for him. Even as a boy, he was desperate to get to America, so it was a dream come true when the Massachusetts Institute of Technology accepted his application. He proposed to my mother in 1960, and later the same year my parents arrived in Boston, knowing not a soul in the country. With only their student scholarships to live on, they couldn't afford heat their first two winters, and wore blankets around to keep warm. My father got his Ph.D. in less than two years and became an assistant professor at Purdue University in West Lafayette, Indiana.

Growing up in the Midwest, my three younger sisters and I always knew that we were different from everyone else. Mortifyingly, we brought Chinese food in thermoses to school; how I wished I could have a bologna sandwich like everyone else! We were required to speak Chinese at home—the punishment was one whack of the chopsticks for every English word accidentally uttered. We drilled math and piano every afternoon and were never allowed to sleep over at our friends' houses. Every evening when my father came home from work, I took off his shoes and socks and brought him his slippers. Our report cards had to be perfect; while our friends were rewarded for Bs, for us getting an A-minus was unthinkable. In eighth grade, I won second place in a history contest and brought my family to the awards ceremony. Somebody else had won the Kiwanis prize for best all-around student. Afterward, my father said to me: "Never, never disgrace me like that again."

When my friends hear these stories, they often imagine that I had a horrible childhood. But that's not true at all; I found strength and confidence in my peculiar family. We started off as outsiders together, and we discovered America together, becoming Americans in the process. I remember my father working until three in the morning every night, so driven he wouldn't even notice us entering the room. But I also remember how excited he was introducing us to tacos, sloppy joes, Dairy Queen, and all-you-can-eat buffets, not to mention sledding, skiing, crabbing, and camping. I remember a boy in grade school making slanty-eyed gestures at me, guffawing as he mimicked the way I pronounced *restaurant* (rest-OW-rant)——I vowed at that moment to rid myself of my Chinese accent. But I also remember Girl Scouts and hula hoops; roller skating and public libraries; winning a Daughters of the American Revolution essay contest; and the proud, momentous day my parents were naturalized.

In 1971, my father accepted an offer from the University of California at Berkeley, and we packed up and moved west. My father grew his hair and wore jackets with peace signs on them. Then he got interested in wine collecting and built himself a one-thousand-bottle cellar. As he became internationally known for his work on chaos theory, we began traveling around the world. I spent my junior year in high school studying in London, Munich, and Lausanne, and my father took us to the Arctic Circle.

But my father was also a Chinese patriarch. When it came

time to apply to colleges, he declared that I was going to live at home and attend Berkeley (where I had already been accepted), and that was that—no visiting campuses and agonizing choices for me. Disobeying him, as he had disobeyed his family, I forged his signature and secretly applied to a school on the East Coast that I'd heard people talking about. When I told him what I had done—and that Harvard had accepted me—my father's reaction surprised me. He went from anger to pride literally overnight. He was equally proud when I later graduated from Harvard Law School and when Michelle, his next daughter, graduated from Yale College and Yale Law School. He was proudest of all (but perhaps also a little heartbroken) when Katrin, his third daughter, left home for Harvard, eventually to get her M.D./Ph.D. there.

America changes people. When I was four, my father said to me, "You will marry a non-Chinese over my dead body." But I ended up marrying Jed, and today my husband and my father are the best of friends. When I was little, my parents had no sympathy for disabled people. In much of Asia, disabilities are seen as shameful, so when my youngest sister Cynthia was born with Down syndrome, my mother initially cried all the time, and some of my relatives encouraged us to send Cindy away to an institution in the Philippines. But my mother was put in touch with special education teachers and other parents of children with disabilities, and soon she was spending hours patiently doing puzzles with Cindy and teaching her to draw. When Cindy started grade school, my mother taught her to read and drilled multiplication tables with her. Today, Cindy holds two International Special Olympics gold medals in swimming.

A tiny part of me regrets that I didn't marry another Chinese person and worries that I am letting down four thousand years of civilization. But most of me feels tremendous gratitude for the freedom and creative opportunity that America has given me. My daughters don't feel like outsiders in America. I sometimes still do. But for me, that is less a burden than a privilege.

5

On Generational Decline

Newborn me and my brave parents,
two years after they arrived in America

One of my greatest fears is family decline. There's an old Chinese saying that "prosperity can never last for three generations." I'll bet that if someone with empirical skills conducted a longitudinal survey about intergenerational performance, they'd find a remarkably common pattern among Chinese immigrants fortunate enough to have come to the United States as graduate students or skilled workers over the last fifty years. The pattern would go something like this:

- The immigrant generation (like my parents) is the hardest-working. Many will have started off in the United States almost penniless, but they will work nonstop until they become successful engineers, scientists, doctors, academics, or businesspeople. As parents, they will be extremely strict and rabidly thrifty. ("Don't throw out those leftovers! Why are you using so much dishwasher liquid? You don't need a beauty salon—I can cut your hair even nicer.") They will invest in real estate. They will not drink much. Everything they do and earn will go toward their children's education and future.

- The next generation (mine), the first to be born in America, will typically be high-achieving. They will usually play the piano and/or violin. They will attend an Ivy League or Top Ten university. They will tend to be professionals—lawyers, doctors, bankers, television anchors—and surpass their parents in income, but that's partly because they started off with more money and because their parents invested so much in them. They will be less frugal than their parents. They will enjoy cocktails. If they are female, they will often marry a white person. Whether male or female, they will not be as strict with their children as their parents were with them.

- The next generation (Sophia and Lulu's) is the one I spend nights lying awake worrying about. Because of the hard work of their parents and grandparents, this generation will be born into the great comforts of the upper middle class. Even as children they will own many hardcover books (an almost criminal luxury from the point of view of immigrant parents). They will have wealthy friends who get paid for B-pluses. They may or may not attend private schools, but in either case they will expect expensive, brand-name clothes. Finally and most problematically, they will feel that they have individual rights guaranteed by the U.S. Constitution and therefore be much more likely to disobey their parents and ignore career advice. In short, all factors point to this generation being headed straight for decline.

Well, not on my watch. From the moment Sophia was born and I looked into her cute and knowing face, I was determined not to let it happen to her, not to raise a soft, entitled child—not to let my family fall.

That's one of the reasons that I insisted Sophia and Lulu do classical music. I knew that I couldn't artificially make them feel like poor immigrant kids. There was no getting around the fact that we lived in a large old house, owned two decent cars, and stayed in nice hotels when we vacationed. But I *could* make sure that Sophia and Lulu were deeper and more cultivated than my parents and I were. Classical music was the opposite of decline, the opposite of laziness, vulgarity, and spoiledness. It was a way for my children to achieve something I hadn't. But it was also a tie-in to the high cultural tradition of my ancient ancestors.

My antidecline campaign had other components too. Like my parents, I required Sophia and Lulu to be fluent in Chinese and to be straight-A students. "Always check your test answers three times," I told them. "Look up every word you don't know and memorize the exact definition." To make sure that Sophia and Lulu weren't pampered and decadent like the Romans when their empire fell, I also insisted that they do physical labor.

"When I was fourteen, I dug a swimming pool for my father by myself with a pick and shovel," I told my daughters more than once. This is actually true. The pool was only three feet deep and ten feet in diameter and came in a kit, but I really did dig it in the backyard of a cabin near Lake Tahoe that my father bought, after saving up for years. "Every Saturday morning," I also loved to harp, "I vacuumed half the house while my sister did the other half. I cleaned toilets, weeded the lawn, and chopped wood. Once I built a rock garden for my father, and I had to carry boulders that were over fifty pounds each. That's why I'm so tough."

Because I wanted them to practice as much as possible, I didn't ask my daughters to chop wood or dig a pool. But I did try to make them carry heavy objects—overflowing laundry baskets up and down stairs, garbage out on Sundays, suitcases when we traveled—as often as I could. Interestingly, Jed had the opposite instinct. It bothered him to see the girls loaded down, and he always worried about their backs.

In imparting these lessons to the girls, I'd constantly remember things my own parents had said to me. "Be modest, be humble, be simple," my mother used to chide. "The last shall come first." What she really meant of course was, "Make sure you come in first so that you have something to be humble about." One of my father's bedrock principles was, "Never complain or make excuses. If something seems unfair at school, just prove yourself by working twice as hard and being twice as good." These tenets too I tried to convey to Sophia and Lulu.

Finally, I tried to demand as much respect from the girls as my parents did of me. This is where I was least successful. Growing up, I was terrified of my parents' disapproval. Not so with Sophia and especially Lulu. America seems to convey something to kids that Chinese culture doesn't. In Chinese culture, it just wouldn't occur to children to question, disobey, or talk back to their parents. In American culture, kids in books, TV shows, and movies constantly score points with their snappy backtalk and independent streaks. Typically, it's the parents who need to be taught a life lesson—by their children.

The House at Tyneford

Natasha Solomons

It's the spring of 1938 and no longer safe to be a Jew in Vienna. Nineteen-year-old Elise Landau realizes her only means of escape is to advertise her services as a domestic servant in England. Fate brings her ad to the attention of Christopher Rivers, handsome scion of the aristocratic Rivers family and master of Tyneford. An anxious Elise arrives at Tyneford and immediately falls under its spell. When Christopher's young son, Kit, returns home, the two strike up an unlikely friendship that will change Tyneford—and Elise—forever. A page-turning tale of family, love, loss, and the power of the human spirit set against the perennially popular backdrop of World War II England. Natasha Solomons's The House at Tyneford _is upmarket romantic fiction at its best._

The Novel in the Viola

Natasha Solomons

'Please treat the church and houses with care; we have given up our homes where many of us lived for generations to help win the war to keep men free. We shall return one day and thank you for treating the village kindly.'

Notice pinned to the door of Tyneford church by departing villagers,

Christmas Eve, 1941.

1.

General Observations on Quadrupeds

When I close my eyes I see Tyneford House. In the darkness as I lay down to sleep, I see the Purbeck stone frontage in the glow of late afternoon. The sunlight glints off the upper windows, and the air is heavy with the scent of magnolia and salt. Ivy clings to the porch archway, and a magpie pecks at lichen coating a limestone roof tile. Smoke seeps from one of the great chimneystacks, and the leaves on the un-felled beech avenue are May green and cast mottled patterns on the driveway. There are no weeds yet tearing through the lavender and thyme borders, and the lawn is velvet cropped and rolled in verdant stripes. No bullet-holes pockmark the ancient garden wall and the drawing room windows are thrown open, the glass not shattered by shellfire. I see the house as it was then, on that first afternoon.

Everyone is just out of sight. I can hear the ring of the drinks tray being prepared; on the terrace a bowl of pink camellias rests on the table. And in the bay, the fishing-boats bounce upon the tide, nets cast wide, the slap of water against wood. We have not yet been exiled. The cottages do not lie in pebbled ruins across the strand, with hazel and blackthorn growing through the flagstones of the village houses. We have not surrendered Tyneford to guns and tanks and birds and ghosts.

I find I forget more and more nowadays. Nothing very important, as yet. I was talking to somebody just now on the telephone, and as soon as I had replaced the receiver, I realised I'd forgotten who it was and what we said. I shall probably remember later when I'm lying in the bath. I've forgotten other things too: the names of the birds are no longer on the tip of my tongue and I'm embarrassed to say that the capital of Paraguay is lost to me forever. And, yet as the years wash everything else away Tyneford remains, a smooth pebble of a memory.

Tyneford. Tyneford. As though if I say the name enough, I can go back again. Those summers were long and blue and hot. I remember it all, or think I do. It doesn't seem long ago to me. I have replayed each moment so often in my mind that I hear my own voice in every part. Now, as I write them they appear fixed, absolute. On the page we live again, young and unknowing, everything yet to happen.

When I received the letter that brought me to Tyneford, I knew nothing about England, except that I wouldn't like it. That morning I perched on my usual spot beside the draining board in the kitchen as Hildegard bustled around, flour up to her elbows and one eyebrow snowy white. I laughed and she flicked her tea-towel at me, knocking the crust out of my hand and onto the floor.

'*Gut.* Bit less bread and butter won't do you any harm.'

I scowled and flicked crumbs onto the linoleum. I wished I could be more like my mother Anna. Worry had made Anna even thinner. Her eyes were huge against her pale skin, so that she looked more than ever like the operatic heroines she played. Anna was already a star when she married my father – a black-eyed beauty with a voice like cherries and chocolate. She was the real thing; when she opened her mouth and began to sing, time paused just a little and everyone listened, bathing in the sound, unsure if what he heard was real or some perfect imagining. When the trouble began, letters started to arrive from Venice and Paris, from tenors and conductors. There was even one from a double bass. They were all the same, *Darling Anna, leave Vienna and come to Paris/ London/ New York and I shall keep you safe...* Of course she would not leave without my father. Or me. Or Margot. I would have gone in a flash, packed my ball gowns (if I'd had any) and escaped to sip champagne in the *Champs Elysées.* But no letters came for me. Not even a note from a second violin. So, I ate bread rolls with butter, while Hildegard sewed little pieces of elastic into the waistband.

'Come,' Hildegard chivvied me off the counter and steered me into the middle of the kitchen where a large book dusted with flour rested on the table. 'You must practice. What shall we make?'

Anna had picked it up at a second hand bookstore and presented it to me with a flush of pride. *Mrs Beeton's Household Management* – a whole kilo of book to teach me how to cook and clean and behave. This was to be my unglamorous fate.

Chewing on my plait, I prodded the tome so that it fell open at the index. '*General Observation on Quadrupeds...Mock Turtle Soup...Eel Pie.*' I shuddered. 'Here,' I pointed to an entry halfway down the page. 'Goose. I should know how to cook goose. I said I knew.'

A month previously, Anna had walked with me to the telegraph offices so that I could wire a 'Refugee Advertisement' to the London *Times*. I'd dragged my feet along the pavement kicking at the wet piles of blossom littering the ground.

'I don't want to go to England. I'll come to New York with you and Papa.'

My parents hoped to escape to New York, where the Metropolitan Opera would help them with a visa, if only Anna would sing.

Anna picked up her pace. 'And you will come. But we cannot get an American visa for you now.'

She stopped in the middle of the street and took my face in her hands. 'I promise you that before I even take a peek at the shoes in Bergdorf Goodman's, I will see a lawyer about bringing you to New York. '

'Before you see the shoes at Bergdorf's?'

'I promise.'

Anna had tiny feet and a massive appetite for shoes. Music may have been her first love, but shoes were definitely her second. Her wardrobe was lined with row upon row of dainty high-heeled shoes in pink, grey, patent leather, calfskin and suede. She made fun of herself to mollify me.

'Please, let me at least check your advertisement,' Anna pleaded. Before she'd met my father Anna had sung a season at Covent Garden and her English was almost perfect.

'No,' I snatched the paper away from her, 'If my English is so terrible that I only can get a place at a flophouse, then it's my own fault.'

Anna tried not to laugh. 'Darling, do you even know what a flophouse is?'

Of course, I had no idea, but I couldn't tell Anna that. I had visions of refugees like myself, alternately fainting upon over stuffed sofas. Full of indignation at her teasing, I made Anna wait outside the office while I sent the telegram:

VIENNESE JEWESS, 19, seeks position as domestic servant. Speaks fluid English. I will cook your goose. Elise Landau. Vienna 4, Dorotheegasse, 30/5.

Hildegard fixed me with a hard stare. 'Elise Rosa Landau, I do not happen to have a goose in my larder this morning so will you please select something else.'

I was about to choose Parrot pie, purely to infuriate Hildegard, when Anna and Julian entered the kitchen. He held out a letter. My father Julian was a tall man, standing six feet in his socks, thick black hair with only a splash of grey around his temples, and eyes as blue as a summer sea. My parents proved that beautiful people don't necessarily produce beautiful children. My mother, fragile blonde loveliness, and Julian so handsome, that he always wore his wire rimmed spectacles to lessen the effect of those too blue eyes (I'd tried them on when he was bathing, and discovered that the lenses were so weak as to be almost clear glass). Yet, somehow this couple had produced me.For years, the great-aunts had cooed, 'Ach, just you wait till she blossoms! Twelve years old, mark my words, and she'll be the spit of her mother.' I could spit but I was nothing like my mother. Twelve came and went. They held out for sixteen. Still no blossoming. By nineteen even Gabriella, the most optimistic of the great-aunts, had given up hope. The best they could manage was 'She has her own charm. And a character.' Whether this character was good or bad, they never said.

Anna lurked behind Julian, blinking and running a pink tongue-tip across her bottom lip. I stood up straight and concentrated on the letter in Julian's hand.

'It's from England,' he said, holding it out to me.

I took it from him and with deliberate slowness well aware they were all watching me, slid a butter knife under the seal. I drew out a creamy sheet of watermarked paper, unfolded it and smoothed the creases. I read in slow silence. The others bore with me for a minute and then Julian interrupted.

'For God's sake, Elise. What does it say?'

I fixed him with a glare. I glared a lot back then. He ignored me, and I read aloud.

Dear Fraulein Landau,

Mr Rivers has instructed me to write to you and tell you that the position of house-parlour maid at Tyneford House is yours if you want it. He has agreed to sign the necessary visa application statements, providing that you stay at Tyneford for a minimum of a twelve-month. If you wish to accept the post, please write or wire by return. On your arrival in London, proceed to the Mayfair Agency in Audley St. W1 where ongoing travel arrangements to Tyneford will be made.

Yours sincerely,

Florence Ellsworth

Housekeeper, Tyneford House.

I lowered the letter.

'But, twelve-months is too long. I'm to be in New York before then, Papa.'

Julian and Anna exchanged a glance, and it was she who answered.

'Darling Bean, I hope you will be in New York in six months. But for now, you must go where it is safe.'

Julian tugged my plait in a gesture of playful affection. 'We can't go to New York unless we know you're safe. The minute we arrive at the Metropolitan we will send for you.'

'I suppose it's too late for me to take singing lessons?'

Anna only smiled. So, it was true then. I was to leave them. Until this moment it had not been real. I had written the telegram, even sent the wire to London, but it had seemed a game. I knew things were bad for us in Vienna. I heard the stories of old women being pulled out of shops by their hair and forced to scrub the pavements. Frau Goldschmidt had been made to scrape dog faeces from the gutter with her mink stole. I overheard her confession to Anna, she had hunched on the sofa in the parlour, her porcelain cup clattering in her hands, as she confided her ordeal, *'The joke is, I never liked that fur. It was a gift from Herman, and I wore it to please him. It was much too hot and it was his mother's colour not mine. He never would learn... But to spoil it like that.'* She'd seemed more upset by the waste than the humiliation. When she left, I saw that Anna had stuffed an arctic rabbit muffler inside her shopping bag.

The evidence of difficult times was all round our apartment. There were scratch marks on the floor in the large sitting room where Anna's concert grand used to sit. It was worth nearly three hundred marks – a gift from one of the conductors at *La Scala*. It had arrived one spring before Margot or I were born, but we all knew that Julian didn't like having this former lover's token cluttering his home. It had been lifted up on a pulley through the dining room windows, the glass of which had to be specially removed – how Margot and

I used to wish that we'd glimpsed the great flying piano spectacle. Occasionally, when Julian and Anna had their rare disagreements, he'd mutter 'why can't you have a box of love letters or a photograph album like any other woman? Why a bloody great concert grand? A man shouldn't have to stub his toe on his rival's passion.' Anna, so gentle in nearly all things, was immovable on matters of music. She would fold her arms and stand up straight, reaching all of five feet nothing and announce, 'Unless you wish to spend three hundred marks on another piano and demolish the dining room again, it stays.' And stay it did, until one day, when I arrived home from running a spurious errand for Anna to discover it missing. There were gouges all along the parquet floor, and from a neighbouring apartment, I could hear the painful clatter of a talentless beginner learning to play. Anna had sold her beloved piano to a woman across the hall, for a fraction of its value. In the evenings at six o'clock, we could hear the rattle of endless clumsy scales, as our neighbour's acne ridden son, was forced to practise. I imagined the piano, wanting to sing a lament at its ill treatment and pining for Anna's touch, but crippled into ugliness. The rich, dark tones of the piano once mingled with Anna's voice, like cream into coffee. After the banishment of the piano, at six every evening Anna always had a reason for leaving the apartment – she'd forgotten to buy potatoes (though the larder was packed with them), there was a letter to post, she'd promised to dress Frau Schneider's corns.

Despite the vanished piano, the spoiled furs, the missing pictures on the walls, Margot's expulsion from the conservator on racial grounds and the slow disappearance of all the younger maids so that only old Hildegard remained, until this moment, I never really thought that I would have to leave Vienna. I loved this city. She was as much part of my family as Anna or great-aunts Gretta, Gerda and Gabriella. It was true strange things kept happening, but at age nineteen nothing really terrible had ever happened to me before, and blessed with the outlook of the soul-deep optimist, I had truly believed that all would be well.

Standing in the kitchen as I looked up into Julian's face, met his sad half-smile, I knew for the first time in my life that everything was not going to be alright, that things would not turn out for the best. I must leave Austria and Anna and the apartment on *Dorotheegasse* with its tall sash windows looking out onto the poplars which glowed pink fire as the sun crept up behind them, and the grocer's boy who came every Tuesday yelling 'Eis! Eis!' And the damask curtains in my bedroom that I never closed so I could see the yellow glow from the street lamps and the twin lights from the tramcars below. I must leave the crimson tulip bulbs in the park in April, and the whirling white dresses at the Opera Ball, and the gloves clapping as Anna sang and Julian wiped away proud tears with his embroidered handkerchief, and midnight ice cream on the balcony on August nights, and Margot and me sunbathing on striped deckchairs in the park as we listened to trumpets on the bandstand, and Margot burning supper, and Robert laughing and saying it doesn't matter and us eating apples and toasted cheese instead and Anna showing me how to put on silk stockings without tearing them by wearing kid gloves and and

'And sit, drink some water.'

Anna thrust a glass in front of me while Julian slid a wooden chair behind me. Even Hildegard looked rattled.

'You have to go,' said Anna.

'I know,' I said, realising as I did, that my luxuriant and prolonged childhood was at an end. I stared at Anna with a shivering sense of time pivoting up and down like a seesaw. I memorised every detail: the tiny crease in the centre of her forehead that appeared when she was worried, Julian beside her, his hand resting on her shoulder – the grey silk of her blouse. The blue tiles behind the sink. Hildegard wringing the dishcloth. That Elise, the girl I was then, would declare me old but she is wrong. I am still she. I am still standing in the kitchen holding the letter, watching the others and waiting and knowing that everything must change.

2.

In the bathtub, singing

Memories do not exist along a timeline. In my mind everything happens at once. Anna kisses

me goodnight and tucks me into my high-sided cot, whilst my hair is brushed for Margot's

wedding, which now takes place on the lawn at Tyneford, my feet bare upon the grass. I am

in Vienna as I wait for their letters to arrive in Dorset. The chronology laid out upon these

pages is not without effort.

I am young in my dreams. The face in the mirror always surprises me. I observe the

smart grey hair, nicely set of course, and the tiredness beneath the eyes that never goes away.

I know that it is my face, and yet the next time I glance in the mirror I am surprised all over

again. Oh, I think, I forgot that this is me. In those blissful days living in the bel-etage, I was

the baby of the family. They all indulged me, Margot, Julian and Anna most of all. I was their

pet, their *liebling,* to be cosseted and adored. I didn't have remarkable gifts like the rest of

them. I couldn't sing. I could play the piano and viola a little but nothing like Margot, who

had inherited all our mother's talent. Her husband Robert had fallen in love before he had

even spoken to her, when he listened to her perform viola in Schumann's *Fairytale Pictures*.

He said that her music painted lightening storms, wheat fields rippling in the rain and girls

with sea-blue hair. He said he'd never seen through someone else's eyes before. Margot

decided to love him back and they were married within six weeks. It was all quite sickening

and I should have been unbearably jealous, if it hadn't been for the fact that Robert had no

sense of humour. He never once laughed at one of my jokes – not even the one about the

rabbi and the dining room chair and the walnut – so clearly he was deficient. The possibility

of a man ever being besotted with my musical gifts was highly improbable but I did need him

to laugh.

I liked the idea of writing like Julian, but unlike him, I'd never written anything other than a list of boys I liked. Once, watching Hildegard stuff seasoned sausage meat into cabbage leaves with her thick red fingers, I'd decided that this would be a fine subject for a poem. But I'd not progressed any further than this insight. I was plump while the others were slender. I had thick ankles and they were fine boned and high cheeked, and the only beauty I'd inherited was Julian's black hair, which hung in a python plait all the way down to my knickers. But they loved me anyway. Anna indulged my babyish ways and I was allowed to sulk and storm off to my room and sob over fairy-stories that I was far too old for. My never-ending childhood made Anna feel young. With a girl-child like me, she did not admit her forty-five years, even to herself.

All that changed with the letter. I must go off into the world alone, and I must finally grow up. The others treated me just the same way as before, but there was self-consciousness in their actions, as if they knew I was sick but were being meticulous in giving nothing away in their behaviour. Anna continued to smile benevolently upon my sullen moods, and slip me the fattest slice of cake and run my bath with her best lavender scented salts. Margot picked fights and borrowed books without asking but I knew it was just for show. Her heart wasn't in the rowing, and she took books she knew I'd already read. Only Hildegard was different. She stopped chiding me, and even when it was probably most urgent, she no longer pressed Mrs Beeton upon me. She called me 'Fraulein Elise,' when I'd been simple 'Elise' or 'pain of my existence' since I was two. This sudden formality was not out of respect at some newfound dignity on my part. It was pity. I suspected Hildegard wanted to give me every mark of rank and social status during those last weeks, knowing how I must feel the humiliation in the months to come, but I wished she would call me Elise, box my ears and threaten to pour salt on my supper once more. I left biscuit crumbs on my nightstand in clear contravention of her no-biscuit-in-the-bedroom policy, but she said nothing, only gave me a tiny curtsy (how I crawled inside) and retired into her kitchen with a wounded expression.

The days slid by. I felt them pass faster and faster like painted horses on a carousel. I willed time to slow, concentrating on the tick-tick of the hall clock, trying to draw out the silence between the relentless beats of the second hand. Of course it did not work. My visa arrived in the post. The clock ticked. Anna took me to receive my passport. Tick. Julian went to another office to pay my departure tax and on his return disappeared into his study without a word and the burgundy decanter. Tick. I packed my travel-trunks with wads of silk stockings, while Hildegard stitched hidden pockets into all of my dresses to stash forbidden valuables, sewing fine gold chains along the seams. Anna and Margot accompanied me on coffee-drinking excursions to the aunts, so we could eat honey-cakes and say goodbye and we'll meet again soon when-all-this-is-over-whenever-that-will-be. Tick. I tried to stay awake all night so that morning would come slower and I would have more precious moments in Vienna. I fell asleep. Tick-tick-tick and another day gone. I took the pictures down from my bedroom wall and slid a knife under the mounting paper, slipping into the lid of my trunk the print of the Belvedere Palace, the signed programmes from the Operaball and my photographs of Margot's wedding; me in my white muslin dress with the leaf embroidery, Julian in white tie and tails, and Anna in shapeless black so she wouldn't upstage the bride and still looking prettier than any of us. Tick. My bags lay in the hall. Tick-tick. My last night in Vienna. The hall clock chimed: six o'clock and time to dress for the party.

Rather than going to my bedroom, I drifted into Julian's study. He was at his desk scribbling away, pen clasped in his left hand. I did not know what he was writing, as no one in Austria would publish his novels anymore. I wondered if he would write his next novel in American.

'Papa?'

'Yes, Bean.'

'Promise you will send for me the minute you arrive.'

Julian stopped writing and drew back his chair. He pulled me onto his lap, as though I was nine rather than nineteen, and clutched me to him, burying his face in my hair. I could smell the clean scent of his shaving soap and the cigar smoke that always lingered on his skin. As I rested my chin on his shoulder, I saw that the burgundy decanter was on the desk, empty once again.

'I won't forget you Bean,' he said, his voice muffled by the tangle of my hair. He clutched me so tightly that my ribs creaked and then with a small sigh, he released me. 'I need you to do something for me, my darling.'

I slid off his lap and watched as he crossed to the corner of the room where a viola case rested, propped against the far wall. He picked it up and set it down on the desk, opening it with a click.

'You remember this viola?'

'Yes, of course.'

I had taken my first music lessons upon this rosewood viola, learning to play before Margot. She took lessons upon the grand piano in the drawing room while I stood in this room (a treat to encourage me to practise) and the viola squealed and scraped. I even enjoyed playing, until the day Margot stole into Julian's study and picked it up. She drew the bow across the strings and it trembled into life. The rosewood sang for the first time, music rippling from the strings as effortless as the wind skimming the Danube. We all drew in to listen, hearing the viola like a siren's song; Anna clutching Julian's arm, eyes wet and bright, Hildegard dabbing her eyes with her duster and me lurking in the doorway, awed by my sister and so jealous I felt sick. In a month all the best music masters in Vienna were summoned to teach my sister. I never played again.

'I want you take it to England with you,' said Julian.

'But I don't play anymore. And anyway, it's Margot's.'

Julian shook his head. 'Margot hasn't used this old viola for years. And, besides it can't be played.' He smiled at me. 'Try.'

I was about to refuse, but there was something odd in his expression, so I picked up the instrument. It felt heavy in my hands, a curious weight in the body. Watching my father, I placed it under my chin and picking up the bow, drew it slowly across the strings. The sound was muffled and strange, as though I had attached a mute beneath the bridge. I lowered the viola and stared at Julian, a smile twitched upon his lips.

'What's inside it, papa?'

'A novel. Well, my novel.'

I peered inside the f-holes carved into the body of the instrument and realised that it was stuffed full of yellow paper.

'How did you manage to get all those pages in there?'

Julian's smile spread into a grin. 'I went to a string maker. He steamed off the front, I placed the novel inside and he glued it shut.'

He spoke with pride, pleased to confide his secret, and then his face became serious once again.

'I want you to take it to England, for safekeeping.'

Julian always wrote in duplicate, writing out his work on carbon paper in his tiny curling hand, so that a shadow novel appeared upon the pages underneath. The top layer on watermarked white paper was sent to his publisher, while the carbon copy on flimsy yellow tissue remained locked in his desk drawer. Julian was terrified of losing work and the mahogany desk held a word-hoard. He'd never permitted a copy to leave his study before.

'I'll take the manuscript with me to New York. But I want you to keep this copy in England. Just in case.'

'Alright. But I'll give it back to you in New York and you can lock it inside your desk again.'

The hall clock chimed the half hour.

'You must go and dress, little one,' said Julian, planting a kiss on my forehead. 'The guests will be arriving soon.'

It was the first night of Passover and Anna had dictated that it was to be a celebration, a party with champagne and dancing like there used to be, before the bad times came. Crying was absolutely forbidden. Margot came round early to dress and we sat in our dressing gowns in Anna's large bathroom, faces flushed with steam. Anna filled the tub with rose petals and propped the dining room candlesticks beside the washbasin mirror, like she did on the evening of the Operaball. She lay back in the tub, her hair knotted on the top of her head, fingers trailing patterns in the water. 'Ring the bell, Margot. Ask Hilde to bring a bottle of the Laurent-Perrier and three glasses.'

Margot did as she was bidden, and soon we sat sipping champagne, each pretending to be cheerful for the benefit of the others. I took a gulp and felt the tears burn in my throat. *No crying.* I told myself and swallowed, the bubbles making me choke.

'Be careful there,' said Anna with a giggle, too high pitched, striking a note of false gaiety.

I wondered how many bottles of wine or champagne were left. I knew Julian had sold the good ones. Anything expensive or valuable was liable to be confiscated, better to sell it first. Margot fanned herself with a magazine and casting it aside, marched to the window, opening the sash to let in a cool breath of night air. I watched the steam trickle outside and the gauze curtain flutter.

'So, tell me about the department in California,' said Anna, lying back and closing her eyes.

Margot flopped into a wicker-rocking chair and unfastened her robe to reveal a white lace corset and matching knickers. I wondered what Robert thought of such exciting underwear and was instantly filled with envy. No one had ever shown the slightest interest in seeing me in my under-things. Robert could be quite dashing in the right sort of lighting, although he always got rather too animated when talking about his star projects at the university. I had once grievously offended him, when I'd introduced him at a party as 'my brother-in-law the astrologer' rather than 'the astronomer'. He'd turned to me with a haughty glare asking, 'Do I wear a blue headscarf and dangling earrings or ask you to cross my palm with silver before I tell you that with Venus in retrograde, I see a handsome stranger in your future?' 'Oh no, but I wish you would!' I replied, and as a consequence he'd never really forgiven me, which was a pity, because before that he used to let me take puffs on his cigar.

'The university at Berkeley is supposed to be very good,' Margot was saying. 'They're saying lots of kind things about Robert. They're so pleased he is joining them and so on.'

'And you? Will you play?' said Anna.

Margot and Anna were the same; they were caged birds if they couldn't have music. Margot lit a cigarette and I saw her hand tremble, ever such a little.

'I shall look for a quartet.'

'*Gut. Gut,*' Anna nodded, satisfied.

I took another gulp of champagne and stared at my mother and sister. They would make friends wherever they ended up. In any city in the world, they could arrive, seek out the nearest cluster of musicians and for as long as the sonata, symphony or minuet lasted, they were at home.

I watched my sister, long-limbed and with golden hair like Anna, falling in damp curls on her bare shoulders. She sprawled in the wicker chair, robe dishevelled, sipping champagne and puffing on her cigarette with an air of studied decadence. A film of perspiration clung to her skin and she smiled at me with dreamy eyes.

'Here, Elsie, have a puff,' she held the cigarette out to me, letting it dangle between her fingers.

I knocked her hand away. 'Don't call me that.'

I hated being called Elsie. It was an old woman's name. Margot laughed, a rich tinkling sound, and at that moment I hated her too and was glad I was going far, far away. I didn't care if I never saw her again. I retreated to the window, unable to breath through all the mist. Despite the heat, I clutched my robe around me, not wanting to take it off in front of them and display my big white knickers and schoolgirl brassiere or the small roll of baby-fat oozing around my middle.

Sensing a round of bickering about to start between Margot and me, Anna did the one thing she could to make us stop. She began to sing. Later that night Anna performed before all the assembled guests, while the garnet choker around her neck trembled like drops of blood, but it is this moment I remember. When I think of Anna, I see her lying naked in the bathtub, singing. The sound filled the small room, thicker than the steam, and the water in the bath began to vibrate. I felt her voice rather than heard it. Anna's rich mezzo tones were inside me. Instead of an aria, she sang the melody to *Für Elise,* a song without words, a song for me.

I leant against the window frame, feeling the cool air against my back, the notes falling on my skin like rain. Margot's glass sagged to the ground unheeded, the champagne trickling onto the floor. I saw that the door was ajar and Julian lingered in the doorway, watching the three of us and listening. He disobeyed Anna's rule for the night. He was crying.

3.

An eggcup of saltwater

The guests arrived for the party. A manservant had been hired for the evening, and he stood in the hallway, collecting coats from the gentlemen and assisting the ladies with their hats and furs. Robert was the first to arrive, he came before eight and I fixed him with a stare to display my disapproval. According to Anna, extreme punctuality was a terrible habit in a guest, although to my irritation, when I complained about Robert, she said that it was acceptable in family or lovers. Some guests didn't arrive at all. Anna issued thirty invitations the week before. But people had started to disappear, and those who remained decided it was best not to draw attention to oneself, to live quietly and not make eye contact in the street. We understood that some would prefer not to come to a Passover soirée at the home of a famous Jewish singer and her avant-garde novelist husband. Anna and Julian said nothing about the missing guests. The table was silently re-set.

We all gathered in the drawing room. Those who had chosen to attend the party had apparently decided by unspoken accord to dazzle in their finest. If coming to the Landau party was dangerous, then they may as well be resplendent. The men were dashing in their white tie and tails. The ladies wore dark furs or dull raincoats down to the floor, but when they removed their chrysalis-coats beneath them they sparkled like tropical butterflies. Margot's dress was shot silk, indigo blue as a summer's night and studded with silver embroidered stars, which twinkled as she moved. Even fat Frau Schneider wore a plum-coloured gown, her white, doughy arms puckered by tight gauze sleeves, grey hair plaited like a crown and studded with cherry blossom. Lily Roth conjured a feathered fascinator from her bag like a magician, and fastened it in her hair, so she resembled a bird of paradise. Every lady wore her jewels, and all of them at once. If in the past seeming garish or extravagant or petty bourgeois had troubled us, now, as we felt everything sliding away into blackness, we wondered how we could have worried about such things. Tonight was for pleasure. Tomorrow we would have to sell our jewels: grandmama's spider web diamond brooch, the gold bracelet studded with rubies and sapphires that the children had teethed upon, the platinum cufflinks given to Herman when he made partner at the bank, so tonight we would wear them all and shine beneath the moon.

Julian sipped burgundy and listened to Herr Finkelstein's stories, smiling easily in all the right places. I'd heard them all – the time he met the Baron Rothschild at the concert, and the Baron mistaking him for someone else, had tipped his head and the Baroness her sherry glass, *'and who on earth would have dreamt there was a smart fellow as bald and round as me. I must find my double and shake his hand.'* I rolled my eyes, bored from a distance. Julian saw me and gestured for me to join them, I shook my head and edged away. Julian stifled a laugh. Margot exchanged pleasantries with Frau Roth, Robert hovering beside her, awkward and incapable of small talk. He could discuss only his passions: astronomy, music and Margot, while Frau Roth's sole topic of conversation was her seventeen grandchildren. I hoped they were not sitting next to one another at dinner.

I knew this was my last party as a guest. I studied the manservant in his black-tie, and impassive face, and tried to imagine myself as one of them, refreshing glasses and pretending not to hear conversation. Pity, I'd never said anything worth eavesdropping upon when I'd had the chance. I tried to think of something now – some profound insight upon the state of the nation. No. Nothing. I smiled at the servant, attempting to convey some sense of solidarity. He caught my glance, but instead of smiling back, glided over.

'Fraulein? Another drink?'

I looked down at the full glass in my hand. 'No. Thank you. I'm fine. All topped up.'

A flicker of confusion showed on the man's face – clearly I had summoned him for my amusement. I flushed, and muttering some apology, hurried out of the drawing room. I lingered in the hallway, listening to the snatches of chatter floating from the next room, *'Max Reinhardt is to leave for New York next week, I hear… Oh? I thought it was London. '*

I closed my eyes and fought against the impulse to stick my fingers in my ears. The kitchen door was firmly shut but emanating from it was a series of clatters and bangs and some of Hildegard's more colourful curses. No one, not Rudolph Valentino, not Moses himself, could have persuaded me to enter the kitchen at that moment.

From my vantage point, I saw Margot and Robert whispering in the corner, hand in hand. I had it on good authority that flirting with one's spouse in public was the depth of ill manners (with anyone else's husband was perfectly fine of course) but once again, Anna informed me, that within the first year of marriage it was quite acceptable. I hoped Margot had written their first anniversary in her diary along with a note to 'stop flirting with Robert'. She would be in America by then, and with something like regret, I realised I would not be able to tell her to behave. I must write and remind her. Although, I mused, it was possible Americans had different rules, and I wondered if I ought point this out to her. At that moment, I was feeling charitable towards my sister. Whilst at most parties, I watched as the men swarmed Margot and Anna, tonight I had caught little Jan Tibor surreptitiously glancing at my bosom, and I felt every bit as sophisticated as the others. In the darkness of the hall, I puffed out my chest, and fluttered my eyelashes, imagining myself irresistible, a dark haired Marlene Dietrich.

'Darling, don't do that,' said Anna, appearing beside me, 'the seams might pop.'

I sighed and deflated. My pink sheath dress had once belonged to Anna, and although Hildegard had let out the material as much as she could, it still pinched.

'It looks lovely on you,' said Anna, suddenly conscious that she may have wounded my feelings, 'You must take it with you.'

I snorted. 'For washing dishes in? Or for dusting?'

Anna changed the subject. 'Do you want to ring the bell for dinner?'

The bell was a tiny silver ornament, once belonging to my grandmother, and tinkled a 'C' sharp according to Margot, who had perfect pitch. As a child, it had been a great treat to put on my party frock, stay up late, and ring the bell for dinner. I would stand beside the dining room door, solemnly allowing myself to be kissed good night by the guests as they filed in for dinner. Tonight as I rang the bell, I saw all those parties flickering before me, and an endless train of people walking past me, like a circular frieze going round and round the room, never stopping. They chattered loudly, faces pink with alcohol, all obeying Anna's dictate of gaiety.

My family was not religious in the slightest. When we were children, Anna wanted Margot and me to understand a little of our heritage and at bedtime told us stories from the Torah alongside tales of 'Peter and Wolf' and 'Mozart and Constanze'. In Anna's hands, Eve was imbued with the glamour of Greta Garbo, and we pictured her lounging in the Garden of Eden, a snake draped tantalisingly around her neck, a besotted Adam (played by Clark Gable) kneeling at her feet. The bible stories had the wild and unlikely plots of operas and Margot and I devoured with them with enthusiasm, mingling the genres seamlessly in our imaginations. Eve tempts Adam with Carmen's arias and the voice of God sounded very much like 'The Barber Seville'. If anyone had asked Anna to choose between God and music, there would have been no contest, and I suspected that Julian was an atheist. We never went to the handsome brick synagogue in *Leopoldstadt*, we ate schnitzel in non-kosher restaurants, celebrated Christmas rather than Chanukah and were proud to be amongst the new class of bourgeois Austrians. We were Viennese-Jews but up till now, the Viennese part always came first. Even this year, when Anna decided we would celebrate Passover, it had to be a party with Margot in her wedding sapphires and me wearing Anna's pearls.

The long dining table was covered with a white monogrammed cloth, the plates were gold edged *Meissen*, and Hildegard had polished the family silver to a gleam. Candles flickered on every surface, a black rose and narcissi posy (rose for love, black for sorrow and narcissi for hope) rested on each lady's side-plate, and a silver yarmulke on each gentleman's. Anna insisted that the large electric lamp be left off and candles provide the only light. I knew that it was only partly for the atmosphere of enchantment that candle glow casts, and more practically to hide the gaps on the dining room walls where the good paintings used to hang. The family portraits remained, the one of me aged eleven in my flimsy muslin dress, dark hair close-cropped, and the images of the sour-faced, thin lipped great-grandparents with their lace caps, as well as great-great-aunt Sophie oddly pictured amongst green fields and a wide blue sky – Sophie had been agoraphobic during life, infamously refusing to leave her rancid apartment for forty years but the portrait lied, re-casting her as some sort of nature loving cloud spotter. My favourite was the painting of Anna as Verdi's Violetta in the moments before her death, bare foot and clad in a translucent nightgown (which had fascinated and outraged the critics in equal measure) her dark eyes beseeching you, wherever you went. I used to hide beneath the dining room table to escape her gaze, but when I emerged after an hour or more, she was always waiting, reproaching me with those mournful black eyes. The other paintings had gone, but they left reminders – the sun-bleached wallpaper marked with rectangular stains, showing the holes where the pictures used to be. I missed most the one of the bustling Parisian street in the drizzle, ladies hurried along a tree-lined boulevard, while men in top-hats clutched black umbrellas. The shop-fronts were red and blue and the ladies pink-cheeked. I had never been to Paris but this had been my window. I shrugged – it shouldn't matter now, whether the paintings were here, since I would not see them. But, when leaving home, one always likes to think of it as it ought to be, and as it was before, perfect and unchanging. Now, when I think of our apartment, I restore each picture to its proper place: Paris opposite the painting of breakfast on the balcony (purchased by Julian as a present for Anna on their honeymoon). I have to remind myself that they had vanished before that last night, and then, with a blink, the walls are empty once again.

The chairs scraped on the parquet floor, as the men helped the ladies into their places, gowns catching on chair legs and under feet, so that the hum of chatter rippled with apologies. We all peered round the table with interest, hoping that ours would be the amusing end of the party and the others did not have better dinner companions. Herr Finkelstein adjusted his *yarmulke*, so it neatly covered the bald disc on his head. The men alternated between the ladies, stark in their black and white, ensuring that none of the women's rainbow dresses clashed beside one another. Anna and Julian sat at opposite heads of the table. They exchanged a look and Anna rang the silver bell once more. Instantly the diners fell silent and Julian rose to his feet.

'Welcome, my friends. This night is indeed different from all other nights. In the morning my younger daughter Elise leaves for England. And in another few weeks, Margot and her husband Robert, depart for America.'

The guests smiled at Margot and then at me, with envy or pity I could not tell. Julian held up his hand, and the hum of conversation dulled once again. He was pale, and even in the half-light I could see beads of perspiration on his brow.

'But the truth is my friends, we already live in exile. We are no longer citizens in our own country. And it is better to be exiled amongst strangers than at home.'

Abruptly he sat down, and wiped his forehead with his napkin.

'Darling?' said Anna, from the other side of the long table, trying to keep the note of anxiety from her voice.

Julian stared at her for second, and then recollecting himself, stood up once more, and opened the *Haggadah*. It was strange, until this year we had always hurried through the Passover Seder; it had become a kind of game, seeing how fast we could race to the end, reading quickly, skipping passages so that we could reach Hildegard's dinner in record time, preferably before she was even ready to serve it, causing her to puff and grumble. This night we paused, and by tacit agreement, read every word. Perhaps the God-fearing amongst us believed in the prayers and hoped that due to their diligence, He would take pity. I did not believe this, but as I listened to stout Herr Finkelstein singing the Hebrew, double chins trembling with fervour, I was torn between scorn at his religious faith (I was Julian's daughter after all) and a sense of congruity. His words licked around me in the darkness, and in my mind's eye, I saw them shine like the lights of home. I pictured Anna's Moses, a hero of the big screen, James Stewart perhaps, leading the Jews into a rose-red dessert and then something older, a glimpse of a story I had always known. As a modern girl, I fumbled with my butter knife, embarrassed by Herr Finkelstein's chanting. He gazed heavenward oblivious to the dribble of *schmaltz* wobbling at the side of his wet lips, and I wanted him to stop, never to stop.

We murmured the blessings over the cups of wine, and the youngest, Jan Tibor, started the ritual of the four questions, 'Why is tonight different from all other nights? Why tonight do we eat only matzos?'

Frau Goldschmidt, pushed her reading glasses up her nose and recited the response, 'Matzos is used during Passover as a symbol of the unleavened bread that the Jews carried with them when they escaped out of Egypt, with no time for their uncooked bread to rise.'

Margot snorted, 'A Jewish household with empty cupboards? Not even a loaf of bread. Seems unlikely to me.'

I kicked her under the table, hard enough to bruise her shin, and I felt a small pulse of satisfaction as she winced.

'Elise. The next question,' said Julian, in his no-nonsense voice. He held up a sprig of parsley, and an eggcup brimming with salt water.

I read from the worn book in my lap, 'Why is it that on all other nights we eat all kinds of herbs, but on this night we eat only maror, bitter herbs?'

Julian placed his book face down on the table, and looked at me as though I had really asked him a question, to which I wished to know the answer. 'Bitter herbs remind us of the pain of the Jewish slaves, and the petty miseries of our own existence. But they are also a symbol of hope and of better things to come.'

He did not glance at the *Haggadah*, and as he continued, I realised that the words were his. 'A man who has experienced great sorrow and then has known its end, wakes each morning feeling the pleasure of sunrise.'

He took a sip of water and dabbed his mouth. 'Margot. The next.'

She stared at him, and then glanced down to her book. 'Why is it that on all other nights, we don't dip our herbs at all, but on this night we dip them twice?'

Julian dipped a sprig of parsley in the pot of sweet *charoset* and leant across the table to hand it to me. I popped it into my mouth and swallowed the sticky mixture of apples, almonds and honey. He bathed a second piece of parsley in the salt water and gave it to me, watching as I ate. My mouth stung with salt, and I tasted tears and long journeys across the sea.

The Death Instinct

BY

Jed Rubenfeld

**From the international bestselling author—
"a sprawling and ambitious literary mystery"
(*The Seattle Times*).**

From a true and shocking event—the bombing of lower Manhattan in September 1920—Jed Rubenfeld weaves a twisting and thrilling work of fiction as a physician, a female radiochemist, and a police official come to believe that the inexplicable attack is only part of a larger plan. It's a conspiracy that takes them from Paris to Prague, from the Vienna home of Sigmund Freud to the corridors of power in Washington, D.C., and ultimately to the depths of our most savage human instincts where there lies the shocking truth behind that fateful day.

ONE

DEATH IS ONLY THE BEGINNING; afterward comes the hard part.
There are three ways to live with the knowledge of death—to keep its terror at bay. The first is suppression: forget it's coming; act as if it isn't. That's what most of us do most of the time. The second is the opposite: *memento mori*. Remember death. Keep it constantly in mind, for surely life can have no greater savor than when a man believes today is his last. The third is acceptance. A man who accepts death—really accepts it—fears nothing and hence achieves a transcendent equanimity in the face of all loss. All three of these strategies have something in common. They're lies. Terror, at least, would be honest.

But there is another way, a fourth way. This is the inadmissible option, the path no man can speak of, not even to himself, not even in the quiet of his own inward conversation. This way requires no forgetting, no lying, no groveling at the altar of the inevitable. All it takes is instinct.

———

At the stroke of noon on September 16, 1920, the bells of Trinity Church began to boom, and as if motivated by a single spring, doors flew open up and down Wall Street, releasing clerks and message boys, secretaries and stenographers, for their precious hour of lunch. They poured into the streets, streaming around cars, lining up at favorite vendors, filling in an instant the busy intersection of Wall, Nassau, and Broad, an intersection known in the financial world as the Corner—just that, the Corner. There stood the United States Treasury, with its Greek temple facade, guarded by a regal bronze George Washington. There stood the white-columned New York Stock Exchange. There, J. P. Morgan's domed fortress of a bank.

In front of that bank, an old bay mare pawed at the cobblestones, hitched to an overloaded, burlap-covered cart—pilotless and blocking traffic. Horns sounded angrily behind it. A stout cab driver exited his vehicle, arms upraised in righteous appeal. Attempting to berate the cartman, who wasn't there, the taxi driver was surprised by an odd, muffled noise coming from inside the wagon. He put his ear to the burlap and heard an unmistakable sound: ticking.

The church bells struck twelve. With the final, sonorous note still echoing, a curious taxi driver drew back one corner of moth-eaten burlap and saw what lay beneath. At that moment, among the jostling thousands, four people knew that death was pregnant in Wall Street: the cab driver; a red-headed woman close by him; the missing pilot of the horse-drawn wagon; and Stratham Younger, who, one hundred fifty feet away, pulled to their knees a police detective and a French girl.

The taxi driver whispered, "Lord have mercy."

Wall Street exploded.

———

Two women, once upon a time the best of friends, meeting again after years apart, will cry out in disbelief, embrace, protest, and immediately take up the missing pieces of their lives, painting them in for one another with all the tint and vividness they can. Two men, under the same conditions, have nothing to say at all.

At eleven that morning, one hour before the explosion, Younger and Jimmy Littlemore shook hands in Madison Square, two miles north of Wall Street. The day was unseasonably fine, the sky a crystal blue. Younger took out a cigarette.

"Been a while, Doc," said Littlemore.

Younger struck, lit, nodded.

Both men were in their thirties, but of different physical types. Littlemore, a detective with the New York Police Department, was the kind of man who mixed easily into his surroundings. His height was average, his weight average, the color of his hair average; even his features were average, a composite of American openness and good health. Younger, by contrast, was arresting. He was tall; he moved well; his skin was a little weathered; he had the kind of imperfections in a handsome face that women like. In short, the doctor's appearance was more demanding than the detective's, but less amiable.

"How's the job?" asked Younger.

"Job's good," said Littlemore, a toothpick wagging between his lips.

"Family?"

"Family's good."

Another difference between them was visible as well. Younger had fought in the war; Littlemore had not. Younger, walking away from his medical practice in Boston and his scientific research at Harvard, had enlisted immediately after war was declared in 1917. Littlemore would have too—if he hadn't had a wife and so many children to provide for.

"That's good," said Younger.

"So are you going to tell me," asked Littlemore, "or do I have to pry it out of you with a crowbar?"

Younger smoked. "Crowbar."

"You call me after all this time, tell me you got something to tell me, and now you're not going to tell me?"

"This is where they had the big victory parade, isn't it?" asked Younger, looking around at Madison Square Park, with its greenery, monuments, and ornamental fountain. "What happened to the arch?"

"Tore it down."

"Why were men so willing to die?"

"Who was?" asked Littlemore.

"It doesn't make sense. From an evolutionary point of view." Younger looked back at Littlemore. "I'm not the one who needs to talk to you. It's Colette."

"The girl you brought back from France?" said Littlemore.

"She should be here any minute. If she's not lost."

"What's she look like?"

Younger thought about it: "Pretty." A moment later, he added, "Here she is."

A double-decker bus had pulled up nearby on Fifth Avenue. Littlemore turned to look; the toothpick nearly fell out of his mouth. A girl in a slim trench coat was coming down the outdoor spiral staircase. The two men met her as she stepped off.

Colette Rousseau kissed Younger once on either cheek and extended a slender arm to Littlemore. She had green eyes, graceful movements, and long dark hair.

"Glad to meet you, Miss," said the detective, recovering gamely.

She eyed him. "So you're Jimmy," she replied, taking him in. "The best and bravest man Stratham has ever known."

Littlemore blinked. "He said that?"

"I also told her your jokes aren't funny," added Younger.

Colette turned to Younger: "You should have come to the radium clinic. They've cured a sarcoma. And a rhinoscleroma. How can a little hospital in America have two whole grams of radium when there isn't one in all of France?"

"I didn't know rhinos had an aroma," said Littlemore.

"Shall we go to lunch?" asked Younger.

———

Where Colette alighted from the bus, a monumental triple arch had only a few months earlier spanned the entirety of Fifth Avenue. In March of 1919, vast throngs cheered as homecoming soldiers paraded beneath the triumphal Roman arch, erected to celebrate the nation's victory in the Great War. Ribbons swirled, balloons flew, cannons saluted, and—because Prohibition had not yet arrived—corks popped.

But the soldiers who received this hero's welcome woke the next morning to discover a city with no jobs for them. Wartime boom had succumbed to postwar collapse. The churning factories boarded up their windows. Stores closed. Buying and selling ground to a halt. Families were put out on the streets with nowhere to go.

The Victory Arch was supposed to have been solid marble. Such extravagance having become unaffordable, it had been built of wood and plaster instead. When the weather came, the paint peeled, and the arch began to crumble. It was demolished before winter was out—about the same time the country went dry.

The colossal, dazzlingly white and vanished arch lent a tremor of ghostliness to Madison Square. Colette felt it. She even turned to see if someone might be watching her. But she turned the wrong way. She didn't look across Fifth Avenue, where, beyond the speeding cars and rattling omnibuses, a pair of eyes was in fact fixed upon her.

These belonged to a female figure, solitary, still, her cheeks gaunt and pallid, so skeletal in stature that, to judge by appearance, she couldn't have threatened a child. A kerchief hid most of her dry red hair, and a worn-out dress from the previous century hung to her ankles. It was impossible to tell her age: she might have been an innocent fourteen or a bony fifty-five. There was, however, a peculiarity about her eyes. The irises, of the palest blue, were flecked with brownish-yellow impurities like corpses floating in a tranquil sea.

Among the vehicles blocking this woman's way across Fifth Avenue was an approaching delivery truck, drawn by a horse. She cast her composed gaze on it. The trotting animal saw her out of the corner of an eye. It balked and reared. The truck driver shouted; vehicles swerved, tires screeched. There were no collisions, but a clear path opened up through the traffic. She crossed Fifth Avenue unmolested.

———

L ittlemore led them to a street cart next to the subway steps, proposing that they have "dogs" for lunch, which required the men to explain to an appalled French girl the ingredients of that recent culinary sensation, the hot dog. "You'll like it, Miss, I promise," said Littlemore.

"I will?" she replied dubiously.

Reaching the near side of Fifth Avenue, the kerchiefed woman placed a blue-veined hand on her abdomen. This was evidently a sign or command. Not far away, the park's flowing fountain ceased to spray, and as the last jets of water fell to the basin, another redheaded woman came into view, so like the first as almost to be a reflection, but less pale, less skeletal, her hair flowing unhindered. She too put a hand on her abdomen. In her other hand was a pair of scissors with strong, curving blades. She set off toward Colette.

"Ketchup, Miss?" asked Littlemore. "Most take mustard, but I say ketchup. There you go."

Colette accepted the hot dog awkwardly. "All right, I'll try."

Using both hands, she took a bite. The two men watched. So did the two red-haired women, approaching from different directions. And so did a third redheaded figure next to a flagpole near Broadway, who wore, in addition to a kerchief over her head, a gray wool scarf wrapped more than once around her neck.

"But it's good!" said Colette. "What did you put on yours?"

"Sauerkraut, Miss," replied Littlemore. "It's kind of a sour, kraut-y—"

"She knows what sauerkraut is," said Younger.

"You want some?" asked Littlemore.

"Yes, please."

The woman under the flagpole licked her lips. Hurrying New Yorkers passed on either side, taking no notice of her—or of her scarf, which the weather didn't justify, and which seemed to bulge out strangely from her throat. She raised a hand to her mouth; emaciated fingertips touched parted lips. She began walking toward the French girl.

"How about downtown?" said Littlemore. "Would you like to see the Brooklyn Bridge, Miss?"

"Very much," said Colette.

"Follow me," said the detective, throwing the vendor two bits for a tip and walking to the top of the subway stairs. He checked his pockets: "Shoot—we need another nickel."

The street vendor, overhearing the detective, began to rummage through his change box when he caught sight of three strangely similar figures approaching his cart. The first two had joined together, fingers touching as they walked. The third advanced by herself from the opposite direction, holding her thick wool scarf to her throat. The vendor's long fork slipped from his hand and disappeared into a pot of simmering water. He stopped looking for nickels.

"I have one," said Younger.

"Let's go," replied Littlemore. He trotted down the stairs. Colette and Younger followed. They were lucky: a downtown train was entering the station; they just made it. Halfway out of the station, the train lurched to a halt. Its doors creaked ajar, snapped shut, then jerked open again. Evidently some latecomers had induced the conductor to let them on.

————

In the narrow arteries of lower Manhattan—they had emerged at City Hall—Younger, Colette, and Littlemore were swept up in the capillary crush of humanity. Younger inhaled deeply. He loved the city's teemingness, its purposiveness, its belligerence. He was a confident man; he always had been. By American standards, Younger was very wellborn: a Schermerhorn on his mother's side, a close cousin to the Fishes of New York and, through his father, the Cabots of Boston. This exalted genealogy, a matter of indifference to him now, had disgusted him as a youth. The sense of superiority his class enjoyed struck him as so patently undeserved that he'd resolved to do the opposite of everything expected of him—until the night his father died, when necessity descended, the world became real, and the whole issue of social class ceased to be of interest.

But those days were long past, scoured away by years of unstinting work, accomplishment, and war, and on this New York morning, Younger experienced a feeling almost of invulnerability. This was, however, he reflected, probably only the knowledge that no snipers lay hidden with your head in their sights, no shells were screaming through the air to relieve you of your legs. Unless perhaps it was the opposite: that the pulse of violence was so atmospheric in New York that a man who had fought in the war could breathe here, could be at home, could flex muscles still pricked by the feral after-charge of uninhibited killing—without making himself a misfit or a monster.

"Shall I tell him?" he asked Colette. To their right rose up incomprehensibly tall skyscrapers. To their left, the Brooklyn Bridge soared over the East River.

"No, I will," said Colette. "I'm sorry to take so much of your time, Jimmy. I should have told you already."

"I got all the time in the world, Miss," said Littlemore.

"Well, it's probably nothing, but last night a girl came to our hotel looking for me. We were out, so she left a note. Here it is." Colette produced a crumpled scrap of paper from her purse. The paper bore a hand-written message, hastily scrawled:

Please I need to see you. They know you're right. I'll come back tomorrow morning at seven-thirty. Please can you help me.

> *Amelia*

"She never came back," added Colette.

"You know this Amelia?" asked Littlemore, turning the note over, but finding nothing on its opposite side.

"No."

" 'They know you're right'?" said Littlemore. "About what?"

"I can't imagine," said Colette.

"There's something else," said Younger.

"Yes, it's what she put inside the note that worries us," said Colette, fishing through her purse. She handed the detective a wad of white cotton.

Littlemore pulled the threads apart. Buried within the cotton ball was a tooth—a small, shiny human molar.

A fusillade of obscenities interrupted them. The cause was a parade on Liberty Street, which had halted traffic. All of the marchers were black. The men wore their Sunday best—a tattered best, their sleeves too short— although it was midweek. Skinny children tripped barefoot among their parents. Most were singing; their hymnal rose above the bystanders' taunts and motorists' ire.

"Hold your horses," said a uniformed officer, barely more than a boy, to one fulminating driver.

Littlemore, excusing himself, approached the officer. "What are you doing here, Boyle?"

"Captain Hamilton sent us, sir," said Boyle, "because of the nigger parade."

"Who's patrolling the Exchange?" asked Littlemore.

"Nobody. We're all up here. Shall I break up this march, sir? Looks like there's going to be trouble."

"Let me think," said Littlemore, scratching his head. "What would you do on St. Paddy's Day if some blacks were causing trouble? Break up the parade?"

"I'd break up the blacks, sir. Break 'em up good."

"That's a boy. You do the same here."

"Yes, sir. All right, you lot," Officer Boyle yelled to the marchers in front of him, pulling out his nightstick, "get off the streets, all of you."

"*Boyle!*" said Littlemore.

"Sir?"

"Not the blacks."

"But you said—"

"You break up the troublemakers, not the marchers. Let cars through every two minutes. These people have a right to parade just like anybody else."

"Yes sir."

Littlemore returned to Younger and Colette. "Okay, the tooth is a little strange," he said. "Why would someone leave you a tooth?"

"I have no idea."

They continued downtown. Littlemore held the tooth up in the sunlight, rotated it. "Clean. Good condition. Why?" He looked at the slip of paper again. "The note doesn't have your name on it, Miss. Maybe it wasn't meant for you."

"The clerk said the girl asked for Miss Colette Rousseau," replied Younger.

"Could be somebody with a similar last name," suggested Littlemore. "The Commodore's a big hotel. Any dentists there?"

"In the hotel?" said Colette.

"How did you know we were at the Commodore?" asked Younger.

"Hotel matches. You lit your cigarette with them."

"Those awful matches," replied Colette. "Luc is sure to be playing with them right now. Luc is my little brother. He's ten. Stratham gives him matches as toys."

"The boy took apart hand grenades in the war," Younger said to Colette. "He'll be fine."

"My oldest is ten—Jimmy Junior, we call him," said Littlemore. "Are your parents here too?"

"No, we're by ourselves," she answered. "We lost our family in the war."

They were entering the Financial District, with its granite facades and dizzying towers. Curbside traders in three-piece suits auctioned securities outside in the September sun.

"I'm sorry, Miss," said Littlemore. "About your family."

"It's nothing special," she said. "Many families were lost. My brother and I were lucky to survive."

Littlemore glanced at Younger, who felt the glance but didn't acknowledge it. Younger knew what Littlemore was wondering—how losing your family could be nothing special—but Littlemore hadn't seen the war. They walked on in silence, each pursuing his or her own reflections, as a result of which none of them heard the creature coming up from behind. Even Colette was unaware until she felt the hot breath on her neck. She recoiled and cried out in alarm.

It was a horse, an old bay mare, snorting hard from the weight of a dilapidated, overloaded wooden cart she towed behind her. Colette, relieved and contrite, reached out and crumpled one of the horse's ears. The mare flapped her nostrils appreciatively. Her driver hissed, stinging the horse's flank with a crop. Colette yanked her hand away. The burlap-covered wagon clacked past them on the cobblestones of Nassau Street.

"May I ask you a question?" asked Littlemore.

"Of course," said Colette.

"Who in New York knows where you're staying?"

"No one."

"What about the old lady you two visited this morning? The one with all the cats, who likes to hug people?"

"Mrs. Meloney?" said Colette. "No, I didn't tell her which hotel—"

"How could you possibly have known that?" interrupted Younger, adding to Colette: "I never told him about Mrs. Meloney."

They were approaching the intersection of Nassau, Broad, and Wall Streets—the financial center of New York City, arguably of the world.

"Kind of obvious, actually," said Littlemore. "You both have cat fur on your shoes, and in your case, Doc, on your pant cuffs. Different kinds of cat fur. So right away I know you both went some place this morning with a lot of cats. But the Miss also has two long, gray hairs on her shoulder—human hair. So I'm figuring the cats belonged to an old lady, and you two paid a call on her this morning, and the lady must be the hugging kind, because that's how—"

"All right, all right," said Younger.

In front of the Morgan Bank, the horse-drawn wagon came to a halt. The bells of Trinity Church began to boom, and the streets began to fill with thousands of office workers released from confinement for their precious hour of lunch.

"Anyway," Littlemore resumed, "I'd say the strong odds are that Amelia was looking for somebody else, and the clerk mixed it up."

Horns began honking angrily behind the parked horse cart, the pilot of which had disappeared. On the steps of the Treasury, a redheaded woman stood alone, head wrapped in a kerchief, surveying the crowd with a keen but composed gaze.

"Sounds like she might be in some trouble though," Littlemore went on. "Mind if I keep the tooth?"

"Please," said Colette.

Littlemore dropped the cotton wad into his breast pocket. On Wall Street, behind the horse-drawn wagon, a stout cab driver exited his vehicle, arms upraised in righteous appeal.

"Amazing," said Younger, "how nothing's changed here. Europe returned to the Dark Ages, but in America time went on holiday."

The bells of Trinity Church continued to peal. A hundred and fifty feet in front of Younger, the cab driver heard an odd noise coming from the burlap-covered wagon, and a cold light came to the eyes of the redheaded woman on the steps of the Treasury. She had seen Colette; she descended the stairs. People unconsciously made way for her.

"I'd say the opposite," replied Littlemore. "Everything's different. The whole city's on edge."

"Why?" asked Colette.

Younger no longer heard them. He was suddenly in France, not New York, trying to save the life of a one-armed soldier in a trench filled knee-high with freezing water, as the piercing, rising, fatal cry of incoming shells filled the air.

"You know," said Littlemore, "no jobs, everybody's broke, people getting evicted, strikes, riots—then they throw in Prohibition."

Younger looked at Colette and Littlemore; they didn't hear the shriek of artillery. No one heard it.

"Prohibition," repeated Littlemore. "That's got to be the worst thing anybody ever did to this country."

In front of the Morgan Bank, a curious taxi driver drew back one corner of moth-eaten burlap. The redheaded woman, who had just strode past him, stopped, puzzled. The pupils of her pale blue irises dilated as she looked back at the cab driver, who whispered, "Lord have mercy."

"Down," said Younger as he pulled an uncomprehending Littlemore and Colette to their knees.

Wall Street exploded.

You Know When the Men are Gone

Siobhan Fallon

"The stories in this volume are, quite frankly, extraordinary...it should not be missed."
—*New York Journal of Books*

Through fiction of dazzling skill and astonishing emotional force, Siobhan Fallon welcomes readers into the American army base at Fort Hood, Texas, where U.S. soldiers prepare to fight, and where their families are left to cope after the men are gone. They'll meet a wife who discovers unsettling secrets when she hacks into her husband's email, a teenager who disappears as her mother fights cancer, and the foreign-born wife who has tongues wagging over her late hours.

In the following excerpt, part of a story called "Leave," a military intelligence officer plans a covert mission against his own home.

LEAVE

Three A.M. and breaking into the house on Cheyenne Trail was even easier than Chief Warrant Officer Nick Cash thought it would be. There were no sounds from above, no lights throwing shadows, no floorboards whining, no water running or the snicker of late-night TV laugh tracks. The basement window, his point of entry, was open. The screws were rusted, but Nick had come prepared with his Gerber knife and WD-40; got the screws and the window out in five minutes flat. He stretched onto his stomach in the dew-wet grass and inched his legs through the opening, then pushed his torso backward until his toes grazed the cardboard boxes in the basement below, full of old shoes and college textbooks, which held his weight.

He had planned this mission the way the army would expect him to, the way only a soldier or a hunter or a neurotic could, considering every detail that ordinary people didn't even think about. He mapped out the route, calculating the

minutes it would take for each task, considering the place-
ment of streetlamps, the kind of vegetation in front, and
how to avoid walking past houses with dogs. He figured out
whether the moon would be new or full and what time the
sprinkler system went off. He staged this as carefully as any
other surveillance mission he had created and briefed to soldiers before.

Except this time the target was his own home.

. . .

He should have been relieved that he was inside, unseen, that
all was going according to plan. But as he screwed the window back into place, he could feel his lungs clench with rage
instead of adrenaline.

How many times had he warned his wife to lock the window? It didn't matter how often he told her about Richard
Ramirez, the Night Stalker, who had gained access to his
victims through open basement windows. Trish argued that
the open window helped air out the basement. A theory that
would have been sound if she actually closed the window
every once in a while. Instead she left it open until a rare and
thundering storm would remind her, then she'd jump up from
the couch, run down the steps, and slam it shut after it had
let in more water than a month of searing-weather-open-
window-days could possibly dry.

Before he left for Iraq, Nick had wanted to install an alarm system but his wife said no.

"Christ, Trish," he had replied. "You can leave the windows and all the doors open while I am home to protect you. But what about when I'm gone?"

She glanced up at him from chopping tomatoes, narrowed her eyes in a way he hadn't seen before, and said flatly, "We've already survived two deployments. I think we can take care of ourselves."

Take care of this, Nick thought now, twisting the screw so violently that the knife slipped and almost split open his palm, the scrape of metal on metal squealing like an assaulted chalkboard. He hesitated, waiting for the neighbor's dog to start barking or a porch light to go on. Again nothing. Nick could be any lunatic loose in the night, close to his unprotected daughter in her room with the safari animals on her wall, close to his wife in their marital bed.

Trish should have listened to him.

. . .

This particular reconnaissance mission had started with a seemingly harmless e-mail. Six months ago, Nick had been deployed to an outlying suburb of Baghdad, in what his battalion commander jovially referred to as "a shitty little base in a shitty little town in a shitty little country." One of his buddies back in Killeen had offered to check on Trish every month or so, to make sure she didn't need anything hammered or lifted or drilled while Nick was away.

His friend wrote:

> Stopped by to see Trish. Mark Rodell was there. Just
> thought you should know.

That was it. That hint, that whisper.

Mark Rodell.

Nick didn't know who the hell that was, but his friend seemed to think he should.

So he called Trish, standing in line at the FOB for an hour and a half for one of the three working pay phones that served over two hundred soldiers.

"Who's this Mark Rodell guy?" he asked as soon as Trish answered the phone.

There was a pause, then her voice, too calm and easy. Too ready. "He's the new gym teacher at Mountain Lion. I told you I wanted a willow tree, for the backyard? Well, he brought it over in his truck."

Nick could hear himself breathing out of his nose. "Is he married?"

"No. Nick, don't blow this out of proportion. He's just a pal. He helps all the teachers who have husbands away."

"I bet." His voice veered too loud so he coughed into his camouflaged shoulder to contain it, then continued in a hoarse whisper, "I bet he is a huge help to all you poor, neglected, stranded wives."

"He is. I don't like the tone of your voice."

Nick shut off the tone, shut his mouth and said nothing, waiting for more of an explanation, for anything, but his wife followed suit and said nothing as well. He could have told her that she was all he thought about during the long patrols or the even longer days at the base, that he had pictures of Trish and Ellie all around his cot so they were the first thing he saw every morning when he woke up and the last thing he saw at night when he shut off his light. He even had a sweat-stained photo of them tucked into his helmet that he would take out and show his interpreters, the local town council, or random Iraqis on the street, just to have an excuse to talk about his wife and child. But instead he said nothing until his time was nearly up, just listened to Trish breathe, knowing that she was winding and unwinding the old phone cord around her narrow fingers and getting angrier with each passing minute.

"How's Ellie?" he finally asked, his voice softening, deciding to salvage a minute or two.

"Damn it—I'm late. I have to get her from Texas Tumblers." And Trish hung up.

Nick pulled the phone away from his ear as if it had bitten him. He stared at it until the sergeant in charge of enforcing the fifteen-minute call limit walked over to him and pointedly glanced at his watch.

From then on, Nick could think of nothing but Mark

Rodell. In the chow hall waiting for a serving of barbecue and bleached-looking green beans, in the Tactical Operations Center, or TOC, where he read reams of intelligence reports, in his weekly review of the latest surveillance video from the Predator Unmanned Aerial Vehicle, otherwise known as "predator porn."

He thought back over the last months of his deployment, to the days Trish forgot to send him one of her quirky e-mails or the nights when a babysitter answered Nick's call, and all of the strained phone conversations in between. She had told him she occasionally went for drinks with her fellow schoolteachers or to the monthly game nights hosted by other military spouses whose husbands were deployed. It had filled him with relief to think of Trish clinking martini glasses with bookish friends or, even better, playing Bunco! with wives wearing their husbands' unit T-shirts. But now he imagined his wife swishing her dark hair in a dimly lit bar, lip-glossed and bare-shouldered, meeting the eyes of a stranger.

Three weeks later, Nick started planning his return.

. . .

He woke at dawn, wide awake but disoriented, as if startled by a mortar attack. He had wedged himself behind a wall of old and crumbling cardboard boxes just in case Trish decided to come down and look for something. It seemed like a great idea at almost three in the morning, but now, with a hint of blue light touching the corners of the basement, he realized that his head and feet were sticking out on either end. The odd noise repeated itself above his head, and he pulled himself into a fetal position, holding his breath. It continued long enough for him to realize that it couldn't be human, and he gingerly got up on his hands and knees, careful not to topple the boxes, and rose to his feet.

He held his Gerber knife ready, expecting a rat, but instead found a cat, an ugly little thing, flecks of brown and orange smudged through its gray fur. It looked up at him, then turned back to its scratching and finally squatted and shat in the corner of a box full of Trish's old college history papers. Nick bit the inside of his cheek to stop himself from barking out a laugh, and reached in to pet its head. He could read its collar: "Anne Lisbeth." It tolerated his touch, then leaped out of the box and wove its way through the detritus of the basement and headed toward the stairs. Nick dropped back down, knocking his head against the cement wall.

Ellie had been asking for a pet for a year now, begging every time they spoke, flip-flopping between cat, dog, chimpanzee. Of course Trish had decided on a cat, not a dog that could watch over them, that could bark or rip out an intruder's jugular. A cat named after Hans Christian Andersen's "Anne Lisbeth": the tale of a mother who abandons her infant in order to become a wet nurse for a count. Her own neglected baby dies and the mother goes mad in the end, haunted by the unloved ghost of her son.

It was just like Ellie to name a cat something so freakishly morbid. She'd become fascinated with fairy tales during Nick's last deployment. And not the Disney fairy tales, oh no, not those wide-eyed, fat-lipped princesses mincing around and breaking out into song. Ellie had gone to spend a couple of weeks with her grandma in Boston two summers ago and came home with a collection of Hans Christian Andersen and illustrated *Grimm's Fairy Tales*. Nick would read them to her every night when he was home. They were full of strange cruelties he wanted to hide from his child: the way Cinderella's stepsisters cut off their own toes in order to fit into her glass slipper; the huntsman giving the queen the still-beating heart of a stag instead of Snow White's; the orphan girl so beguiled by her red shoes that she is cursed to dance in them until her legs are chopped off with an ax. Whenever he tried to skip or edit any of the ghoulish bits, Ellie corrected him, staring at him with her mother's huge and serious eyes, disappointed with his omission.

Then Nick heard the faraway tinkle of his wife's alarm playing the Bizet CD it always did. He hid behind his boxes, listening as she waited for two tracks, probably doing her morning yoga stretches, and then rose from the bed, the springs gasping. He felt his gut loosen a little when he realized that she was alone; no voices, muted laugher, or heavy steps followed his wife's tread into the kitchen. Her slippers scraped along the hardwood floors and headed directly to the coffeemaker. He could see her clearly: her hair held up in a messy ponytail on the top of her head so it didn't get in her eyes when she slept. One of her mother's old robes draped across her narrow shoulders. Sweatpants loose on her hips. A Brown University T-shirt tight across her breasts, which still looked damn good for a woman who breast-fed Ellie until she was two.

He suddenly wanted to walk up those basement stairs as easily as the cat. This was his home, she was his wife, his baby girl was still asleep in her pink-comfortered bed. He was a fool. Then he heard Trish back in the bedroom, probably rooting around for her sneakers, putting on her running shorts and a tank top that showed off her nicely sculpted shoulders, getting her body firm for Mark Rodell.

The coffee machine buzzed above and Nick reached for a warm Gatorade. No, he wasn't ready to go upstairs yet. He couldn't let himself break. He needed to listen, to find out, to know.

Nick quickly unpacked while Trish was out running. He had fourteen MREs jammed into his assault pack—one for every day. There were also a few shelves of dusty canned goods in the basement laundry room that he could eat: peaches, pineapple rings, kidney beans, tuna fish. He had a two-quart CamelBak of water and three large Gatorade bottles that he would drink and then use as a urinal when his wife was home, and that he could dump when she wasn't. He also had his sleeping bag liner, not too soft but at least it was something, a set of civilian clothes in case he needed to go out into the world like a normal person, and a backup set of black clothing in case he didn't.

It seemed like every little bit of training for the past seven years had led him to this moment, to hiding in his own basement, his intestines tight with fear in a way they had never been in Iraq. Every minute he had spent in Baghdad, sifting through lies, brought him back to this, to his home, his wife, the entirety of his life. While he organized his possessions against the basement's damp wall, he thought about the TOC, all those intelligence reports, how difficult it was to discern truth from exaggeration and ambiguity. He interviewed informers and interrogated suspects, watched the blinking eyes, twitching hands, the sweat on their foreheads, knowing that every word was suspect, each sentence could be loaded with mistruths, familial vengeance, jihadism, fear, self-preservation, and maybe, just maybe, innocence. It was difficult to determine if someone was one-hundred-percent guilty, but nearly impossible to find someone one-hundred-percent innocent.

When Nick showed up for an interrogation, his soldiers would say, "Here comes Chief Cash, we're about to hit the jackpot," or "With Chief Cash dealing, we're gonna win us some old-fashioned Texas Hold 'em." Nick ignored them; he wasn't any luckier than anyone else. But he did happen to be paired with an interpreter, Ibrahim, who used to be a

Baghdad taxi driver and knew every street and shred of gossip in the city. They were a good team, Nick and Ibrahim, listening, waiting, knowing how to be patient and how to ask the right questions, and occasionally it led to something, like a dozen rocket launchers hidden in a hole under a mayor's refrigerator. But most of the time it led to nothing.

Nick understood the slippery nature of his task. Sources lied. Eyewitnesses missed crucial facts. Even the intel experts stateside regularly screwed up. So when his buddy offered to check on Trish more often, he told him no. Nor did Nick grill his wife about the details of her evenings out when they spoke on the phone, to search for cracks and split them open. Nick knew that his friend wouldn't be able to get at the truth no matter how many times he stopped by the house. And the thousands of miles of static and dropped calls separating Nick from Trish made it impossible for him to find out if she lied. There was only so much that could be gained from talking. He knew from experience that the only way to prove anything beyond a reasonable doubt was to get inside the suspect's house, to find the sniper rifle under the bed, the Iranian bomb-making electronics in a back shed, the sketches of the nearest U.S. military base in a hollow panel of the wall.

The only thing to do was to find out for himself. To go home in a way that didn't give Trish enough notice to hide the evidence.

To go home and catch her in the act.

. . .

Forty-seven minutes after her alarm had gone off, Trish returned from her run, the latch on the front door clicking shut. At the same instant, Nick heard his daughter wake up—heard her jump down off her bed and her bare feet slap along floors, heard the high-pitched screech of her voice, "Anne Lisbeth! Anne Lisbeth!"

Nick winced; that ugly cat did not look like the cuddling kind. Knowing Trish, they had gone to some "no-kill" shelter and deliberately found a cat that no sane person in the world would adopt. He imagined Ellie with scratches on her face and bite marks on her hands and Trish gingerly putting peroxide on the wounds rather than admit she couldn't rehabilitate a fey cat. It felt good to create this jittery resentment against his wife just when the sound of his child's footsteps was starting to make him yearn for her small arms around his neck.

"Mommy, where's Anne Lisbeth?" Ellie's voice screamed from the kitchen, probably a few feet away from Trish, who must be wiping sweat from her lean face, starting in on her second cup of coffee in order to put on a smile for her early morning whirling dervish. Nick was amazed he could hear her voice so clearly; he would have to be careful about every noise he made.

"Maybe she's in the basement," Trish replied. Nick quickly scanned the dim room and spotted Anne Lisbeth sitting on her haunches a few feet away, staring at him.

The cat lifted a paw and indifferently licked. Nick made as if he was going to kick it and it shot off, a blur of raccoon gray, bursting up the stairs, and he heard his daughter's shout of happiness.

. . .

When Nick's mid-tour leave came up at six months, he just didn't tell Trish. He said he wasn't coming home; he said a private's wife was having severe complications in her pregnancy and Nick gave his leave to him.

"There isn't some single soldier who could make the sacrifice instead?" Trish asked. Then, when Nick didn't say anything, "Fine, be the good guy. That's what I'll tell Ellie. You can't see your daddy because he's being the hero again." She didn't sound angry or even that upset, just giving him shit because lately she always gave him shit about something.

"Anything you want to tell me?" he asked calmly. "Anything at all?" He wasn't sure what he was getting at, if he was asking for a confession or a fight.

There was a long silence, as if Trish wasn't sure what he was getting at either, and then the predictable talk of Ellie: A's in the first grade, her most recent piano recital and the birthday party he had missed, all the milestones and transformations that had passed Nick by.

"She misses you," Trish said softly, as if she didn't want their daughter to hear. Nick imagined Ellie paging through her *Grimm's* in the living room, arching a thin eyebrow when her mother's voice dropped low, knowing the way all children do when their parents are talking about them. Nick waited for Trish to say that she missed him, too, but she hadn't said that in months.

Trish continued, "Last night, during prayers, she asked God to blow up the bad guys before they could blow you up."

Nick tried to laugh but instead closed his eyes and pressed his forehead against the hot metal of the pay phone and felt like all the gravity of the world was pulling on his rib cage.

"Kiss her for me," he whispered, and two hours later he was boarding a plane for home.

. . .

Nick, being Nick, had every step planned out. When he was sure, absolutely sure, that his wife wasn't cheating on him, he would leave the basement. He would wait until Ellie and Trish went to bed. Then he would jog the four miles to the Travelodge just off Indian Trail and get a room. He would take a really long shower, shave, brush his teeth, make sure there wasn't any dirt under his nails, eat a hot meal, get a few hours of sleep in a bed. First thing in the morning he would change into the uniform that was carefully folded in his assault pack. Then he'd call Trish, catch her before her run, and tell her he was on his way, that he had gotten leave after all at the last minute and had to jump on a plane, that he hadn't had a chance to contact her when they stopped over in Kuwait, but he was here at the Killeen Airport, he was home, he was about to get into a cab and he couldn't wait to see her and Ellie. He would say that he loved them, he was sorry, he was everything and anything he ought to be. Then he'd hang up, tell the cab-driver to stop at a florist, and Nick would buy a huge bouquet and whatever stuffed animals he could get his hands on.

However, he did not know what he would do if he found out that Trish was indeed cheating on him.

. . .

The scrape of the car keys, the corralling of Ellie out the door, time for first grade, time for Trish to go to work at that Montessori School in the ritzy neighboring town of Salado, finger painting to Mozart, prints of freaky Frida Kahlo with monkeys in her hair gazing down at the kids. Nick started to go up the stairs and then hesitated, sat down on the dim bottom step and waited. Then the front door opened again and he heard the click of Trish's shoes moving quickly from the hallway to the kitchen. Ellie must have decided she needed something—a juice box or an apple or maybe her favorite Maggie doll. Something forgotten, always something, and then Trish was gone. The old Volvo pulled out of the driveway and Nick tiptoed into the civilian world.

The first thing he did was walk into the kitchen and look out at the backyard.

Sure enough, there was a willow tree sitting right smack in the middle of the lawn. A frail, spindly spider sort of thing. But big enough that it wouldn't have fit in Trish's car. Nick took a deep breath. So at least part of Trish's story was true. That was a good liar's smoothest trick, to plant bits of reality into the subterfuge. It was the untold that Nick watched for. The slipup. The contradiction. The nervous hands touching a cheek, an ear, the smile or frown that seemed forced, the desire to change the subject. Such obvious signs.

The cat stepped in front of Nick, weaving between his legs as if deliberately trying to trip him.

"Shoo!" Nick stamped his foot and the cat hissed and ran.

He opened the fridge and stared at the shelves of plenty: a gallon of organic milk, a block of sharp cheddar cheese, fresh squeezed orange juice, and weirdly hourglass-shaped bottles of pomegranate juice. Nick hadn't seen such vividly colorful food for more than six months. He poured himself a cup of orange juice, careful not to take enough to be noticed. He did the same with the milk and savored it, full fat and fresh. Then a handful of blueberries, cherries, grapes. The garbage bag was new and empty so he put the cherry pits in his pocket. He shaved a few slices off the cheese with his Gerber knife and let it melt in his mouth.

Then he noticed the two bottles of white wine, both

opened. His wife always drank red. Did that count as proof or had his wife just started drinking something new? Maybe she had a girlfriend over one night who had brought the wine, maybe they watched movies, painted their nails, told themselves how good their hair looked, or did whatever women did when their men were away.

He carefully washed and dried his glass, made sure everything was put back perfectly in the fridge, and left the kitchen.

He went directly to the master bedroom and stood in the doorway. He had picked out this furniture set of dark mahogany, choosing it because the headboard had a pillow of leather pegged into the wood with medieval-looking brass nails. Trish said it looked like the Inquisition but that was what Nick liked—the bed seemed like it was made for history, that it would be fixed in their lives forever.

The room was immaculate. No strange baseball caps or sneakers, no boxers or tightie-whities in the laundry basket, no new lingerie in Trish's top drawer. His relief hit him hard enough that he had to sit down on the mattress. It felt like it always did, the bed, the room, the house; it felt like it was *his.*

On his way back to the basement, he walked through the living room and, like the bedroom, it was the same, the family photos spaced nicely around the flat-screen TV, an abstract oil painting over the fireplace, a few charcoal sketches perfectly accenting the black leather sofa. He ran his hands along the cushions as if he could channel who had sat on the leather from its soft touch. They had fought over it. Trish had whined and whined, wanted an ugly stuffed corduroy couch with clawed feet like an old bathtub, but Nick had won. Now the leather leered at him, so soft, so sexy. He had wanted it because he imagined making love to Trish on the supple length and then somehow they never had, she was a bedroom-only kind of girl, but now he wondered if, like the white wine, she had developed new tastes.

. . .

There was a day at the forward operating base, a day like any other, the guys coming in from their latest mission empty-handed, unsure if not finding a cache of guns at the local imam's house was a good or bad thing. They were exhausted, hungry, the Humvee's AC busted again, and they knew they had missed DFAC's one hot meal of the day. They exited the Humvee, snapped off their forty pounds of Kevlar, took off their dusty Oakley sunglasses, and wiped the sweat from their eyes.

A private was sitting on a folding chair cleaning his rifle and drinking Wild Tiger, an Iraqi energy drink reputed to be laced with nicotine, the radio at his feet blasting Stephen Stills's "Love the One You're With." He was singing along, intent on the greasy insides of his gun.

Nick stood listening and thought of Trish's hips sashaying

to the refrain, *When you can't be with the one you love, love the one you're with.* She grooved on all those long-haired seventies sounds, Bee Gees, Rod Stewart, Eagles, whipping out her old high school cassette tapes when feeling frisky.

Then Nick heard a hissed "Motherfucker." He glanced up in time to see Staff Sergeant Torres, one of the most laid-back guys he knew, walk straight over to the private and stomp the radio to smithereens.

The private leaned back in his chair to get away from flying bits of plastic. Nick and two other soldiers moved in close, ready to pull the men apart if Staff Sergeant Torres planned on smashing the private's face as well.

Instead Torres looked down at the shards under his boots. "I'll pay for that," he said, then turned and walked back to his tent.

None of the men looked at each other, as if refusing to acknowledge what they had witnessed. They knew there was only one thing that would make a guy snap like that, make him want to crush those words out of existence, and it didn't have a damn thing to do with life in Iraq.

. . .

By the time Trish and Ellie returned from school, Nick was firmly ensconced and almost comfortable with his setup. He had shoved some of Ellie's discarded stuffed animals into an old pillowcase and propped it against the wall as a cushion for his back. He had dug through the boxes he could reach and found a few of his books. Maybe not his favorites, his *How to Eat Soup with a Knife, Personal Memoirs of Ulysses S. Grant,* and *Crime and Punishment* were still in his office upstairs, but here were the books he had liked before he joined the army, his Grisham and Clancy and *Black Hawk Down.*

A couple of Ellie's fairy tales were here, too, a yard sale version of Hans Christian Andersen and a lesser known collection of Grimm. He picked the Grimm up gingerly, as if he were touching his daughter's hand. He wondered if she was finally over her obsession, if she was listening to ordinary stories now with happy endings, stories that other children liked, the fluff that made Disney worth millions. He opened it and started reading a story titled "Child in the Grave," whose first sentence stated: *It was a very sad day, and every heart in the house felt the deepest grief; for the youngest child, a boy of four years old, the joy and hope of his parents, was dead.* He closed the book and shut his eyes.

That was life. The motherless Hansel and Gretel, starving and lost in the forest, arriving at the cannibal witch's gingerbread cottage. The little mermaid rescuing her prince from the stormy sea, then giving up her voice and her fin for painful legs only to watch him fall in love with the woman he mistakenly thinks saved him from drowning. The young army corporal, a mere three days from going home to his wife and newborn, gets hit by a sniper. Such vicious twists dealt to the undeserving.

And those were the stories people knew about. The ones that stayed silent could be almost just as bad: the everyday horrors of lonely and quietly disappointed wives, of husbands deployed to the desert for years and years, missing their children's first steps, spelling bees, scraped knees.

. . .

Nick stretched; his neck and back ached from sleeping contorted on the hard cement. It was day three and he was starting to smell; as soon as his girls left for school he would risk a shower. And he desperately needed to dump the latest bottles of urine; even the cat shit above couldn't mask the acid and meaty stench of his slightly dehydrated, over-proteined piss. Trish hadn't been grocery shopping so he couldn't eat much of the dwindled-down fresh food but he could eat a can or two of tuna. She wouldn't miss a couple of tablespoons of mayo or slices of bread. Nick might even turn on the TV for an hour or two to see what was happening in the world.

So far there had been no sign of this Mark Rodell—maybe Trish had told him the truth, Nick thought, letting himself feel hopeful. Maybe he really was just a pal.

Or maybe he planted the willow in the backyard and then planted something else. Nick took a deep breath and told himself he could live with that. He could forgive. He could handle it as long as Trish's feelings hadn't changed toward

Nick, as long as she still loved him, and this . . . this *aberration* faded with time until it was nothing but a memory overshadowed by anniversaries and vacations and Ellie's high school graduation. He could do it, he could, if it meant keeping the life they had, the beautiful life of Trish next to him, her hip pressed against his in the night, her hands tracing the bones of his spine, her body pulling him toward her, against and inside her, to a place he knew and longed for, safe with her and home.

But what if, what if, damn it, the *what-ifs* burned his brain and he pushed his filthy hands against his eye sockets. What if it had happened in his bed, on his couch, in the newly redone tub of the master bathroom? Relax, he told himself, relax, don't kick the wall or kill the cat. Then he thought of the sergeant busting the radio to bits, how good it must have felt, that release and revenge, in crushing that sound into nothing.